DARK TRIALS

The Vickie Chronicles
Dark Trials
Written by I. Savage

Published by Improvisation News LLC / IN Studios

Copyright © 2024 Israel Savage

All rights reserved. No part of this publication may be reproduced, distributed, or transmitted in any form or by any means, including photocopying, recording, or other electronic or mechanical methods, without the prior written permission of the publisher, except in the case of brief quotations embodied in critical reviews and certain other noncommercial uses permitted by copyright law. For permission requests, contact the publisher, addressed "Attention: Permissions Coordinator," at the email address below.

ISBN: 978-1-959791-10-2 (Digital)
ISBN: 978-1-959791-11-9 (Paperback)
ISBN: 978-1-959791-12-6 (Hardcover)

Library of Congress Registration Number: Pending

This book is a work of fiction. Although inspired by real events, any references to historical events, real people, or real places are used fictitiously. Specific names, characters, places, and events are products of the author's imagination, and any resemblance to actual events or places or persons, living or dead, is entirely coincidental.

Edited by Suzanne Purvis
Continuity Edits by Kylie Maron-Vallorani
Cover, chapter and part page design by Katarina Prenda
Author photo by Ismael Fernandez

Improvisation News, LLC / IN Studios
Suite 5B
New York, NY 10031
https://thesavagebooks.com/
thesavagebooks@gmail.com

The
VICKIE CHRONICLES
BOOK 0

DARK TRIALS

I. SAVAGE

The Vickie Chronicles

Dive into the thrilling series prequel, *Dark Trials*, and be among the first to experience *Dark Masks* and *Dark Chains*—book one and two, available now on Amazon.

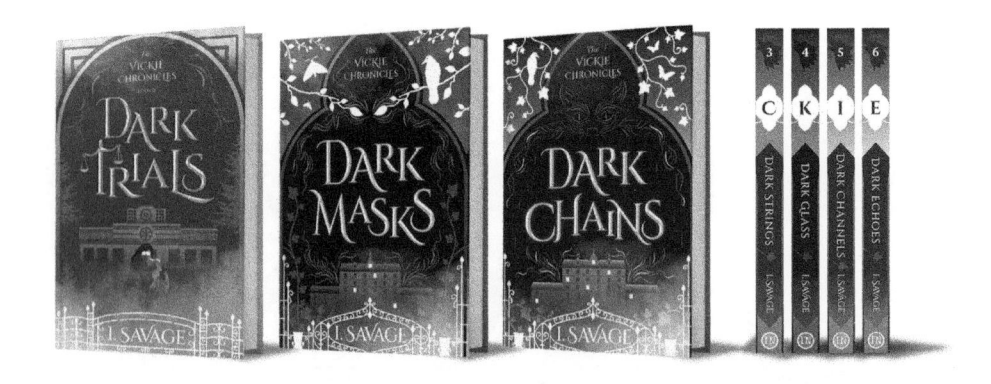

ORDER HERE

SCAN ME

DEDICATION

To Candy, my adopted, childhood dog

To Mozelle, my adopted grandma who gifted him to me

And to found families everywhere.

Trials and Temptations

Consider it pure joy, my brothers and sisters, whenever you face trials of many kinds, because you know that the testing of your faith produces perseverance. Let perseverance finish its work so that you may be mature and complete, not lacking anything.
James 2:1-4

Inspired by Real Events

TRIAL ONE

DARK KEY

CHAPTER 1
Suicide Blue

Queens, NY
1949
DASHER

Detective Max Dasher sits at his desk. A lazy ceiling fan stirs the hot summer air, and the smell of stale cigarettes, a testament to long nights and lost sleep, coats the walls. A black rotary phone, its cord tangled like Dasher's thoughts, waits for the next call.

The light from a green-shaded brass desk lamp shellacs the room and its crevices. There aren't any windows in the basement office of Suarez Enterprises, but Dasher doesn't need windows to know he's being watched.

A car full of goons has been following him the past three evenings, likely parked on the corner of what old-timers would call Lorraine Street. People from the neighborhood, like him, call it Linden Avenue on account of the trees that bloom with creamy white, sweet-smelling Linden blossoms, always swarming with bees that savor the nectar and transform it into white honey.

He knows every crack in the pavement, every brick and alley of this neighborhood, every whisper of the wind through the fire escapes. It's his beat, his turf, his home.

His schedule's no secret; neither is his mission. The Argentinians hired him to protect the building and the key with his life.

He pours Old Forester whiskey into a heavy, chipped, lowball glass. Gonna be a long night.

The basement entrance door creaks open. Could be the wind, but he knows better.

Clicking footsteps traverse the long hallway. Long strides, steady, light. Female.

He draws his gun and aims at the door. His heart pounds a rhythm that never quite settled since the war.

The footsteps stop. His door inches open.

First the shadow. Then her legs. And then, those suicide-blue eyes.

Marlena.

She steps into the room; her belted beige Burberry trench coat, slick with rain, clings to her figure. And her wind-tousled dirty-blonde hair hugs her delicate features.

She smiles at the sight of his cocked gun. It's a slow, deliberate curve of her lips, a predatory promise wrapped in velvet, which sends a shiver down his spine. The good kind of shiver, awakening memories he'd buried under layers of regret and whiskey.

"I see you were expecting me." Her seductive German accent slices through the fog of his thoughts.

His pulse thrums in his ears. He's not ready for this, for her. Not now, not ever. The years haven't dulled her effect on him. If anything, they've sharpened it, made her more dangerous.

He uncocks the gun and places it on his desk. Seeing her again, after so many years, stirs bittersweet thoughts. "So, Glotto sent his girl to do the dirty work." He picks up his glass of whiskey, swirling the amber liquid.

"I'm nobody's girl. You of all people should know that." She glides across the room. Her movements barely disturb the air.

He stands, walks to her, and an electrical storm whirls between them. As the inches close, he's unsure how his body will respond when he's next to her.

She undoes her coat. Her delicate red-tipped fingers dance along the buttons.

He extends a hand to take her trench coat and she turns in toward him, a practiced ritual. Her damp hair grazes his nose. Tickles.

He helps her out of the first sleeve, lingers in her scent—Guerlain's Shalimar. His lips are millimeters from the nape of her neck.

Men have auctioned their souls for less than these few seconds with her. A moment longer and he'd pay the price. A too-high price.

He's not strong. Never pretended to be. Just a man. And he's right back to who he was when he first met her. Heart throbbing. Palms sweating. Back on the front lines of their short romance.

She watches him over her shoulder. Wicked amusement in her eyes. She moves her purse into her opposite hand so he can slide off the other sleeve. Water droplets hit the floor.

He positions the coat on the coat rack by the door, next to his black fedora. They look good side by side. Like they belong.

"Been a long time, Detective Dasher."

All she has to do is wag a treat at him. Call his name. She trained him that way. Not a bad gig, from what he remembers, being her plaything. Not a reliable gig. No job security. He shakes off the returning fantasies. He's nobody's bone. Anymore.

Hard to turn his back on her, walk away, even the short distance to his desk. But he does. "I heard you were in town." He adjusts his tie, the fabric a deep-burgundy silk, and attempts to keep his voice even. Every part of him wants to believe she's here for him, but he knows better.

Her heels Morse code across the wooden floor, a message of remorse, longing, love, a message only for him. Not likely. She joins him at his desk. "And what else have you heard?" Her fingers brush the leather-bound notepad filled with his scribbles about Glotto, the man that ruined his life and his home.

"That Glotto put the fix on me." He taps on the desk, his eyes narrow, trying to squeeze her out of his mind. Too late for that.

"The joke's on Glotto. There's no fixing you." Her laugh is soft, musical.

"Makes two of us—unfixables." He doesn't laugh with her. Not his style.

She sits across from him; her black silk dress caresses her the way he wants to. Close. She always liked the finer things. And always found a way to get them, even during the war.

She fingers through the inside of her purse, and his hand instinctively moves to his gun.

She pulls out a cigarette, shows it to him, then brings it to her lips. She waits, an invitation in her eyes.

He slips his hand inside his jacket pocket and retrieves a silver cigarette case, monogrammed MCD. Maxwell Colton Dasher. A silver disk next to the matches glistens. He lights her cigarette, their faces close enough to feel each other's breath. The past and present collide in the flicker of the match flame.

She holds his hand, sucking in the fire.

He extinguishes the match flicker with a wave. "I came back for you. As soon as the war was over. I thought you were dead."

"What makes you so sure I'm not—dead." She releases his hand, and sits back into the creaky wooden chair.

"Guess I'm not surprised that you're still playing both sides. You were always good at that." He pours another glass of whiskey. The bitterness he feels is familiar, brings comfort. The bitterness of the whiskey and of their last missed encounter five years ago.

"That's a fault you have. You should know better. There's only one side I play." Her relentless, teasing eyes never leave his.

"Is that so, Ms. Waltz." He takes a sip, a soothing burn in his throat. The woman sitting before him is both a dream and a resurrected nightmare.

"That's not my name and you know it." Her voice is sharp, a knife's edge.

"It fits. You waltz in here and try to charm me. But I see Glotto's shadow one step behind you. Lingering like the scent of your fancy French perfume." He sets the glass down, the sound a final punctuation to his statement.

He refills his glass with a two-finger pour. "I'd offer you a drink, but I only have one glass."

"We've shared much more intimate things than a glass." She runs her finger up the side of the glass, gathering a meandering drop on her pinky, and tastes it. "But I prefer to keep a clear head when I'm with you."

Dasher retracts his body back into his seat. "The past always catches up, no matter how fast you run."

"You have it all in reverse. Glotto is a shadow like you said, but not mine or yours. He's the shadow of something bigger than us." She exhales a cloud of smoke through the side of her mouth. "And you and me, we're both hiding. You in this basement office and me, well, I'm hiding somewhere you'll never find me."

The detective sips, a distraction from her intoxicating pull. "You're playing a dangerous game."

"I'm playing an innocent game of smiling. Something you don't do very often." She caresses the edge of his oak desk.

"I don't mix business and pleasure. Especially on my face."

She glances at an open folder and he closes it, lifts a rock on top of papers eight inches high, tosses the folder on top, and returns the rock to its duties. A paperweight keeping things in place.

Her left leg slides over the right, the smooth silk of her stockings catching light. "You're wrong. I could tell by your face, the minute you saw me, this business meeting of ours would lead to pleasure—yours anyway." She flicks a sly smile.

He runs his thumb around the rim of his glass. "You've always been good with words. But those are ideas coming out of your mug. Just cause you say 'em don't make 'em true. And what business do we have?"

"Patience, Detective. Can't a girl enjoy her cigarette before we get into boring details?"

He notices the lipstick stain on her cigarette, a deep red. The small detail holds his attention. And the way she brings the cigarette to her lips, the slow exhale of smoke— mesmerizing. Every movement, a calculated seduction.

She glances at the rock, pinning the folders. "The rock on your desk. Where's it from?" Her hand traces its jagged edges.

"The Blue Grotto."

"The Blue Grotto in Capri? I know it well. What I wouldn't give to be somewhere warm on a cold and wet night like this."

"No. The Blue Grotto Bar off Linden Avenue. The rock's a souvenir from a bar fight." He remains stone-faced.

The muscles around her eyes ease. "I've thought of you. Wondered what became of the strong, idealistic, young American soldier I fell in love with."

"He never made it out of Germany." His voice is a low rumble.

She relaxes into the chair. "Then who is this handsome man in front of me? Detective Max Dasher? Is he like his pet rock? Silent. Heavy. Smashing people. Smashing hearts of lonely girls everywhere."

"I am who I am. Do what needs doing to get the job done. Smash those who cross me." His eyes bore into hers, searching for the answers, searching for questions, searching for the woman he loved.

"We're not so different. I am crystal, you are rock. Both from the underground. Hardened by life and time. Together maybe we can make some changes around here." She runs her fingers along the strap of her handbag.

"I'll leave the changes to the nuns and priests and do-gooders. I want justice. To take down Glotto. He's torn this town apart." The whiskey sloshes in turbulent waves when he raises his glass to his lips.

"And he's the reason you're not a cop anymore. A part-time private dick with a basement office. Playing security guard for a bunch of Argentinians." Her words sting, but ring accurate. Her flavor of truth has a way of hurting.

"Guess you know me after all." He sets down his glass with a decisive thud.

"And you think you can take down Glotto. Delusional as ever." Her gaze glides and grazes, like she's guarding against unseen threats.

"I thought you said idealistic."

"Same thing. And even if I could help you, what's in it for me? Besides a one-way trip six feet under." Marlena crosses her legs.

"For you? I'll work on my smile. And maybe take you somewhere warm." He squirms in his collared shirt and tie and squeezes out some breathing room around the neck with his finger.

"I've been everywhere warm. Nowhere new you can take me." She shakes her head; the sadness in her eyes deepens.

"Then I'll take you back somewhere you've been." His body relaxes and tenses all at once.

"I wish we could go back. The two of us. To how we were. I think we loved each other. In our way. But we were young." Smoke circles her and wafts over to him.

"Wasn't that long ago." His voice is rough, the pain refreshed.

Her knuckles whiten, her left hand tightening on the arm of the chair. "That's because you're measuring the years in time. I'm measuring in bruises."

"A lot of hard knocks for us both." He breathes in her smoke the way he wants to merge with all of her.

"Do you think you could love me again?" Her tone is vulnerable, a rare crack in her armor.

He turns the extinguished match in his fingers. "Who says I ever stopped? But, like you pointed out, I'm delusional."

"And like you said, I like to play dangerous games. Match made in heaven." Every word out of her mouth is like a dance, and her eyes swirl him into a whirlpool of memories, sweet and bitter.

"Match made in hell is more like it."

She finishes her cigarette and puts it out in an ashtray. She reaches in her purse, and he flinches for his gun—again.

"You can trust me." Her voice is consistent reassurance.

The way she moves, the way she looks at him—a siren call he knows he shouldn't answer. But he can't help himself. He never could resist her.

She slowly removes a pen and paper.

He relaxes, but his guard's still up.

She jots something on the paper and slides it to him. "Let's get down to business. I need you to perform an act."

"Is that so?" He reads the note, the words blurring in his mind.

"Need to get into a building."

His fingers tighten around the paper. "For Glotto?"

She looks under the desk and under her chair.

"What are you looking for?"

"Glotto. He's not here. No one's in this room but you and me, yet he's all you think about. Talk about. "

"What building is it you want to get into?"

Both her hands caress the arms of the chair. "This one."

"Mission accomplished." He folds the note, finds a home for it in his inside jacket pocket.

"You know what I mean. Word on the street is you're guarding a key to a basement vault with enough dirt on Glotto to put him away." She taps the arm of her chair like she's playing an instrument. The way she'd like to play him.

"The street has a big mouth. Tell Glotto he's not getting the key." He lifts his glass, takes a long sip.

She slides one leg over the other; the fabric of her dress gives up a rustle. "Glotto doesn't take no for an answer."

The floor creaks outside the door. She slips her hand inside her purse.

He grips the handle of his gun.

Gaze unflinching, her eyes hold his. "Trust me."

Relaxation embraces him and he nods.

Her hand hovers, hesitates.

1. SAVAGE

She flashes a broken smile and pulls out a gun, blue eyes both bright and bleak.

His hand twitches towards his own piece, but he knows he's at her mercy. She's always been faster, colder, more relentless.

The cold glint of metal she holds jolts him like a shot of bad bourbon. His mind races; a storm of memories and regrets get caught in his circling cigarette smoke. He braces for the familiar scent of gunpowder and blood, muddled with her fancy French perfume. "Marlena."

She fires three times, the smoke from the barrel curling around her like a serpent.

CHAPTER 2
The Burning Bloom

Marlena

Marlena stands in the hallway on the other side of Dasher's door. The silence from his office screams in her ears. The bitter scent of gunpowder on her hands, she tightens the belt on her coat, the silk lining cool against her still damp skin. Like crossing a one-way bridge, she made her choice, and so did Dasher.

The plan's set. She must manufacture a look of composed calm.

She risks a glance at her reflection in the large mirror hanging on the hallway wall. Nothing has changed in her appearance since she entered the building, but she's not the same.

Noodles's nefarious figure navigates near, a dark shape behind her in the mirror's murky reflection. His were the footsteps Dasher heard.

Dasher.

If only there had been another way.

Noodles's reflection is a jarring contrast to her effortless elegance. Barely out of his teens, yet already looking worn down by life. Skinny, greasy, slimy. A perfect minion for Glotto. His hair gleams, slicked back with too much Brillo creme.

She's always found him repulsive, a necessary evil in this dark game. The way he licks his lips nervously, the way he rubs his hands together like a sewer rat, causes creeping chills to cascade down her spine. But tonight, she needs him.

As if expecting danger to leap out, his beady eyes dart from nook to cranny.

She smooths her hair and ties a scarf around her head with practiced precision, the satin soft and luxurious. "You know what to do." Her fingers linger on the knot, ensuring it's just right. She walks through the outer basement door, the sound of her heels pinging.

Up a few steps to street level, the heavy, dark rain greets her. The city lights glisten like jewels, hers for the taking. She pulls her coat tighter, and steps onto Linden Avenue, every pore on high alert.

Rain cascades in heavy drops and creates a rhythmic drumbeat on the roof of a black luxury limousine. A 1949 Cadillac Series 75, parked in front of Suarez Enterprises, the Argentinians' shadow empire.

The driver opens the back door for her.

Inside, rich, supple leather seats, polished wood trim, and the faint scent of cigar smoke lingers.

Glotto, obese and bald, sits in a smug pool of arrogance, petting Mimi, his big-eyed, hairless Chinese Crested dog. The dog's eyes glisten like polished onyx, its delicate collar studded with tiny diamonds. Mimi curls up on Glotto's lap, burying her head into his side. The dog's tiny body trembles.

Glotto, his bulk obscene and out of place in the luxury car, is a monster, but a necessary one. Fear claws at Marlena's insides every time she sees him, but she masks it. He can never know the power he holds over her.

"Poor Mimi. Daddy's here. She hates thunderstorms." Glotto's voice is low, almost tender. He strokes his pet.

"It's done." Marlena's voice is even, but inside, her nerves pulse.

Glotto's eyes pin her like a butterfly on a card. "I heard the shots. Three. You really did hate him as much as me."

Her palm grips the silver cigarette case. "More."

Noodles climbs into the back, shaking off the rain. He wears his threadbare trench coat, too big for his frame, and a hat that swallows his head. His collar turned up, hiding the sharp angles of his face. She can almost smell the desperation on him, a mix of cheap aftershave and sweat. He looks even more nervous than usual. She hopes he doesn't break.

"How did she do?" Glotto's question is directed at Noodles, but his eyes are on her.

Noodles fiddles with the brim of his hat. "A real pro."

"I don't like being checked up on." She raises Dasher's silver cigarette case. Sleek, polished, engraved with intricate patterns.

Glotto grabs for it, but she pulls back her hand.

Glotto motions to Noodles, who throws a sack of cash at her.

She catches it, then hands over the cigarette case. Inside the case, there's a circular disk with grooves etched into its surface. The key Glotto sent her to kill for. The one Dasher unintentionally flashed when he lit her cigarette.

Glotto lifts it like a jewel. His eyes spark, captivated. "Those Argentinians never cease to amaze me. Marvelous."

Noodles extends a hand to give Mimi a rub, but the dog bares its tiny, sharp teeth.

Glotto throws the disk to Noodles, discarding the case to the side.

"Once you're in the vault room, destroy the files. In fact, Noodles, burn the entire building down." Glotto caresses the shiny fur of his pet. Glotto's sinister smile unfurls. "That's a message even those Argentinians can understand."

Minutes later, the building goes up in flames so intense the sky's rainy tears don't stand a chance. The onslaught of water droplets sizzles to nothing in the inferno.

Marlena thinks Glotto's plan is madness. Destroying the files is one thing, but burning down the entire building? It's reckless, a display of power that could draw unwanted attention. But Glotto thrives on chaos and control. She feels a pang of guilt about Dasher—brief, sharp, and quickly buried.

She's caught in a quicksand of her choices. The money is good, the protection better. But the price she pays gnaws, a gnawing that never fades.

Her gaze careens upward to the flames, the reflection flickering in the car window, a dance of destruction. She clutches the discarded cigarette case, a reminder of the price of betrayal.

The Suarez Enterprises sign warps and twists in the heat. Metal groans, smoke billows, and dark plumes blot out the stars. White blossoms from the nearby trees drop to the ground.

The fire's mesmerizing, a violent ballet of destruction. She knows Glotto is watching her, studying her reactions. She keeps her face impassive, a technique she's perfected. She's learned to hide her fear, her doubts, her humanity.

Her thoughts drift to the future, uncertain and perilous. Every step she takes is a gamble, every decision a potential pitfall. But she's survived this long, and she'll keep surviving. She has to. The Linden tree outside the building sparks into flames, sending its blossoms flitting through the circling wind.

She toughens up. Regret is a waste of time. Her choices are written in ink. The journey's a murky trail, but her life primed her for it.

DAY ONE

CHAPTER 3
The Great Detectives

1998
6:00 a.m.
VICKIE

I'm parked in Nona's back room, cross-legged on a cozy, faded floral armchair. Cushions sag from when Papa Bartolucci was alive; Pop-Pop was my name for him. This room was his escape hatch. Now it's mine. The worn fabric cradles me like a hug from an oversized stuffed animal. The orange-and-brown afghan wrapped around me completes the cozy embrace.

My focus fixes on the hulking 1990s stereo, a JVC beast with dual cassette decks and speakers big enough to rattle the windows. Worn buttons, flickering digital display, it reliably belts tunes like a champ. The cassette spins, the dramatic music swells, and the male radio announcer's voice kicks in. "Tune in next week for another episode of *The Great Detectives*, inspired by the series of books written by M. Dasher."

I blew through two episodes this morning. Dying to know what the deal is with that weird key and why Marlena killed Dasher.

"Vickie, come say hi to your uncle Aldo." Ma's voice completes my reentry into reality. Almost forgot it's a school day. Tried to forget anyway. Such is life for a twelve-year-old, un-emancipated minor.

I eject the cassette, and click it back into its case.

Walking down the hall into the living room with the afghan around my shoulders; the smell of Nona's baked bread is its own afghan for my heart.

Nona sits in her rocking chair with a scrapbook and boxes of old photos around her, a gentle smile on her face as she flips through the memories.

Uncle Aldo kisses Nona on the cheek, sets his cop hat on the doily-covered coffee table. "Sorry I'm late." He sips from his mug. "Good coffee, Ma."

Uncle Aldo is a small mountain, broad shoulders and sturdy frame bulging at the belt, a testament to years on the force, junk food at late-night stakeouts, and Italian family dinners. His hair's now more salt than pepper, but his eyes remain sharp, observant, and always looking out for us.

"Morning, Uncle Aldo." My voice is groggy.

"Morning, kiddo." He adjusts his uniform, smoothes out a wrinkle.

Ma, with her puffy hair, wears her pink waitress outfit; the frilly matching apron sits on the couch next to Nona. "Thanks again for letting Vickie stay over, Ma. Hopefully, I won't have so many late shifts next week."

"I told you I can stay by myself." I pull the afghan tighter around my shoulders. "I'm not a baby. I've handled things on my own plenty of times."

"Then how would I get to spend quality time with my granddaughter?" Nona positions a photo into the scrapbook, her hands steady and precise.

Uncle Aldo plops in the recliner with the newspaper. "Was that *The Great Detectives* you were listening to?"

"Yeah." I sit down beside Nona. She adjusts her glasses, squints at a faded photo. "Found those cassette tapes in the back of the closet in a box of old photos." She looks over the rim of her glasses at Uncle Aldo. "Remember when we gave them to you for your birthday a few years back?"

Uncle Aldo looks up from the paper. "Yeah. Those brought back lots of memories of when we would gather around the radio, you, me, and Pa, and listen to all kinds of shows. How old was I?"

Nona flattens the plastic sleeve over the photos situated on the pages of the scrapbook. "Five, maybe six, I think. This is how we learned English. By listening to the radio."

1. SAVAGE

"*The Great Detectives* was my favorite because it was based on locations right here in Queens. And they said the writer was a woman. But that didn't come out until years later. I never believed it, though." Uncle Aldo's foot taps on the decorative rug, a Persian pattern worn thin in spots from decades of footsteps.

"Why couldn't the writer have been a woman?" Ma folds her apron and places it on the arm of the couch where it's less likely to get mussed.

"Yeah, why's that?" I shuffle through a stack of photos so old I don't recognize anyone.

Uncle Aldo folds to a new section of the paper. "The series was gritty. And you never heard of women writers back then telling stories like that."

"Stories like what?" Ma prods, grasping for a family photo, sipping from the pink coffee cup she always drinks from.

"Macho. Detective Dasher. World War II. You can learn a lot of history from those stories," he says.

Nona's eyes are their own history lesson waiting to happen. "Real history is not all wine and roses and happy endings. Not for us in Italy. 1941." She removes her glasses like she means business. "Police everywhere checking our identity. You could see what was coming. These home invaders. This is why we leave. Your grandfather and me, may he rest in peace."

It's hard to believe she left everything behind; her neighborhood, her home, her friends. The kind of strength Nona has. Her voice carries the weight of stories passed down and memories kept alive.

Nona holds my gaze. "Can you imagine, Vickie? Just picking up and leaving. You should never know such pain. Leaving to stay safe."

Ma squeezes Nona's hand.

Nona lays a photo of Papa Bartolucci in the album. "So handsome. I wish you knew him then. Free spirit like you, Rosie."

Ma lights up like a little girl at the nickname Nona uses for her — Rosie.

"Your father was changed man after we leave home. Drank to drown memories. In a way, Nazis killed him." Nona stands and twists the position of a potted plant to catch the changing light.

"Better to look ahead and not back." Ma sips from her cup of coffee.

"No. We must remember. Always." Nona's seated again and back to stroking the pages of the scrapbook.

"But you said being forced to leave home's what changed Papa. Wouldn't remembering make things worse? " Ma sinks back into the couch cushion.

Nona rubs her own hands together in a comforting massage. "Your father didn't lose himself because he remembered. He lost part of himself because he tried to forget. The world needs more scrapbooks. More reminders."

I feel my face scrunch. "I always thought you loved Queens, Nona."

"When we move here. Some things nice. Some not so nice. Families here from similar areas of Turin. Nice. Neighborhood full of crime and gangs. Not so nice."

Uncle Aldo and Ma both agree with a nod.

"And outside the neighborhood we were called things. WOP. Your grandfather, may he rest in peace, was beat up for being Italian." Nona runs her fingers over a photo of a much younger Papa. "Make fun of our accent. Some of our friends never learn to speak English. Afraid to try." Both Nona's hands tremble into fists. "I would go to grocery and ask for milk and eggs. And they would throw the money at me. My money not as good as theirs. Same money. But we had this apartment. We had each other. We play cards together. Share stories."

Uncle Aldo laughs, grips the La-Z-Boy lever, pulls, and sends himself shooting backward. "Ma used to do the laundry with ladies in the neighborhood in washtubs behind the apartment building. One time, me and Luigi had to undress and hide in the back room of the apartment."

Nona's laugh bubbles like boiling pasta. "Cause your uncle only had one pair of clothes. He was filthy, what he run around in. And Aldo hated baths."

"Some things never change," Ma teases, folding Nona's glasses, sitting between them, rescuing them from a descent in between the cushions.

"Get outta here. I was as fresh as a summer breeze. Always." Uncle Aldo puts the paper aside.

I get up, pull my backpack onto one shoulder—that's how the cool kids wear it. "Better get going."

"Isn't it a little early for school?" Uncle Aldo glances at Nona's cuckoo clock—6:10 a.m.

"You know me. I like to get settled." I shift my lopsided shoulder and thrust my other arm into the strap; the backpack is now square on my back. Much more comfortable. I don't care what the cool kids do.

"No breakfast?" Ma rises, both hands around her coffee cup.

"I ate," I lie, and give each sleeve of my sweater a tug.

"Make sure you've got snacks in your bookbag. Always carry snacks." Nona's voice is soft but firm.

Leaving Nona's feels like stepping out of a safe haven. Detention waits for me at school. But I'm not ready to face that yet. There's a pit stop I need to make.

CHAPTER 4
Syrup and Sass

The morning creeps across the windows of Sal's Diner. My pit stop. I hop onto the round red stool and rotate — a 360 spin. The regulars are like the hands of a clock, ticking away their mornings in their seats. And the staff's as predictable. Two waitresses, Vina and Geraldine, and the owner, Sal, are on duty. Ma's working the lunch shift. Won't be in until later.

Vina reminds me of Sal's milkshakes, a sweet kind of ditzy, mostly air. Geraldine, on the other hand, is a full serving of pancakes, syrup, and sass. And Sal's that grumpy grandfather you like to needle just for kicks.

People come to Sal's Diner for the same reason they watch a rerun on TV: same script, familiar characters, no surprises.

But today feels different. Maybe it's me. Maybe it's the way the light hits the linoleum, making everything look sharper, more real. Or maybe change is in the air, masquerading as the scent of bacon and coffee, my favorite blue-collar cologne.

Vina sorts through the customer suggestion box a couple seats down from me. Sal sweats over a grill, slides orders through the short-order window to the kitchen.

Geraldine's eyes twinkle like Texas stars on the other side of the counter. "What can I get you, shug? Usual?" Her trailing twang tickles my ears.

1. SAVAGE

"Make it a double." I tap a restless rhythm on the counter.

Geraldine wraps her hand around a glass faster than a quick-draw gun battle. "Straight up or on the rocks?"

I lemon twist my head. "What do you think?"

She winks, screws the cap off the milk jug. "Straight up." She gurgles the milk into the glass, gives it three squirts of chocolate syrup, a stir, and sets it in front of me.

"Detention again?" Sal's voice, a rough rumble, reaches me from the pass-through window.

"All week." I stab my straw into the glass of chocolate milk.

Sal flips a pancake; his spatula clinks against the griddle. "What's wrong with those teachers?".

Geraldine leans on the counter, taps her pen against the order pad. "What did they get you for this time? Fighting?"

I swirl the straw, watching the chocolate whirlpool. "Wasn't much of a fight."

Sal slides a plate of pancakes onto the pass-through ledge. "That a girl."

Geraldine's laugh is light, but her eyes are serious. "It's all right to fight when you have to, but a lady's also got to know how to talk her way out of things."

"School's full of bullies. I've got seven fifth-graders under my protection." I tear the straw wrapper into little pieces.

A rare smile twitches Sal's lips. "Kid's either gonna be a mobster or a cop."

Geraldine pops the gum she chews. "Don't limit your options. You're young enough to try both."

Vina still sorts through the suggestion box, but then looks up at me. "Geraldine's kidding. What do you mean they're under your protection?"

I loop-de-loop my eyes. "I'm not a bully, but I'm built like one. I'm leveraging my assets. Watching out for the runts." I tear the paper from my straw into pieces.

Geraldine pats her puffy hair. "I understand. I developed early, too, but in different spots." She slaps her hips. "I've been leveraging my assets ever since."

"If your mouth is one of your assets — it's over-leveraged." The sound of Sal's laugh is like gravel underfoot.

"Shove it, Sal." Geraldine tosses a dish towel over her shoulder and delivers my pancakes to me. "Does your mother know about detention?"

"No. She gets stressed out." I arrange the little pieces of paper into a nonsensical pattern. "So I'm handling it. What are you working on, Vina?" My attempt to change the subject.

Vina doesn't look up. "Customer suggestion box."

Geraldine dips her head toward Vina. "Any good ones, Vina?"

Vina squints at a slip of paper. "No more cheap toilet paper."

Geraldine claps her hands. "You hear that, Sal? No more one-ply. The customers are complaining. You know what they say, happy wipe, happy life."

Sal throws a sausage patty into the sizzling grill grease. "Paper products won't make you happy."

"My ass would be a lot happier serving this slop if it wasn't chapped because you're trying to save a penny." Geraldine takes a pen from her apron and writes something on a slip of paper.

An elderly woman alone in a booth sits reading the newspaper. "I'd be happy with another cup of coffee," she says.

"Be right with you, Marge." Geraldine checks the industrial coffee maker, gives it a couple whacks on the side to speed up the brewing process.

Sal checks the order tickets pinned up above the griddle. "Besides, one-ply is a cost savings I can apply to the quality in other areas."

Geraldine and Vina's eyes meet in a silent chitchat.

"Like where?" Geraldine plants her hand on her hip like a flag on the moon.

"The cuisine." Sal flips a charred sausage patty, and waves away the smoke .

Geraldine's and Vina's laughs spritz like a sprinkler.

"They can't say you don't have a sense of humor, Sal." Geraldine wipes the counter with her wet rag.

"I'm getting too old for this abuse. I need to retire." Sal places an order in the window and balls up the finished ticket. Vina grabs the plates and delivers them to a table near the back.

I glance back at the elderly woman alone in a booth, reading a newspaper. "I've seen her in here every day for the past couple weeks."

Geraldine's gaze trails mine. "Marge?" Geraldine grabs the coffee pot. "From out of town. Her husband died. She's here to clear out their old apartment. Feel sorry for her. Be right back. Gotta get that tough old goat some coffee. And maybe throw some more suggestions in the box." Geraldine walks around the counter, fills Marge's cup, and tosses a piece of paper into the suggestion box on her way back.

I whirl around to follow Geraldine. "The toilet paper suggestion was from you, wasn't it?"

Geraldine elbows me in the shoulder. "I love seeing Sal worked up." She heads to the back section. "Have a good day, sweetie."

I slide off the stool; my sneakers hit the floor with a synchronized thud.

"Hey, short stuff. Next time, if you beat somebody up, try not to get caught." Sal's gruff voice follows me to the door.

My grin leaps over my shoulder. "You got it, Sal."

CHAPTER 5
Italian Vampires

I stroll down the street, passing an abandoned lot on my way to school. It's fenced off with eight-foot-tall green plywood, a small window cut out in the middle. I peek through the manmade peephole. Inside, the overgrown weeds and wildflowers reclaim the space like nature's rebellion. It's almost beautiful in a forgotten, scrappy kind of way.

Two shifty guys lean against the fence that lines the sidewalk, puffing on cigarettes, darting their eyes, looking for trouble. I'm an island, isolated from their shady schemes.

A familiar rattling sound, the low hum of a car engine slowing, approaches. Uncle Aldo's police car pulls up, the window sliding down with a smooth buzz. "Get in, kid. I'll give you a lift."

I adjust the strap of my backpack. "School's only a few blocks away."

"Best not to risk it. Don't want you to get detention for being late to detention." He grips the steering wheel. "Don't make me turn on the siren and embarrass you."

I climb into the passenger seat, toss my backpack onto the floor—the seat leather is cool and comforting. "How'd you know about detention?" I tug at the seat belt, click it into place.

Uncle Aldo twists the rearview mirror. "I'm a cop. I know things. But more than that, I'm your uncle, and I know you."

A small smile breaks on my face.

His gaze narrows to the shifty guys. "I'm going to have the station post a license checkpoint for a couple nights. Don't like the look of those guys." He watches them in the rearview mirror. "So, you like to get to school early to settle in, huh? You shouldn't lie to your mother."

"That wasn't a lie." I pick at a loose thread on my backpack strap.

"Also wasn't the truth."

I fiddle with the seat belt buckle. "I didn't mean to hide it. But you know Ma. She's been doing so good and she's been so happy with the new job. I don't want to wreck it."

"Well, I'd be lying if I didn't 'fess up that I had detention a time or two when I was in school." Uncle Aldo's eyes soften. "When I was a boy, they made you beat the chalk dust out of erasers. What do they have you doing?"

"Scraping gum from under the desks." I gaze out the window, but see Uncle Aldo reflected in the glass.

He wrinkles his nose. "That's disgusting."

"Not really. Most of it's mine." I snicker at my own joke.

Uncle Aldo rubs the back of his neck. "It's no secret this isn't the best neighborhood, but that doesn't mean your surroundings have to seep into you."

"I know that." I pick up my backpack and put it in my lap, so I get out as fast as possible.

"A lot of people leave before it gets into them."

"You stayed." I challenge him with a stare.

"Yeah, well, I'm made of steel. Like Superman." He gives me a soft jab in the shoulder. "Kidding. But there's only one way to protect yourself. Want to know the secret?"

I lift my shoulders.

He sweeps the air with an open palm. "Where's the enthusiasm?"

"What do you want, a pep rally?" My tone is as dry as a desert.

"I do the jokes. This family's only got room for one comedian. Capiche?" He ruffles my hair.

I'm not the kind of girl that's afraid my hair's gonna get messed up. Some days I forget to comb it. Still, I swat his hand away. "Capiche."

"So, here's the secret. Do something with your life. Wards off all the neighborhood vampires like garlic."

"It's an Italian neighborhood. Garlic would be like a dinner bell." I lock my arms across my body.

"How'd I end up with such a smart-aleck for a niece?"

"Apple doesn't fall far from the shopping cart." I nestle my elbow on the armrest.

"Guess so. Good talk." He pats the steering wheel.

"Good talk. Mind dropping me off here?" I point to the curb.

"Two blocks from school?"

"It's the cop car. You'll ruin my reputation."

Uncle Aldo pulls over. "Didn't you hear anything I said?"

I hop out.

"Hey, kid. I'm proud of you." He rests his arm on the open window.

"For what?" I bend so I can meet him eye to eye.

"For being Vickie Bartolucci." He salutes me.

"Thanks, Uncle Aldo." I salute back.

CHAPTER 6
Family Matters

ROSEMARY

Rosemary bursts into Sal's Diner and is hit with the lunch rush like a bug splatting against the windshield. She throws her purse down behind the register and scans the room.

Marge always claims her lunch table at noon and she's halfway through her pastrami on rye, which means Rosemary is at least twenty minutes late. She grabs her apron and ties it tight. "Sorry. The bus—"

Geraldine shoves a coffee pot into Rosemary's hand. "I did my best to cover for you, but we're slammed. Sal's furious."

"Thanks, Geraldine. I owe you one." Rosemary hides the panic in her gut. She needs this job. Rent's due, gotta keep it together.

Geraldine's all business, pointing to the chaos. "Move through section A and top off everyone's coffee. Then check on the large table in the back. Mr. Handsome has been asking for you."

Rosemary grips the coffee pot, weaves through the tables, fills cups with a shaky hand. She sneaks a glance at Sal through the order window. He's got that stern look, the one that makes her stomach twist. He's tough but fair. Mess up too many times, though, and he'll find someone else. Can't let that happen. Not now. She reaches Marge. "More coffee, Marge?"

The older woman offers a polite smile. "Please, dear."

Rosemary steps to the large table in the back; her nerves buzz.

Niko's eyes are a dark cup of joe that hold hers. Her heart's wild and quiet. Mr. Handsome is a nickname that fits, but she's done with men. Time to focus on her new job.

"Hey, Rosebud." Niko's voice is smooth. Too smooth.

Rosemary's cheeks heat, but she stays icebox cool. "How's everyone doing?"

Niko's hand settles on the table like a large cat curling up in the sun. "Much better now that you're here. Thought you were sick or something."

"Just one of those days." She swirls the pot, only a half cup left. "What can I get you, boys? More wine? More coffee?"

"Top it off." Niko's thick and short sidekick, Frank, slides his cup over. She holds up the pot. "Not much left. You know what? There's a fresh pot brewing. Be right back." She saunters away, feels their eyes on her, but doesn't turn back.

NIKO

Niko sits at the head of their usual table for six in the back of Sal's Diner with Frank on his right. Four hired guns, Mickey, Dom, Carmine, and Victor, are clustered at the other end of the table, deep in their own conversation. The group's on their second lunchtime bottle of wine. Frank's only having coffee. He never drinks before five o'clock. Like that makes him more self-controlled, more superior than the rest of them.

Niko twists the gold watch on his wrist, his eyes locked on Rosemary, who's grabbing a fresh pot of coffee behind the counter. The watch carries a weight, heavy with memories. It belonged to Pops—Three Fingers, they called him, after he lost a couple digits taking down one of the most notorious capos in Queens. Pops always wore that watch on his mangled hand, a constant reminder to everyone who was boss and what he was willing to do to keep it that way. Niko swirls the wine in his glass, hearing Pops' voice in his head, telling him to be a man, to take what's his.

"Watch looks good on you." Frank butters a piece of bread.

"Had to let it out a little. Pops was skinny his whole life right until the end."

The watch is more than just a piece of metal. It's Pops's legacy, a reminder to stay on top, to never let his guard down. And to do whatever it takes to get the job done, even if it costs a few fingers.

Frank sips from his water glass. "Thanks for giving Mickey a chance."

Mickey's middle-aged, too much hair grease, and he's not gonna win any awards for his brainpower. But guys like Mickey got their uses. Easy to control, 'cause they're so dumb. And that's what Niko needs with the Argentians moving in on his territory, guys who follow orders without a side of questions.

Niko cuts into his steak; the knife slices clean. "You enjoying your chicken parm down there, Mickey?"

"Yeah, boss." Mickey twirls spaghetti on his fork, a Coney Island Ferris wheel of pasta.

"Hear that everybody? Boss. Finally some respect." Niko wipes his mouth with his napkin. "I like that. How about you, Frank? You think you can show me the same respect you showed my father?" Niko eyes Rosemary with his side vision.

Rosemary's got a spark in her that he thinks Pops woulda liked. Doesn't fall over herself trying to get to Niko and what he's got. He needs someone like that.

Frank leans forward, his fork poised over his plate. "Of course I respect you, Niko."

Niko reclines back in his chair. "That's funny. 'Cause I heard you been saying things."

Frank's always running his mouth. Thinks he knows everything.

He was loyal to Pops. But that doesn't mean he'll show Niko the same courtesy. Niko's got to keep his guard up now more than ever. Pops always said, "Keep your friends close, and your enemies in the family."

Frank pushes his plate aside. "We're cousins. Family. I respect you. Just gotta get used to you at the head of the table."

"Good, 'cause I thought you was trying to show your mushroom." Niko runs his finger around the rim of his glass. Frank's big everywhere, but nothing special below the belt. Niko knows from the literal pissing contests they had as kids.

Frank drags his plate back toward him and goes in for another bite of pasta. "You know me. If I got something to say or something to show, I put it in your face."

Niko's hand tightens around his wineglass. "Keep it to yourself. 'Cause nobody needs to see your baby-button mushroom."

Frank scoots his chair closer. "I'll be honest with you. This ain't the usual way. You don't become a capo before you do the grunt work. First you got to shovel shit."

Niko twists his cufflinks. He wasn't as interested in the family business as Frank. But Pops is dead and the torch is passed, like it or lump it. "I'll be honest with you: That little tongue you're wagging can get cut out at any time."

"I got a big tongue. And a big mushroom. You don't believe me, go ask your mother." Frank balls his napkin in his fist.

Niko tosses his fork on the table. "My mother? My mother is your aunt, stupid. That's why I let you get away with that mouth of yours. 'Cause you're so stupid you can't even sling an insult without hitting yourself in the face."

Rosemary approaches, meek as a mouse, fills Frank's coffee cup. Niko smiles down to his bones. His face feels as warm as the cup. She's the type of girl that's beautiful inside and out.

Frank folds his arms, a challenge in his eyes. "From cousin to cousin. Watch yourself. And don't get distracted. Transitions can be unsettling times."

Rosemary moves on to another table, a young couple done with their meal, arguing over who gets to pay.

Niko rubs his stubble, staring at Rosemary. "I got my eyes straight ahead."

Frank follows Niko's stare like a bloodhound on a scent. "I know where you got your focus. How many times that waitress got to turn you down before you take a hint. Trouble with you is you are quick to put all your eggs in a basket you're not even holding."

Niko raises his glass in a mock toast, his focus now fully on Frank. "Then let's talk business already. What kind of skill set does Mickey bring to the table?"

Frank takes a deliberate bite of his food, and chews slowly, then swallows. "We served some time together. He was in for pickpocketing and arson. But he's the right kind of desperate and just dumb enough so we can mold him how we like."

Niko turns to Mickey, calculating his prospects. "All right. That's what I was thinking. Hey, Mickey. You up for some work?"

Mickey pours a sugar packet down his throat. "Sure thing, boss."

Niko flicks a breadcrumb off the table. "I got about 200 pounds of Argentinian beef I need taken care of."

Rosemary's gaze brushes Niko from across the room, then jumps away like it got burned.

Mickey straightens his menu, still in front of him from when they ordered. "Don't worry, boss."

Frank removes a toothpick from the pocket of his jacket, twirls it between his fingers. "Mickey. You still got that truck with the special compartment in it? For large cargo?"

Mickey rubs his hands together like he's tryin' to start a fire. "Still got it."

"And you know where we dispose of the meat that's gone bad?" Niko crosses his arms, evaluating Mickey.

Mickey splits the meatball with his knife, juices spillin' like secrets. "Frank told me."

"All right. Show us what you got. Tonight. Frank'll give you details." Niko slicks his hair with his hand; his eyes linger on Rosemary.

"So, we'll touch base tonight." Frank pushes his chair back.

Niko stays seated.

"You coming?" Frank's tone is like he's telling Niko what he should do.

Rosemary's back with a soft shuffle of her shoes.

Niko tugs and tucks his shirt into his pants. "Nah. I'm going to stay for some—"

"Apple pie?" Rosemary refills the sugar packets on the table.

"You know me so well." Niko takes another sip of wine.

Frank buttons his suit jacket. "So, we'll touch base tonight, Don Juan."

"You see the kind of bullshit I put up with." Niko places his fork and knife on top of his plate, making it easier for her to remove.

Frank, Mickey, and the rest if the crew leave.

Rosemary clears plates, dropping them at a bussing station in the corner.

Niko's mom was a waitress, met his old man in a joint like this. Hard worker, always on her feet. He wonders if Rosemary's life is just as tough. Probably. She's got that same fire his mother had, the kind that keeps a family going. Makes his palms sweat just thinking about asking Rosemary out again. "You look especially beautiful today."

"I look the same as always. Same makeup. Same hair. Same uniform." She stacks plates.

"It's that inner glow you got." He places his elbows on the table, clasps his hands under his chin.

"I'll get you that apple pie. Two scoops of gelato on the side?" She stacks the water glasses.

"I have a confession to make." He fidgets with his watch. "I hate apple pie."

"You order it every day." She wipes her hands on her apron.

"It's just 'cause it gives me a chance to stick around and something to talk to you about. Our secret thing, like we know each other." He swirls a last swig of wine.

"A smooth talker like you doesn't need any help conversing." She gathers knives in one hand, spoons and forks in the other.

"You make me nervous." He tugs on each of his shirtsleeves.

"I make you nervous? You? What did your friend call you? Don Juan?" She wipes the table with a damp cloth.

"I feel more like a Don Zero with you. I know you're too good for me. But if you just give me a chance." His right leg shakes under the table.

"Look, I've got my mind on other things. I'm a mother." She clutches the top of her uniform.

"I know that. I've seen your kid. Cute. Smart mouth on her. But I respect that." He picks up a stray sugar packet and puts it back in the holder.

She retrieves a dinner napkin that fell to the floor. "And I'm still new at this job. Trying to get the hang of it."

"I get it."

"Thank you for understanding. So, no pie. Another glass of wine?" She grabs the house-wine carafe next to the bussing station.

"Sure." Niko slides his glass toward her.

She's close enough that he catches a whiff of her perfume, a subtle flower scent that makes his head spin. He clenches his jaw, fighting the urge to reach out and hold her hand. He's supposed to be smooth, in control, but she's got him all contorted inside.

She pours.

"Rosemary." Sal's voice booms from the kitchen.

Rosemary jumps, spilling wine on Niko's shirt.

Sal dings a little bell.

"I'm sorry." She uses the towel on her shoulder to dab at Niko's collar.

"Don't worry about it." Niko brushes her hand away.

"On your silk shirt." She keeps dabbing at the stain.

"It's okay." He steadies her hands with his. Their eyes padlock onto one another.

She pulls away and walks to the pickup window.

He wants to ask her out again, but knows he'll get rejected. Being shot down six times would clip any man's wings.

But he doesn't care if he's a chump. There's something about her. Innocent. Kind. She's a fresh breeze in a city full of smog. She's got this strength, this resilience. Just like his ma.

Geraldine breezes by, balancing several plates on her arm.

"Rosemary. Five orders up here getting cold." Sal's voice is as sharp as a butcher's cleaver.

"Pipe down, Sal. We're taking care of it." Geraldine sets down plates at a nearby table.

Sal's spatula clanks against the grill. "Stop covering for her. If Rosemary can't cut it, she can't cut it."

Geraldine refills water glasses at the next table. "We just wanted to give the customers one last chance to change their minds about eating here."

Sal exits the kitchen into the dining area. "This is not your first warning, Rosemary. You're screwing up every time I turn around."

"I'll get better. I really want to learn. I'm all ears." Rosemary's now at the register, drops her order pad, bends to pick it up.

"That's the problem. You're all ears. But what about hands. And feet. And brains." Sal's spatula stabs the air for emphasis.

Niko approaches, ready for the action. "Hey. Sal. Who taught you manners? You don't talk to a lady like that."

Rosemary straightens her tickets in her pad. "Niko—"

"Sal, you can't tell me you never made a mistake? 'Cause I've tried your meatballs." Niko's face twists in a revolted display.

Geraldine throws her head back in a laugh. "He's got a point."

Rosemary's glance bounces between Sal and Niko like a nervous ball. "It's okay, Niko."

Niko claims the counter as his territory with his arm. "Maybe she needs better training. You ever thought of that, Sal?"

Sal's stern stance shows stubborn strength. "I'm cooking back there. And I got to put out her fires out here."

Niko's pops was a living myth. Everybody knew not to mess with him. He had respect, power, everything Niko's tryin' to get. Never backed down from a fight either. Always stood his ground. But Rosemary's watching. He can't get too rough. Has to use his soft touch. He puts a hand on Sal's shoulder. "I'd consider it a personal favor if you gave her one more shot."

Sal shrugs Niko's hand off. "With all due respect. My place. My rules."

Niko slings his arm around Sal and walks him over to the corner. "My family's been watching out for you and this place for years. Right? Just asking you to do me this one personal favor. All right?"

Sal sighs, then stomps over to the kitchen door. "One more chance. I'm too old for this. I've got to retire." He pushes through the swinging door.

"I can't believe you did that for me." Rosemary nervously twists a napkin. "All right. Yes."

"Yes, what?" Niko's eyelids stretch tight.

"I'll go out with you." Her voice is a quivering string tugging on his heart.

"Yeah?"

"Yeah."

"Tonight?"

She clicks her pen a few times. "It's girls' poker night."

"I didn't know you played poker."

"I don't. Not really. Me and the girls are learning."

"Then let me take you for a drink after." His finger grazes her arm as light as a moth's wing.

"I don't drink." Her hair obeys her smooth touch.

"How about Shirley Temples?" He frictions his hands together warming up in Rosemary's flame.

She writes her address on the back of a ticket and hands it to him. "Pick me up at nine."

"Deal." He tucks the ticket into his pocket.

Niko can't mess this up. He needs to be perfect for her. Pops would want him to impress. Maybe a new suit. Definitely a haircut. Gotta look like a winner. A man she can be proud to have on her arm. She deserves it.

CHAPTER 7
High Stakes and Heartaches

VICKIE

I'm in the living room, working on a puzzle, pieces scattered over the coffee table. Keeps me from worrying about Ma. When she's stressed about work or the bills or her love life, her thoughts go swervy and she forgets to do the basic things, like eating.

It's Wednesday evening. Girls' night. Vina, Geraldine, and Ma play a round of Texas Hold 'Em at the kitchen table. Vina's wearing a frilly pink dress with a little-girl lace ribbon in her hair. Geraldine's in her faded flannel shirt and jeans, her hair pulled back in a messy ponytail, with her cat-eye glasses. Ma's got on her pretty dress and extra makeup. She looks like a polished pearl in a pile of pebbles. All this to impress Niko, the guy from the diner, picking her up in a couple hours. Ma swore she'd take a break from men, but she's back for another round of dead-end dating.

I don't like him. He's got everyone fooled with that slime smile. But not me. And he's always hanging out with those thugs at Sal's. Ma deserves better.

Watching Ma, Vina, and Geraldine pretend to know how to play cards is funny. I'm waiting for them to notice you can see everyone's hand in the big mirror behind the couch. At least they know better than to play for real money.

Vina swigs from her beer bottle. "I have a terrible hand."

"You're not supposed to say that out loud." Ma squints at her cards.

Geraldine pushes a few chips into the pot. "Too late. Thanks for the tip, Vina. I raise you one."

Vina's holding her cards like they're made of gold. She's not bluffing, just doesn't know what she's doing, if her hand's good or bad. She looks at her cards and then at Geraldine. "I see your one. And I raise you two. And raise you one."

"You're raising against yourself? And I thought you said you had a terrible hand." Geraldine pushes her chair back. "I'm out. It's too easy. I like a challenge."

Vina grins, shows her cards. Two and a seven from different suits. One of the worst hands you can have, but Vina seems unaware, all smiles. Ignorance is happiness. She turns to Ma. "What've you got?"

"That's not how the game works." Ma shakes her head. "Maybe we should try blackjack?"

Geraldine gets up and opens the fridge, grabs another beer. "You sure you don't want one, Rosemary?"

"I'm fine with Diet Coke." Ma takes a sip through a big straw.

Geraldine uses the edge of the counter to crack the top off her beer bottle. "How anyone can work at Sal's without a nip here and there is a mystery to me."

"My father was a drinker." Ma's smile fades when she talks about Papa. As a grandfather, he was a good guy. But I never expected anything from him, so I was never disappointed. Ma's different. Full of hope even when it doesn't make sense. "All his binges always started with a nip. I'm a lot like him."

"I'm like that with cheesecake." Vina spins a poker chip on its side. "I make my slices extra thin, but I end up eating nine thin slices instead of one regular one."

"Vickie, you doing all right over there?" Ma's mellow murmur makes it to me.

"Making progress." I fit another piece into place. The left eye of a golden retriever.

"I've got a surprise. I got us each a lotto ticket." Vina waves four lotto tickets around like they're magic wands. "Jackpot's up to ten million."

"I wouldn't know what to do with all that money." Ma's eyes drift to the icebox like fridge magnets and land on the cosmetology flyer stuck to the door.

My heart aches for Ma's delayed dreams. She saves a little, but then she gets laid off or she gets distracted with a shiny new guy. Niko's only going to send her on another detour.

Vina fans herself with the colorful tickets. "I'd get a boat. And park it in Florida."

"You can't even swim." Geraldine's always cracking jokes, always up for a good time, always looking out for me and Ma.

"That's why I'd get a boat." Vina's different. She's unintentionally funny. Vina's golden heart glints with goodness.

Geraldine pours a bag of pretzels into a bowl. "I'd open my own restaurant."

"How about you, Rosemary?" Vina stacks her chips in little piles.

"I'd send Vickie to a better school, and start a college fund for her." Ma shifts in her seat.

"And what about your cosmetology license?" I shuffle through my puzzle pieces. Every piece is a tiny victory, a small win in a chaotic world. Finding the corner pieces first, like setting the boundaries of my life. It's funny how pieces that seem to fit perfectly don't, just like some people. Like Niko.

"Getting my license would be nice. Imagine me and Vickie both in school." Ma's hand rests on her heart. "But that's just a silly dream."

"Those are the best kind." Geraldine's eyes bridge to Ma's land of dreams delayed.

Ma's face lights up like she just found a hidden twenty-dollar bill in her old jeans whenever she talks about the Queens Institute of Cosmetology Arts. She wants to make people feel beautiful, and helping someone makes her feel beautiful and useful. I want that for her.

"What would you do if you had a winning ticket, Ms. Vickie?" Geraldine walks the pretzel bowl over to me and holds it out.

"I'd hire a body double so I didn't have to go to school anymore and get a platinum 7-Eleven card for unlimited Slurpees. And I'd help Ma get her cosmetology license." I grab a handful of pretzels.

"You've got a good head on your shoulders, kid." Geraldine's got that look like she's been through it all and come out tougher. She got Ma the job at the diner. She didn't ask, she told Sal to hire her. I think Sal's afraid of Geraldine or respects her, or both. "Want to play another hand of something?"

"I don't know." Ma flicks her eyes at the thrift store clock on the wall. The second hand jerks forward with each tick, like it's struggling to keep up. "My mind's somewhere else."

Geraldine gives Ma an elbow nudge. "I know what your mind is on." Ma's got that dreamy look, the one that spells trouble. Niko's a wrong number that won't hang up.

"Thanks for staying with Vickie until I get back, Geraldine." Ma glances at me and I glare back.

"I can take care of myself. I don't need a babysitter." I shove a twisty pretzel in my mouth and crunch.

"I'm the one that needs a babysitter. You're doing me a favor, kid." Geraldine's laugh is like a fistful of bang caps hitting concrete. "This is my third beer. Someone stop me."

Vina collects the cards into a neat pile. "Niko's so handsome, Rosemary."

"I know." Ma's voice is almost day-dreamy. "What am I doing? My track record isn't the best."

When it comes to men, Ma's always looking for diamonds in dumpsters. It's like watching a slow-motion tumble down the stairs, each bounce a new bruise.

Vina's arms are propped on the table; her palm cradles her chin. "I think he really likes you."

Ma's cheeks flush. "Makes my heart race. Never met a man like him."

"It's your body telling you to run. It's called stranger danger." I stretch my legs out. My left foot's going to sleep like Ma's brain.

Ma puts her head in her hands, crumpling like a tin can in an elephant stampede. "Vickie's right. My life's finally on track. A steady job. Vickie's doing better in school. Why do I need a man to mess it all up?"

"Especially a sneaky man." I snap another puzzle piece into place.

"What makes you say that, Vix?" Her eyes are full of hope, and it kills me to crush it.

"I've seen him at the diner, whispering to those friends of his like they're planning a big surprise party. And he smells like cigar smoke and trouble."

"That's my kind of man." Geraldine leans back and takes a long sip of beer. "Listen, life's a game just like poker. You can't sit down at the table and say you only want the aces. You never know what you're going to get. But if you're lucky, you get more hearts than clubs."

"Niko's a world-class joker." I earn a round of laughter.

CHAPTER 8
Drinks and Dreams

ROSEMARY

Rosemary sits across from Niko at the bar of The Velvet Lounge, a place with just enough polish to feel fancy without being uptight. The bar's got leather stools that don't squeak and a mirror wall lined with expensive-looking bottles. Soft jazz plays from the speakers, the kind of music that makes everything feel like it's gonna be all right. Rosemary's nervous, but she hides it well, focusing on the drink in front of her.

Niko's suit looks new, tailored. The dark fabric hugs him like it's afraid to let go. Not flashy, but quality. Every look from him is a tiny spark, lighting her up from the inside. He swirls the straw in his glass; his eyes never leave hers. "How's your Shirley Temple?"

"Good. Yours?" Rosemary traces the side of her glass with her long nails.

Niko savors a sip, watches her over the rim of the glass. "Top notch."

She's got this flutter in her chest, like she swallowed a bunch of butterflies. "Just because I'm not drinking doesn't mean you can't." She twirls the straw in her glass.

He's got that smile, the one that makes her forget her own name. Focus. She's got a job, a daughter, responsibilities.

Vickie's words echo in her head. Run. But there's something about him, something that makes her want to trust him, something that makes her want him to be different than the rest.

Niko spins his tiny umbrella between his fingers. "Who needs alcohol? When I'm with you I feel drunk. I still can't believe you're here with me. A nice girl like you."

"Come on. You're one of my nicest customers." Rosemary fingers trace the edges of the cocktail napkin under her drink.

Niko looks at her like she matters. Like she's more than a mother, a waitress, a screwup.

Niko fiddles with his shiny silver cufflinks. "Being nice to you is easy. But my job isn't something that everybody can handle. You know what I do?"

"I heard you talking in the diner." She jiggles her glass, the cubes clink together.

Niko slides his drink and body closer. "And you don't mind."

"It's not like I'm a vegetarian or something." She picks up a peanut from a bowl and examines it, avoiding his gaze. The nut feels rough in her fingers, like her daydreams when they hit reality. She wonders if taking a chance on him is smart or stupid, probably both. She's scared he'll see the mess underneath her makeup and smiles. But maybe it's what she needs. It's frightening to be seen, but it's also the best kind of thrill.

"There's more to my job than that." Niko swivels on his bar stool.

"Sounds important." She wipes a drop of condensation from her glass. Her thoughts slide.

A family business. She gets it. Rosemary's trying to build something for Vickie. Something better than what Rosemary had growing up. "Your family means a lot to you. I think that's noble. I've got a big family. I only have one sister and one brother, Mariucci and Aldo. My sister lives in Maine. But I've got lots of cousins. We're loud when we all get together." Rosemary rattles the ice in her glass. "I was nervous about tonight. I still am."

"Hope I didn't do anything to make you feel that way." Niko's hand slides across the bar, closer to hers. Her heart does a little flip, caught between anxiety and anticipation. She feels like she's standing on the edge, ready to jump.

"No, you didn't do anything. It's me. I don't really trust my judgment. Lots of bad decisions." She looks down, wishing she could smooth out her past mistakes with men like she does wrinkles in her dress.

"I've made a few of those type decisions." Niko's hand detours to the bowl of nuts. Cracks a pistachio from the bowl.

"Well, here's to making better choices." Rosemary raises her glass.

"I'll drink to that." He raises his glass and clinks hers. "Who is this Shirley Temple anyway? Is that a real person?" Niko's eyes sparkle like a pair of disco balls at Webster Hall.

Her giggle is a release valve of stress. "You don't know who Shirley Temple is? *The Little Princess, Bright Eyes, Curly Top*?"

"Sounds like I'm looking at Shirley Temple right now from that description." Niko's grin gleams, giving her a glimpse of his playful side.

"Those are movies she was in." Rosemary's cheeks burn; the warmth spreads through her. Every time she looks at Niko, she sees a chance, a chance to feel something more than just tired.

Maybe this is the start of something good and the end of a long string of bad luck.

MICKEY

Sitting behind the wheel of his truck, Mickey flicks on the radio and bops to "Gettin' Jiggy wit It." The truck's parked on a side street in Queens, shadows playing hide and seek with the streetlights. He's outside Swank's, the late-night dive where whispers and deals flow easier than the booze. The sidewalks are empty, littered with yesterday's news and a stray cat prowling for scraps. Overhead, the L train rattles by, a ghostly serpent slithering through the night. A neon sign flickers on a closed pawn shop, its promise of "CASH FOR GOLD" faded and worn. The air smells of rain on pavement and stale cigar smoke, a mix that clings to clothes. Mickey's eyes dart to the rearview mirror, watching, waiting.

His custom truck cost him a fortune at Dick's Chop Shop, but worth every dirty dime. The shop, a hole-in-the-wall joint near the docks, stinks of oil and broken dreams. It's a place where whispers linger and the past is buried beneath layers of grime.

The engine roars, all muscle and menace under the hood. Custom-built, no questions asked. A Frankenstein monster, cobbled together from hot parts from all around town. A cherry-red '97 Ford, the color like a candy apple, but with a bite. Tires from a Chevy, doors from a Dodge— each part a secret, a lie. Took a week to build, paid in cash and favors, a deal made under the hum of fluorescent lights.

And best of all, the secret compartment for large, dead cargo. Perfect for tonight's assignment. The compartment's hidden under the truck bed, a steel coffin lined with silence. Just like the ex-cons at Dick's promised. Cops never guess the compartment's there, hidden in plain sight.

Frank's taking a chance on him, putting in a word with Niko.

He met Frank in jail, a friendship forged behind bars from bad decisions. Mickey was the guy with the smokes, the one who knew how to get things done. Frank was the scrappy newcomer, hungry for a taste of the life. They traded stories and cigarettes, secrets whispered between cell bars. Jailhouse bonds are stronger than blood, tied with knots of desperation and need.

He looks at the shiny gold watch on his wrist. Niko's watch. Shouldn't have swiped it, but it's so shiny, pretty.

Impulse control. Got to remember to get some of that.

It's okay. Just can't flash it around Niko.

Focus.

On this job.

He takes a swig from the bottle of Jim Beam on the seat next to him and then caps it.

His gaze darts to the Persian carpet spread out in the middle of the deserted street. It's three a.m. Most bars are closed, but Swank's isn't a legal joint. His heart pounds a wild beat, echoing in the quiet. A weaselly laugh escapes.

A two-hundred-pound Argentinian guy stumbles out of the dive bar, heads for his car, a black '98 Mercury, sleek and shiny, built for speed and style. Mickey holds up a photo he's carrying and compares. It's the target.

Mickey's fingers clench the steering wheel, knuckles white as bones. Adrenaline spikes, setting fire to his nerves.

The guy stops right in the middle of the carpet. A man with broad shoulders and a gut to match. His eyes squint in confusion, like he's just realized he's the punchline to a bad joke. A gold chain glints at his neck, a flashy promise of status. Gotcha.

"Here we go." Mickey cranks the engine and slams the gas. The truck roars toward the guy. Like a mouse stuck to sticky paper, he doesn't move.

Surprise.

The impact is brutal. The Argentinian crumples. The truck jumps like a wild horse, bouncing over the body with a sickening thud. Mickey's thrown against the seat, the jolt rattling his teeth. He laughs again, a high-pitched squeal. Not over yet. He reverses to run over the guy a second time. The wheel jerks in his hands, fighting the violence of the impact. Tires thump over flesh and bone, the sound echoing in the still night. The cab shakes, a metal beast devouring its prey. Bones crunch, loud as a bag of chips.

Mickey jumps out. His heart sings, a twisted melody of triumph and terror.

Blood seeps through the carpet, a dark stain spreading like ink on paper. Mickey looks down at the lifeless eyes, wide open and staring at nothing. The guy's face is twisted, caught in a final moment of shock and fear. Mickey snatches the necklace and holds it up, examining it in the moonlight, then slips it in his pocket.

He lowers the back gate on the truck, rolls the body in the carpet, hands shaking in delight, then drags the bundle into the secret compartment, under the truck bed. Not easy.

Mickey climbs in the cab of the truck and drives.

He loves his job.

He's good at it.

Or at least not as bad at it as he is at normal jobs, the nine to five kind normal people do who live normal lives.

Frank gave him instructions for what to do next.

Drop off the body at the secret location.

A few minutes later, Mickey's truck approaches the block as instructed. The abandoned lot. Boarded up. But two cop cars are parked in front. A line of cars snakes by, the cops checking licenses, probably looking for drunks.

His wet palms slip on the wheel. He cups his mouth and smells his alcohol-soaked breath. No way he'll make it through the checkpoint.

Panic claws at his insides. The world narrows to a pinprick, closing in on him.

Just before his turn in the checkpoint line, panic seizes him. He floors the gas and the truck lurches onto the sidewalk, jumping the curb, tires screaming against the concrete.

Mickey checks the rearview mirror. One of the cops runs to his car. Red and blue lights flashing.

Mickey swerves around a corner. The truck lurches, bouncing over potholes. He ducks his head, trying to make himself smaller, invisible.

"Oh no, oh no. This is bad. Real bad." Mickey's voice rattles. He can't get caught. Can't go back to prison. Think. Every alley, every side street is a possible escape route. A couple blocks away and around the corner, he stops and presses a button, opening the back compartment. He climbs out and rolls the body, still in the carpet, onto a pile of trash bags, then drives away. Safe for now.

DAY TWO

THE GREAT DETECTIVES

CHAPTER 9
Slimy and Limp

1949

MARLENA

Marlena stands at the door of a rundown fourth-floor apartment in Queens. The hall walls, a faded beige, bleed blotches from decades of leaks. Floors creak like old bones, and the smell of boiled cabbage ferments in the air. A single flickering bulb casts jittery shadows.

She tightens her coat, the rain still dripping from its edges. Her burgundy scarf's snug around her loose blonde curls, protecting them from the damp. She glances over her shoulder, making sure she's alone, and knocks with her spare hand. Her purse is in the other. Locks click, and Noodles opens the door to a dim room.

"What took you so long?" Noodles scurries back to a small table set for two in the shoebox of a kitchen. He sits and hunches over a plate of spaghetti, sauce dribbling from his chin, staining his dingy undershirt.

"Had to make sure I wasn't tailed." Marlena closes the door. She notices the wear and tear of the apartment. The stained checkered tablecloth, the old stove, the mismatched chairs, all scream of a life lived on the margins. This isn't her world, but she's willing to step into it, use it, if it means getting what she wants. The stakes are high, and she can't afford to blink. "Anyone know about this place?"

"Nah, just us. Inherited it from my aunt, God rest her soul." Noodles waves a forkful of spaghetti. "I rent it to hookers when I'm short on dough."

She slips off her coat. Drapes it with care over a torn leather chair.

The sounds of a couple arguing on the street slide through the open window. "Charming place." She pulls the drapes closed, her purse still in her hand.

He grins, sucking a spaghetti strand through his teeth. "I don't make good decisions on an empty stomach. I love a steaming bowl of pasta. Bet you thought they call me Noodles on account of me being all skin and bones."

She removes the scarf on her head and places it on top of her coat. "No. I thought it was because you go slimy and limp when things get hot."

"It's 'cause I like psghetti." The way he pronounces the word revolts her. He slurps wine from a Mason jar glass. "And I haven't let you down yet. But can I count on *you*?"

She walks to the kitchenette. A hum from an old icebox vibrates the floor. "You can trust me." She places her purse on top of the fridge.

Marlena's come too far to let someone like Noodles mess things up. He's a rat, plain and simple. But tonight, he's her pet rat. She needs him to play his part, and play it well.

He points his fork at her. "Trust, huh? You throw that word around like you're Babe Ruth. Don't mean nothin'." He waves the fork like it's a magic wand. "Means nothin'."

She leans against the vibrating icebox, arms crossed. "Why so nervous?"

"I don't normally work with others. Don't pay to count on people who let you down. Once bitten, twice shy. Read that in my fortune cookie once." He wipes his mouth with a dishcloth.

"Who bit you?" His greasy hair, his nervous lip-licking, his nasal voice—makes her skin prickle.

"There's a list that goes around the frickin' block. You better not be gettin' in line."

He has no class.

No finesse.

Just like those Germans she knew during the War, climbing up from nothing, clutching at power with greasy fingers. They'd do anything to hold on to it, to feel like they mattered. And Noodles is no different. He thinks he's important because he's got a little bit of information, a little bit of leverage.

But she knows better. She knows he's just a pawn in a much bigger game she's playing. "Changing things up can be good." She picks up the bottle of wine, turning it in her hands. "Like switching from cheap wine to — less cheap wine."

"Change is change. It's people who are good or bad." He stands, takes the near-empty bottle of chianti from her. Gestures for her to have some.

Marlena shakes her head.

He swigs down the last swill from the bottle.

Every glance, every movement, every word she makes all has to be calculated, precise. She can't let him see her fear, or disgust. She has to stay calm, composed. The plan is in motion, and she needs him to play his part like a key in a lock. No room for mistakes, no room for error.

"So, where is he?" Marlena's gaze pans the room.

Noodles belches. Loud. "On the phone in the back. Guy's a control freak. Don't need him breathing in my ears. Looking down on me. But nobody's trying to scrape me off the bottom of their boot when they got a dirty job that needs doing."

Marlena watches him closely, every movement, every twitch. "We're all in this deep. Don't forget that."

Pacing footsteps echo from the back room. Her heart races. What happens next is crucial to her plan to take down Glotto.

1. SAVAGE

She glances at her reflection in the window. Lips losing their stain. Smudged eyeliner. No. Not eyeliner. Soot. From the fire.

The door to the back room of Noodles's apartment opens. The stakes are a tightrope, and one misstep could send Marlena for a swan dive.

CHAPTER 10
Trash and Treasure

VICKIE

I pause on the corner, a few yards from my morning pit stop at Sal's Diner. "What the frick?" Vina and Geraldine stand on the curb. They don't see me.

I press stop on my Walkman, a sleek silver Sony WM-FX290W, my sidekick since fifth grade, all beat up but still spinning. *The Great Detectives* cassette sputters to a standstill.

Vina's dark hair is in a tight bun, and Geraldine's big hair's a wild auburn sunrise. The color's wiped off Vina's and Geraldine's faces.

They stare at the trash heap, like they're in a zombie trance. Beside the trash cans, two legs, in a scissor pose, draped in dark slacks, stick out of a rolled-up fancy rug like a pig in a blanket. I remove my headphones.

"Maybe it's a mannequin." Vina wrings her hands out like a dishrag.

"Maybe it's not." Geraldine chews a wad of gum in slow motion.

Vina nudges Geraldine. "Poke him."

Geraldine shakes her head. "That's not in my job description."

I shove the headphones into my backpack. Possibilities ping-pong. Mannequin or dead guy, somebody's gotta do something. Looks like today I'm the somebody. And if I've learned anything from crime shows on TV and *The Great Detectives* cassette in my backpack, whatever I do, I can't disturb the body. Or the evidence.

I need gloves.

I stride behind Geraldine and Vina, an invisible wisp, and push through the diner's glass door. The familiar scent of frying bacon and freshly brewed coffee is the hug I needed.

I head straight to the kitchen, grab a pair of rubber gloves from the sink. No sign of Sal. He must be in the bathroom.

I head back outside to the curb. Geraldine and Vina see me.

"Vickie. Don't touch that." Geraldine takes a half-step forward, her hand out.

Too late. I bend down, and with my gloved hand, pull up the pant hem of the left leg protruding from the rug. Skin already pale.

Not a mannequin. A hairy calf. Reality smacks me in the stomach.

"It's a real guy. Dead." I strip off the gloves, toss them into the trash. "Got a quarter?"

Geraldine digs into her apron, holds out her hand.

I go to the nearby pay phone, slide the quarter into the slot—the metallic clink echoes. The pay phone's receiver is cold and heavy. The dial tone buzzes. I punch in the numbers. The operator's voice crackles to life, efficient and detached. "911, what's your emergency?"

I explain. Body. Trash. Sal's Diner.

The operator's tone shifts, professional urgency replacing calm. "Help is on the way."

Help for who? Not the dead guy. Whoever he is. Was.

I clunk the receiver into place.

Vina crumples the bottom of her apron with both fists. "Good thing we weren't busy this morning."

A thought flashes through my skull and I grin. "You think this is going to get me out of school today?"

Geraldine's backbone snaps straight. "I'd say finding a dead body in the trash should get you excused through third period at least. Come on inside. I'll pour you some chocolate milk. You earned it." The door slings shut behind Vina and Geraldine, but I spy a glimmer in the gutter and I detour to the curb, crouch down, close my fingers around a gold watch. Street juice drips from its polished surface. I shake it, hold it to my ear. Still ticking, probably wasn't there long.

I stand, polish it on the side of my sweats, and fasten it around my wrist. It dangles loose, but I like it.

No school. New watch. Day's turning around.

I head inside. My first glass of chocolate milk goes down smooth. Not even finished with my second when the police arrive, then the paramedics, and then the camera crews. News trucks swarm like buzzards circling for their last meal, the air thick with the hum of curiosity and opportunism.

I wander outside. Hard to ignore the excitement of the flashing lights.

Microphones thrust at my face. "You found the body?" one scrawny reporter asks.

"That's right." I squeeze the watch on my wrist.

"Say and spell your name for us," an even scrawnier, hungrier reporter says.

"Vickie Bartolucci. V-I-C-K-I-E."

Later that evening, me, Uncle Aldo, and Ma sit in silence. On the screen, my face looks back at me. The TV casts a blue glow in the dim living room of our apartment. My interview replays for the city to see. I'm famous.

Uncle Aldo's eyebrows ball up tight like fists. His voice breaks through the crackle of newscasters. "What the frick."

"That's what I said." I sink deeper into the couch.

He gets up and paces. "What were you thinking, Vickie?"

"You're always telling me to do something. So I did something."

Ma's eyes stretch to the ceiling. "So there's a murder and you touched a dead body."

"I had on gloves. So I wouldn't contaminate any evidence."

Ma's body shudders. "Gives me the heebie-jeebies. A murder right there where I work."

Uncle Aldo freezes, looks right at me. "If there was a murder, then there's a murderer out there. Who, by the way, knows your name, Vickie."

I stand. "I'm going to my room."

"Wait just a second." Ma's voice chases me down the hall.

"I've got homework." In my room, I dig the watch out of my bag. I put it there for safekeeping so it wouldn't fall off at school. I inspect it, turn it over. There's an inscription on the back I didn't see before. *For Niko, From Pops.*

Niko.

The shady guy from the diner who has the hots for, Ma? It's got to be the same guy. And his watch and a dead body inches from each other can't be a coincidence.

I turn the watch over, but drop it. The back pops off. Looks broken. I pick up the pieces. Not broken. A secret compartment. And some sort of round disk is inside. Feels heavy for its size. I run my fingers over the designs in the disk, ovals splintering from the center like a flower petal. If the watch hides secrets, then Niko probably has even bigger secrets to spill. Questions buzz in my brain. I've stumbled into something. A mystery worthy of Detective Dasher.

NIKO

Niko's mansion's decorated like the lobbies of the fancy hotels in Manhattan his pops used to show him. Italian leather couches, pristine and expensive, sit on either side of a glass coffee table that holds a crystal decanter half-filled with whiskey. A large TV flickers on one side of the room. Niko hovers by his large, ornate, never-been-lit fireplace. He's dressed in a dark, tailored suit, the kind that speaks of new money and his desire to impress and intimidate.

Frank flanks the chair that holds Mickey.

A bead of sweat rolls down Mickey's temple. Mickey's knee bounces a frantic dance, the rhythm of panic.

Niko lifts his crystal glass from the coffee table, swirls the whiskey, then takes a deliberate sip. Niko's mind swims in the amber liquid, the burn a familiar friend, pulling to mind old lessons.

Trust ain't easy.

He watches Mickey with the kind of calm that tells you something's about to break. Deep down, he knows how he handles the screwup is a test and Frank's watching. This isn't just business; it's personal, and personal means blood. "I trusted you, Frank."

Frank fiddles with a cigarette he's just lit, angles his head down, and glares at Mickey. "And I trusted you, Mickey."

Niko puts the glass down; the crystal clinks against the glass table. "You recommended this punk, Frank." Niko's frustration is a fire that feeds on broken promises. Every mistake's a chip in the armor, and Niko's feeling exposed. He's starting to question if loyalty means turning a blind eye or cutting ties before the ties strangle you.

Frank flicks the ashes off his cigarette.

Niko glares. "Where are your manners?"

Frank turns over a crystal glass and flicks ashes into it, then bends close to Mickey's ear. "You screwed up. And I told you exactly what to do."

Mickey's gaze darts, looking for an escape that he isn't going to find. He wipes his likely sweaty palms on his knees. "Cops were on the corner. I panicked."

Niko steps close. "And you stole my watch." Mickey's eyes are wide, pupils dilated like a junkie's. Niko can almost hear the tremor in Mickey's heartbeat.

Anger flashes across Frank's face. He takes a drag from his cigarette.

"Are you that stupid, Mickey? Give him back his watch. It's important. It was his father's."

Mickey shakes his head. "I don't have it."

Niko pulls back his jacket, reveals the grip of a sleek Beretta. He taps the gun. "You're lying. I know you took it." Niko feels the power in his hand, cold steel promising justice. Mickey's chin quivers. "I mean I had it. But I lost it."

"You lost—" The TV catches Niko's attention. Vickie and a reporter appear on the screen. "Hey, that's Rosemary's kid." Niko notices right away his gold watch on Vickie's wrist. Niko's gut twists, a sickening reminder of carelessness. Vickie's face, innocent yet defiant, stares back at him, complicating things.

Frank points to the TV. "Check out what's on her wrist. You see that?"

"We found your watch. That's good news, right?" Mickey's attempt at finding a silver lining in his otherwise dark predicament.

Niko inches closer to the screen. "No, not good news. My future girlfriend's kid found the watch that you stole and then lost, and she found the body you were supposed to dispose of." Niko's head spins. His future plans with Rosemary, already on shaky ground, are quaking. He's gotta act fast, stitch this wound before it bleeds out.

Frank rubs the back of his neck. "How you going to explain that to Rosemary?"

Niko tears his gaze from the TV, and focuses on Frank. "I'm not going to explain anything. You're going to fix this. And this time, do it yourself. You can start by cleaning up the mess." Frank's loyalty is on trial, and Niko's the judge, jury, and executioner. The stakes are high, the price of failure too steep to pay. This ain't just about saving face; it's about survival, about maintaining control in a world that's threatening to slip through his fingers.

Frank swallows hard, like he's trying to choke down a meatball the size of Staten Island. "What mess?"

Niko pulls the gun, pulls the trigger, and shoots Mickey in the head.

The sound of the gunshot shakes the crystal on the coffee table.

Niko lowers the gun. "That mess."

Splatters of blood slide down the TV screen across Vickie's face.

DAY THREE

CHAPTER 11
Encounters

VICKIE

Elbows resting on Sal's counter, I sip chocolate milk. The sweetness cuts the taste of mint toothpaste still in my mouth.

Uncle Aldo sits beside me, nursing a black coffee. "You only have three days of detention left."

"Yep." I swirl the creamy chocolate with a straw.

Uncle Aldo runs a hand through his salt-and-pepper hair like a gardener tending to a weathered lawn. "Listen. Sorry I was harsh yesterday. I worry about you, and your Ma too." He pats my shoulder with a gentle thud.

"I know." I trace a crack in the counter with my finger.

The vinyl seat squeaks beneath Uncle Aldo as he shifts positions and hopefully changes the subject. "How's *The Great Detectives*? Got to the twist yet?"

"I'm up to the part where Marlena's working with Noodles." I pat my backpack and the Walkman inside. "Got sidetracked with the real-life dead body."

Marge, the only other customer, gets up from her booth and walks to the coffee station near the register, cup in hand. "Where is everybody this morning?" She pours herself a coffee. "Sometimes a girl's got to take matters into her own hands." She looks at me, her eyes crinkling at the corners. "I saw you on the news. That was a brave thing you did."

I give a rebel shrug. "Some people think it was a stupid thing." I quick-glance at Uncle Aldo.

"Brave people need folks like your uncle in their lives. Keeps them alive." Marge glides back to her booth.

Uncle Aldo checks his watch, which makes me think about the watch I found. Maybe there's a way to get Uncle Aldo's help without mentioning the watch.

"I've got to get to work," he says. "You sure you don't want a ride?"

"I'm good." I unzip the front pocket of my backpack. "One more thing. Have you ever seen anything like this in one of your cases?" I present the disk I found in the watch.

"Where'd you get it?" He inspects it closely.

"Found it." I brace for more questions.

"Not sure what it is. Looks old though." He flips the disk in his hand like a coin and slides it back to me across the counter. "Have a good day, kiddo." He ruffles my hair. He leaves, and Niko and the guy that's always with him enter. They pass Uncle Aldo. Niko nods. Uncle Aldo glares like he's got history with Niko. Niko takes the seat beside me and his buddy sits a few down.

Marge's gaze flicks between us.

Niko picks up a napkin and wipes away Uncle Aldo's coffee ring. "You're a little young to be wandering around so early in the morning, Shorty." His voice is smooth like oil.

"You're a little old to be talking to a preteen girl, Shifty." I stir my milk. Niko's body is a confident ooze on his stool.

"You know who I am?"

"I know who you are." I pinch the straw. "The guy who's been sniffing around my mom."

"How about I call you Vickie, and you call me Niko."

"So, does your brain choke on all that hair grease? Shifty." My arms are a barrier, keeping his charm at bay.

"I would never guess a woman with such a lovely disposition as your mother would have a kid with so much attitude." Niko straightens the sugar packets in their container.

"Everybody's got baggage. Yours is probably a bunch of dead bodies in the trunk of your car." I don't buy his "let's be nice and friendly" act.

"I know what you're missing. A father figure. A strong hand. Some guidance. Some discipline. Can you imagine me talking to my father that way, Frank?" Niko angles his gaze to his buddy, Frank.

Frank chuckles. "It's this generation."

Niko leans closer to me. "Let me tell you something. Your mother and I are an item. And that's gonna be what it's gonna be. I'm here for a long time."

He thinks he can just muscle in and take over our lives. Not happening.

I crumple the straw wrapper. "Let me tell you something. Blood is thicker than hair grease. I stick to my mother like super glue. You'll slime right off after a good rinse."

His smile is a crooked path, leading nowhere good. "That's a lot of mouth for a ten-year-old."

"I'm twelve. And this is me holding back." I toss the crumpled paper onto the counter, like a pitcher throwing a curveball.

He flicks a stray menu, sending it into a spin. "Give your mother some space to breathe. She gave up everything for you. Let her be happy for a bit."

This guy's got the nerve of a cockroach scuttling out in broad daylight. Telling me what to go fetch. Ma could never be happy with him.

Ma rushes in, tying an apron around her waist. She spots Niko, Frank, and me. "Niko, what are you doing here? And Vickie, I thought you left for school." She doesn't know about detention.

Niko rises like a tsunami coming in. "I just wanted to see your pretty face. Start my day right."

"That's a sweet thing to say. But you can't just stop by. I'm working. And I'm not exactly Sal's favorite employee." Ma glances at the kitchen door.

"What's Sal gonna do?" Niko slinks closer to Ma.

"You're distracting me. I need to focus on my job." Ma irons her apron with her hand.

That's right. Focus on your job, Ma. And keep an eye on this creep.

"Then when can I see you?" Niko is close enough to practically kiss her.

Ma twists her focus to me. "That reminds me, Vickie. I'm working a double. So you're going to stay at Nona's tonight."

"I don't need a babysitter."

Niko brushes his hand through his slicked-back hair, flashing fangs like he's got it all figured out. "You got to eat, Rosemary. Why don't I pick you up and take you somewhere for your dinner break?"

This guy doesn't understand the word no.

Ma gives him a smile. I get it. She likes the attention. She deserves the attention. "All right. That sounds nice."

Wake up, Ma. This guy's not nice.

Niko tosses a couple of bills on the counter. "Nice chatting with you, Vickie. Chocolate milk's on me. And I'll see you later, Rosemary." He runs his hand along Ma's arm. "Come on, Frank."

I don't like the way he talks about my mom like he owns her. Makes it even more urgent I get to the bottom of what this guy's really about.

CHAPTER 12
Apple Pie

ROSEMARY

Rosemary sits at a table in the nicest restaurant she's been to in years, sitting across from the nicest guy she's been out with in years. A candle flickers in the middle of the table, throwing soft light on the Shirley Temple Niko had waiting for her.

Looking around at the fancy velvet seats, the big, shiny chandeliers, and the tables draped with starched linens, she feels outta place.

Her uniform's scratchy and stiff, a reminder of the double shift she's working. Her reflection in the window shows tired eyes and drooping shoulders. She's exhausted; her muscles ache from carrying trays and rushing around the diner. The day has been long, and all she really wants is to collapse in bed. But here she is, parked in a restaurant, dressed like a slob, with a man who doesn't seem to mind that she looks like yesterday's special. "I didn't know we were going to such a nice place."

"That smile of yours is classing up the joint. Just what it needed. What I needed." He's got a build that fills up the space. His dark hair's all slicked back, shining in the lights, and that smile of his has got a mix of charm and trouble. The way he sits, all confident and easy, makes heads turn, even in a place this fancy. The things he says and the way he looks at her make her feel like she's the only woman in Queens.

The room smells of rich Italian food, a comforting aroma that contrasts with her unease about the dinner rush waiting for her when she returns to Sal's. "Sorry, I don't have long." She tucks a loose strand of hair behind her ear.

"That's okay. Just a few minutes with you is worth it." He stretches across the table and takes her hand; his touch sends a warm burst through her, like when you sink into a tub of water after a long day. "I enjoyed my chat with your daughter. But I don't think she likes me very much."

"Sorry about that. It's hard for her. It's just been the two of us for so long." She doesn't want Vickie feeling left out.

She and Vickie have got each other's back, even when it's tough. Being a single mom's not easy, but she's gotta do right by Vickie, no matter what.

He squeezes her hand. Their palms linger together. There's a part of her that likes him, but her body's sending mixed signals, all stop and go. She's got butterflies, but it's hard to trust them. Her heart's racing, and she don't know if it's excitement or fear.

Every time he looks at her, he pulls her closer.

She wriggles her hand free, and picks up her water glass, takes a sip to calm her nerves. "That's why my job is so important. I want to get Vickie in a better school. Give her as much opportunity as I can."

He leans back in his chair. "My sister, Gina, works at a Catholic school, St. Hilda's School for Girls. It's real nice. Maybe I could pull some strings."

She's grateful for the offer, but it's too much, too soon. It's a nice gesture, though, and she doesn't get many of those. Still, she knows nothing comes free, especially not from guys. It feels like a lifeline, but she doesn't wanna grab it and get tangled with strings.

"I'm still a hundred double-shifts away from being able to afford private school." She sets the glass down and fiddles with the cloth napkin in her lap.

"They got scholarships. I could put in a word." He rotates his water glass a half a turn. His face lights up with a genuine smile, eyes crinkling at the corners like he means it.

"You'd do that for me and Vickie?" A hesitant hope flutters in her chest.

"Yeah. And if you were my girl, I'd protect you and Vickie with my life." There's a confidence in his look, like he's sure of what he wants, and it's her. His expression is open, no walls up, just honesty staring back at her. The intensity of his gaze makes her feel like he sees her, really sees her, and it's both terrifying and exhilarating. He extends his hand across the table again, his fingers brushing hers.

Strings. Everything comes with strings. Every offer, every nice word, there's always something attached. She's learned that the hard way, trusting too easy and getting stuck in promises.

"What if I don't want to be your girl?" Her heart races, because she wants to be his girl more and more, with each moment he looks at her. But she's tired of having men puppet her around.

Skepticism is hard to shake. She's lost count of the times she's been fooled by sweet talk and good looks. Her and Vickie's lives are a delicate balance, and she's scared to tip the scales again.

"I'd still protect you even if you weren't my girl. If you'd let me. I like you, Rosemary." He picks up his fork and plays with his salad.

Salads.

She didn't even notice the waiter bring them. What's Niko doing to her? Messing with her mind? What are these tingly feelings rising up, energizing her tired body? And what else besides the salads is she overlooking because his pull is so magnetic and distracting?

"I like you a lot. How much apple pie has a guy got to eat to prove it?" He unfolds his napkin in his lap.

"A girl doesn't need blush when you're around. I'm turning red over here." Despite her lingering doubts, she lets herself feel good, just for a moment. It's a reminder that she's more than just a mom and a waitress; she's a woman. She stares into the candle, its light dancing on the silverware and glasses. She decides to take a risk, reaching across the table and giving his hand a gentle squeeze, letting herself believe in the possibility of something good.

If Niko works out, maybe life gets a little easier. Maybe she and Vickie won't have to do it all alone.

Rosemary wipes away the double-shift sweat and grime on her forehead. No matter how hard she scrubs, there remains a layer of grease on the appliances closest to the kitchen in Sal's Diner.

She pushes through the swinging door to the kitchen.

Sal's out picking up supplies at the depot. A part-time cook sweats over a basket of fries and eight cheeseburgers cooked at various temperatures for a table in her section.

The cook's frazzled and doesn't speak much English; she dares not disturb him and heads to the large industrial fridge for the vat of french dressing. The one teenager at her eight-top table ordered a salad. French dressing. And of course, the smaller french dressing dispenser needs refilling.

The five-gallon container perches on the top shelf. On tiptoes, she claws at it, hoping to get a grip.

The vat tips, and the contents lava down her uniform and onto the floor. Someone, maybe her, didn't screw the top on tight. The orange dressing quickly soaks through the cheap fabric of her uniform.

"Oh, come on!" she yells, kicking the fridge in frustration.

Vina witnesses the catastrophe, grabs rags, and rushes over.

"Oh my god. I can't let Sal see me like this." Rosemary's on her knees, pushing the dressing into a big glob before it seeps under the refrigerator. "Sal's gonna blow an artery." She tugs at the soaked fabric, trying to peel it away from her skin. "I've got an extra uniform at home. If I hurry, I can be back in twenty minutes."

"Go. I'll clean up." Vina's got a heart as big as Niagara Falls.

Rosemary hurries out of the kitchen, snatches her purse from her locker, and scuttles through the front door.

She walk-jogs, her shoes slapping the pavement, leaving a faint trail of orange on the sidewalk.

She arrives at her 127-unit apartment building, an old red-brick structure held up by rusty fire escapes. The rickety elevator takes her to the fourth floor, and she sprints to her door, fumbles with her keys, breathing hard, hands shaking. She finally unlocks the door. Inside, her bedroom's a mess, clothes everywhere. She digs through her closet and fishes out the extra uniform.

Sounds of shuffling come from Vickie's room. But Vickie's at Ma's. Rosemary detours.

Vickie's bedroom door is cracked open, and the corner of a "Keep Out" sign Vickie made in third grade dangles. Maybe the sign made the sound she heard. She straightens it.

Without a sound, a large hand covers Rosemary's mouth and nose from behind. The scent of aftershave and leather from the gloved hand invades her senses.

Panic surges.

Her nostrils flare and her heart slams against her ribs, a wild animal trapped in a cage.

She tries to pull in air, her chest tightening.

She twists and turns. The grip tightens, and she's pulled backward into the living room. She tries to scream, but the hand muffles her cries.

She struggles harder. Tears prick her eyes and she flings her head back and forth, catching a glimpse of dark, focused, familiar eyes.

CHAPTER 13
Shattered Peace

VICKIE

I push open the door of the apartment. The deli bag swings like a wrecking ball at my side and the smell of greasy fries and burgers makes my taste buds twitch.

I'll get in serious trouble for not going to Nona's to spend the night. But trouble is becoming my sidekick. Staying home alone is how I prove I don't need a babysitter.

The overhead light beams bright. Ma must've left the living room light on this morning. She was likely in a hurry, running late.

I step inside and drop my keys on the table by the door. There's supposed to be a bowl there to catch them. The bowl's on the floor in pieces. I put down the takeout bag.

A muffled moan.

I step farther inside and Ma's in the middle of the living room, tied to a kitchen chair with cut-off lamp cords. My stomach flips like a fish that jumped out of the tank and I gulp for air. I rush over to her. My fingers fumble, peeling the tape off her mouth.

She winces. "Vickie. What are you doing home?"

My mind races. A burglar? Who would want to break into our comfy but crummy apartment? "What's going on, Ma?"

"Shhh. He's still here." Ma's gaze flicks to the hallway that leads to my room. Shuffling, scuffling sounds. "Who's still here?" My voice is a low tremor. I struggle to untie Ma, but the knots are twisted too tight.

"I don't know who it is, but he's tearing the place apart looking for something." She glances down the hallway.

"What could anyone want from us? We've got next to nothing." I don't have time to ask more questions. My mind screams at me to move faster. Only one guy and Ma's in danger. And he's in my space. I need to protect my room, my stuff. I snatch a bat from the coat closet; the metal's cold.

"Vickie, go, get out of here." Her hands convulse.

"I've got this, Ma." I have to protect her.

"Vickie. Don't."

"Stay here," I tell her, even though I know she doesn't have a choice. She's still tied up.

I sneak down the hall. The sounds from my room grow louder—drawers yanked open, things hitting the floor. With each crash I flinch.

I peek around the cracked-open door. The window's shattered, letting in a chill breeze. My room's turned upside down, like my life's being ripped apart. Papers flutter across the floor. My desk chair's upside down, and the mattress is crooked. Stuffed animals mixed with school books, and that cheap lamp's knocked over.

A big guy dressed in black with a ski mask pulled over his head has his back to me, rifling through the nightstand. This is my chance. I might not get another one. I need to be brave.

I take a couple steps inside, swing the bat at the back of his head. It connects with a satisfying crack. My hands tingle. The impact jolts up my arms, my muscles straining.

He screams, drops the gold watch I found. His knees buckle and he folds to the floor.

I swing again, but he clutches the bat. We struggle, I fall, the vase on my nightstand shatters. My back hits the floor, my breath knocked out. Shards scatter around us and pain shoots through my side, but I keep fighting.

I claw at his face and his ski mask slips.

I glimpse part of his face. His eyes are familiar, but no time to figure out why.

He's on the floor, hand reaching for the bat. I grab a shattered vase shard. We're only feet apart, and I lunge forward. I slash his hand.

He yells, scrambles backward.

The burglar snatches the gold watch and hoists himself out the broken window, clattering down the fire escape.

I run back to the living room, breathless.

Ma's eyes are wide with fear and relief. "Vickie. Are you all right?"

My fingers work like a pickpocket at a street fair. I manage to loosen one knot, then another, but it takes all my remaining strength to pull them free.

"You're supposed to be at Nona's." With her arms freed, we hug.

"You're supposed to be at work." I squeeze her tighter.

We cling to each other like Velcro. "What would I do if something happened to you?" Ma's voice is a whisper in my ear, and she's shaking all over.

My breath comes fast, adrenaline still pumping.

An hour later, Uncle Aldo's in our living room and Ma's in a bathrobe. Showers relax her.

I can smell the Wella Balsam on her damp hair. Her hands still tremble, clutching the glass of water she's sipping.

My fingers tap against my leg, restless.

"What did Sal say? Was he mad?" Ma's big eyes are like open windows. "He's short-staffed."

Uncle Aldo puts his hand on her shoulder. "You were attacked. He'll make do. Did the guy take anything?" His voice is calm, but there's an angry edge, reserved for the guy that broke into our home.

Ma's gaze spins around the apartment. "What do we have that anyone would want? A bunch of second-hand furniture. Doesn't make sense."

She's right. We've got nothing of value. Except for one thing. The watch I found. I don't want to say anything about it. Not yet. Or the piece that fell out of the watch that I still have.

Uncle Aldo's face hardens, a protective gleam in his eyes. "I'll feel better if you stay at Ma's tonight. Grab your stuff, I'll take you." He's not asking. He's telling. Now I'm happy to go to Nona's.

I pack the essentials — clothes, schoolbooks, the detective-series tape.

Outside the air's cool and fresh compared to the stale fear inside our apartment. The night feels too calm after what happened.

Uncle Aldo drives us away, and I look back. The building doesn't feel like home anymore. The thief took more than a watch. And I'm going to make sure he gets what's coming to him. Whoever he is.

DAY FOUR

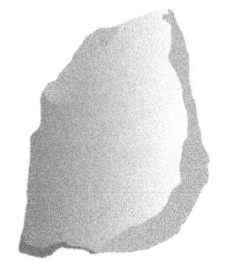

CHAPTER 14
Lucky Strikes

VICKIE

My old sneakers strike the pavement. I shift my backpack. The straps dig into my shoulders, but it's a familiar discomfort—one I can handle. Sal's Diner and school's just a few blocks away, but this morning, it's like trudging through wet cement.

The weight of the bat in my hands, the sound of it connecting with the burglar's head, the image of Ma tied up, her fear face, is like a movie playing on repeat in my head, and no matter how many times I hit Pause, it keeps going.

I stop at the crosswalk, wait for the light to change, then hurry across. Uncle Aldo's words from last night ricochet in my mind. "Stay at Ma's tonight." As if hiding away at Nona's could fix anything. The truth is, no matter where we go, the danger follows because Niko's got something to do with the break-in. He's in deep with something, and it's dragging us down with him. I remember the shiny gold watch that's got his name on the back.

My thoughts skip to the disk. What did Uncle Aldo say? "Looks old." Yeah, no kidding. It's like holding a piece of a puzzle that doesn't fit anywhere. I need to figure out what it means. It's a lot to mull over before I've even had my morning chocolate milk.

1. SAVAGE

I reach into my backpack and pull out my Walkman, rewind *The Great Detectives* cassette a few twirls. The narrator's voice crackles to life, fills my ears, and pushes out the memories of last night.

1949

MARLENA

The door to the back room of Noodles's apartment opens. The stakes are a tightrope, and one misstep could send Marlena for a swan dive.

Footsteps creak from the other room.

Dasher enters. A smile splays on his lips.

Her heart's snared, his presence a balm and a thorn, soothing yet sharp. Memories of their past dance in her mind, vivid as a Technicolor dream. First kiss. First dance. First lie. Last lie.

He moves with the confidence of a man who's seen it all and lived to tell the tale. Pats down his jacket pockets and winks at her.

She removes his cigarette case from her purse on the fridge and tosses it to him. He takes out two cigarettes and offers one to her and lights it for her. Their fingers brush in an electric rush.

Noodles, seated at the table, pulls a near-empty pack of Lucky Strikes from his inside jacket pocket. "Don't worry about offering me one. I got my own smokes. Jeez. It's like I'm not even here." His words burn with sarcasm. "Who was on the phone?"

Dasher's been in the back since Marlena entered Noodles's apartment. She couldn't make out any of the conversation, but heard Dasher's tense pacing.

Dasher tucks the cigarette case in his inside jacket pocket. "That was my contact at the precinct. They'll give you what you asked for, Noodles."

Relief relaxes Noodles's face. "Great. Immunity for me and my guys."

Marlena takes a drag from her cigarette; the smoke curls into a protective shroud around her. "What guys? I thought you worked alone."

Noodles shoves his plate aside. "It's crowded at the bottom of the food chain. Dash, did you tell them I want the building, too?"

Dasher's gaze is a bridge between their two islands. "You've got a lot of demands."

Marlena places her cigarette in the ashtray on the kitchen counter. "Suarez Enterprises building? There's nothing left but debris."

Noodles's focus darts back and forth, a caged animal searching for escape. "I'm sticking my neck out to hand Glotto over to you. Without me, you got nothin'."

Marlena's heels click a staccato rhythm toward Noodles, marking time in the tension. "We want to see the files you held on to from the vault at Suarez Enterprises."

"No dice. Those files are my insurance policy. You keep me alive and I'll come through." Noodles slides his chair back. "I'm gonna hit the head. Don't touch my pasta." He slimes his way to the bathroom and closes the door.

Dasher's and Marlena's shoulders touch in an accidental graze, as delicate as a whisper shared in the dark. Her body tilts, seeking his closeness. "When this is over you're taking me to the Blue Grotto to celebrate."

His lips part in a soft sigh, warmth taking form. "In Capri?"

"No. The Blue Grotto off Linden Avenue. First round's on you." Her words are as playful as a kitten batting at strings.

"You think we can pull this off?" His voice drops like a velvet curtain.

She places her hand in his. "We've come this far."

His gaze digs into her. "I want to thank you."

"For what?" Her heart pounds in her chest. Having him this close invites her body to relax and tense at the same time.

"For being such a terrible shot." Dasher's voice softens. "I've been thinking about what you wrote in the note you passed me."

She tilts her head like a curious sparrow. "The part about Glotto's men being outside?"

"The part after that. 'Love always trusts.'" He strokes the hair out of her eyes. "Same thing you said to me last time I saw you overseas."

Her chin rises, a banner declaring independence. "Trust seems to be a topic on everyone's mind."

"Trust's important. But this time I'm talking about the first two words in that phrase." He places his arm around her waist and gives her a gentle squeeze.

"'Love always.'" Her voice is soft as the rustle of silk sheets.

"I'll never stop loving you." He cradles Marlena's cheek in his hand.

"I know." Their breath mingles, close enough to kiss. The world fades, leaving only the two of them in a shared moment. For the first time in years, hope blooms like a stubborn flower breaking through concrete.

"You always did see right through me." Dasher gives her arm a warming rub. "You're trembling."

"That's because me and you is the most dangerous game I've ever played." Her fingers trace the lines of his face.

"The most dangerous game *we've* played. You're not in this alone. So, how about it?" He holds her hand behind her back, their bodies pressed into one another. "The two of us. For life."

"What are you saying?" Marlena puts her head on his shoulder. His warmth seeps into her, a soothing balm against the chill of uncertainty.

The sound of the toilet flushing shakes the bathroom wall.

"Ahh. Sounds like Noodles is playing our song." Her smile snaps into a soft pucker of contentment. "A toilet flush."

They laugh in each other's arms.

Noodles opens the bathroom door, rolls his eyes as he walks back to the table. "Get a room."

CHAPTER 15
Nine Lives

VICKIE

I walk down Linden Avenue, the voices from *The Great Detectives* cassette drowning out the city ruckus.

"Get a room." Noodles's words make me chuckle. And phew, Dasher's alive. Maybe that's the twist Uncle Aldo was talking about.

The faded letters spelling *The Blue Grotto* on the top of a building pull me to a halt.

I yank off my headphones and I read the name again. "The Blue Grotto." Dasher and Marlena's Blue Grotto?

My two worlds blur together. Can't be the same joint from *The Great Detectives*. Can it?

I never noticed it before, hiding in plain sight.

The building's brick exterior is worn, the paint's peeling. Vines cling. A sagging, faded blue awning hangs above the entrance and a line of down-and-out people curves around the building. Hollow eyes, weathered faces. The smell of desperation sticks to them like kitchen grease.

The windows are as grime-streaked as the people in line. I walk to the front door. A handwritten sign reads:

Soup kitchen hours:

Breakfast 6AM - 9AM, Lunch 12PM - 2PM.

7. SAVAGE

I push open the door.

"Hey, you can't break the line," a voice grumbles, rough like rocks.

"I'm not here for breakfast." I stride inside. Shadows cling to the corners. A man ladles oatmeal into bowls, his movements almost mechanical.

The large bar area stands out, a relic of past glory. The limestone countertop is missing a chunk from the corner. My fingers graze the jagged edge. The cold stone grounds me and convinces me The Blue Grotto is real and not a nostalgic daydream.

"Can I help you?" the man asks, wiping his hands on a stained apron. His face is lined with years of hard work, eyes tired but kind.

"I don't know. I'm looking for someone." I trace the chipped edge of the counter.

"Who's that?" Curiosity glimmers on his worn face.

"Detective Max Dasher." The name feels silly in my mouth, like grown-ups who talk about superheroes as if they're real people.

"There's a name I haven't heard in a long time." He hands his ladle to a nearby woman. She's younger, and moves with purpose, efficiently taking over his task.

"I'll be right back," he says to her, then walks to me. He offers his hand. "Who'd you say you are again? I'm Sandy."

"Vickie." I shake his rough hand.

"Used to be a bartender here." He glances around the room.

I follow his gaze. "A lot has probably changed."

"Some things haven't. This place still draws the down and out. I'd rather be serving food than booze, to tell you the truth."

"What happened to this corner of the bar?" I tap the damaged edge.

"Bar fight. Detective Dasher took out a whole chunk with his face. Nobody thought he'd get back up. But he did. I swear that man had nine lives." Sandy's tone is tinged with admiration.

"What happened to him? To Dasher?" I ask like I'm a detective looking for a missing person.

"Don't know. Stopped coming in. Decades ago. Do you know him?" Now Sandy's the curious one.

"No, just heard stories. Never noticed the place before." I've got an urge to take a souvenir, some token from this place to prove I didn't imagine it. But the shelves behind the bar are empty. Nothing suitable for taking. Maybe the memory's enough.

"I'd better get back to work. Long line this morning. Good to meet you." Sandy marches back to the energetic girl and picks up his ladle.

On my way out, I scan the faces standing in the even longer line and decide to leave something instead of taking.

I open my backpack and offer up the snacks I packed to a few people. Nona always reminds me to never leave the house without snacks. Maybe, not just for me, but in case someone else needs them, too.

I return to the cracked sidewalk and make my way to school. If the Blue Grotto is real, what else from the world of *The Great Detectives* might be? After school I'm going to find out.

CHAPTER 16
Maps and Mysteries

I stand at the front desk at the library with the office phone pressed to my ear. The building smells like old paper and dust, with the faint, comforting mustiness of countless stories tucked away in corners. The elderly librarian eyes me over her reading glasses.

I angle my back away from the nosey woman and speak into the phone. "I'm glad you're feeling better, Ma."

"How was school?" Ma's voice drips with concern like syrup over a stack of pancakes, sticky and impossible to ignore.

"Boring as usual. Just at the library. Have to work on something." I shuffle through the microfiche cards I asked the librarian to get from the back.

There's a pause on the other end of the phone. "Be careful."

I twist the cord in between my fingers. "Are you sure you're okay to work today?"

"I have to." Ma's still worried about her job. "Don't stay out late."

"I'll be back at Nona's before nine." My voice is steady, but my mind races, juggling my deceptions like a pro.

I hand the phone back to the uptight librarian. "Can you set me up on a microfiche machine?" I hold up the microfiche cards. She points to the back room. "Third machine on the left," she says, her voice flat.

I sit on a wooden chair in front of the bulky device, its surface polished smooth by decades of use. The room is lit with only the light from the machine and a few old-fashioned desk lamps.

The old maps from 1949 flicker on the screen, projected from the microfiche film; each frame's a step back in time. The machine whirs, its ancient insides struggling to keep up with the modern world.

My fingers scroll through history, piecing together my new puzzle. Every smooth edge of the film card displays a forgotten street.

The newspaper headlines whirl past. One catches my attention. "Fire Guts Suarez Enterprises." A photo of the Suarez Enterprises building pops up on screen. My fingers trace the screen, the plastic cool under my touch. Just like in *The Great Detectives* tapes.

I look closer at the former address, which would put it right where the abandoned community garden is today, a couple blocks from Sal's Diner.

The librarian's silhouette looms in the doorway. "The microfiche room closes in ten minutes." Her voice breaks my concentration.

I shut down the machine, gathering my notes, and drop the cards off at the front desk.

The librarian watches as I head for the exit. It's like she thinks I stuffed the humongous microfiche machine in my backpack.

I step out into the cool early evening air, the pieces of the past fitting snugly into the present.

Time to dig up some ghosts.

I crouch behind the shrubs across the street from the community garden. My first stakeout.

It's dark outside. I'm not going to make it home by nine p.m., but as long as I'm at Nona's by the time Ma gets off her shift, she'll never know.

The eight-foot green plywood that surrounds the garden is covered with defaced flyers of long-past events and colorful graffiti.

No activity in the garden, but I keep my eyes trained on the abandoned plot, waiting for something, anything.

I decide to search my backpack for any old leftover snack I didn't hand out at the soup kitchen. Nothing but an old peppermint. The kind Nona keeps in a dish by the door during the holidays. Probably in my backpack since Christmas. Better than nothing. I unwrap it and pop it in my mouth.

I press play on my Walkman, and through the headphones, *The Great Detectives* intro music floods my ears, something to focus on while I wait.

The Blue Grotto. Suarez Enterprises. Both real. Even Detective Dasher wasn't made-up. History's all around me.

CHAPTER 17
Bon Appétit

1949

DASHER

Dasher sits at a table big enough for twenty-four guests in Glotto's formal dining room. A black eye blooms across his cheek and his bloody lip seeps. Every bruise and ache screams at him, a bodily map of missteps. Dasher sorts through his mind's maze for the rat that double-crossed him. Noodles? A cop? Or worse—Marlena.

Rich mahogany paneling lines the dining room walls, interrupted only by the occasional gilded family portraits. The chandelier glitters with countless crystals, spewing fragmented light. The long, polished table dominates, topped with only four place settings of fine silver and china.

Glotto sits at the head, a king on a crooked throne. Several of his goons stand guard around the perimeter of the room, dressed in dark suits, ready to pounce.

Dasher is parked halfway down the table. A battlefield dressed in fine china and deceit stretches between Dasher and Glotto. Empty chairs are ghostly placeholders, an unnerving setup. Glotto's bald head glistens with sweat and his eyes flick to Dasher.

Dasher's hands rest on the edge of the table, his posture tense, every muscle coiled and ready.

1. SAVAGE

The door opens and Marlena enters. Her wind-tousled dirty-blonde hair frames her face, and those blue eyes pierce through the smoke and mirrors of the space. She's got on that killer smile, the kind that promises everything and nothing at the same time. Her face is an iron mask. Even Dasher can't tell whose side she's on. The words she scribbled in his office anchor him: *Love. Always. Trusts.*

Glotto's smile prowls across his face. "Marlena. So kind of you to accept my dinner invitation."

Marlena surveys the fine china and silverware. "You didn't leave me much choice."

Dasher's mind races, retracing their steps, each choice leading them to this elegant trap. Marlena's on his side.

Glotto slips off his silver napkin ring. "I believe you've met Detective Dasher. Many times."

Marlena glances at Dasher; her expression remains unreadable. Her fingers trace the delicate pattern on the china. She's most likely surveying the table for the best weapon and calculating her odds against a room full of killers. "What do you want, Glotto?"

Glotto twists his cufflinks like screws. "I want to enjoy a lovely meal. You never know when it might be your last. Just ask Noodles."

Dasher shifts in his seat, winces with the pain from his injuries. A reminder of the jeopardy he's in. "You wouldn't kill Noodles without the files," he says.

The air in the large room is suffocating with the scent of expensive food and malice. The flickering flames in the fireplace suck up the oxygen.

"True. But it's getting chilly, don't you think?" Glotto motions to a goon. Glotto's voice grates on Dasher's nerves, every word dripping with smug superiority. The man thinks he's untouchable, surrounded by his hired muscle and wealth.

A goon opens a box and then feeds the fire a couple of file folders. The flames roar, consuming the documents with a ferocious hunger.

Dasher feels the heat, smells the burning paper. The warm flames send a chilling message of lost evidence and opportunities. The files shrivel to ash, and his jaw tightens. "You got Noodles. The files. So what's this dinner all about?"

Glotto leans back like a cat playing with a mouse, savoring the game. "Sometimes things are not as clear cut as they seem. You would know all about that, wouldn't you, Marlena?"

Marlena's eyes are as sharp as ever, cutting through Glotto's bullshit with a single glance.

Glotto dabs the sweat from his forehead. "I got *some* of the files. But how can I be sure I got them all? Hence this dinner party."

Dasher's focus narrows. "Then Noodles is still alive?"

Marlena's fingers finesse the fork, fine-tuning her facade of control, perhaps choosing her weapon. "Where is he?"

Dasher connects the dots in his mind, each revelation another bullet in the chamber. Noodles isn't dead yet, but every second ticking by is a second closer to the grave. The files, the dinner, the taunting—they all form a pattern, a deadly dance orchestrated by Glotto. Dasher senses the trap, its jaws closing slowly but surely around them. He sees the game for what it is—a high-stakes gamble where the chips are human lives.

Glotto waves a dismissive hand. "First, we eat."

Three servants enter; each takes a silver cover off their plate, revealing steaming dishes, one for Marlena, one for Dasher, and one for Glotto. The fourth setting glares at Dasher like an unsolved riddle, a ghost at the feast. Its emptiness speaks louder than words, a silent invitation or a threat. That empty seat nags at him, a reminder that nothing is ever what it seems.

"Linguine with an Italian ragu in honor of Noodles. Eat." Glotto picks up his fork and luxuriates in his first bite.

Dasher pushes the plate away. "I'm not hungry."

Glotto nods, and two goons flank Dasher, their presence a silent threat.

Dasher picks up the fork, his hand shakes, and he tastes the dish. The ragu is rich and savory, its flavors mocking his twisted stomach. Each bite is a battle, the pasta a slippery serpent slithering down his throat. The tang of tomatoes mingles with the metallic taste of fear, creating a bitter concoction.

"Some wine for my guests. To wash it all down with." A woman with sleek black hair and a no-nonsense uniform pours wine into crystal glasses.

Dasher raises his glass in a mock toast; his eyes are twin torches, lighting a path through Glotto's dark, tiring game.

Glotto raises his glass. "A toast. To love. I must say, you have renewed my faith, Marlena. If you can fall victim to Cupid's arrow, there's hope for the rest of us."

Marlena's face flashes with impatience. "Where's Noodles?"

"Right here." Glotto masks truth beneath a smile.

"Stop playing games." Dasher slams his hand on the table, rattling the silverware. "Where is he?" His fierce calm erupts, a quiet explosion of control lost.

Glotto's eyes dance with malicious delight. "So close you can taste him."

Dasher stirs the ragu. Two fingers peek out from under the mountain of pasta. His stomach lurches in a queasy groan, and he heaves into his napkin. He retches, the taste of horror mingling with the rich sauce.

Glotto's guffaws grip the room, gruesome and grating. "Too gamey for you, Detective? Perhaps we'll have something sweeter for dessert," Glotto taunts, and glares at Marlena. "So much fun, and we're just getting started."

Glotto's head bobs and two goons bring in Noodles, minus two fingers on his right hand. His features sag, weary and worn. They shove him into a chair at the table in front of the empty place setting.

Tension tightens like a noose.

Marlena's glare drills into Glotto. "How did you figure it out?" Her glare targets Glotto, her eyes twin daggers demanding truth.

"I have friends in high places." Glotto dabs his forehead with the napkin.

"My contact at the precinct." Dasher's tone is a shattered mirror, trust broken.

Glotto nods. "You mean *my* contact at the precinct.

"And now to the matter at hand." Glotto holds up his palm, folding two fingers in. His eyes glitter with amusement. "Too soon?" Glotto chuckles. "We threatened Noodles, tortured him, and he gave us some of the files. But not all of them. He insisted that both of you be here before he handed over the rest."

"Noodles, if you give him what he wants, he'll kill all of us," Dasher, his voice tense, warns.

"What's going on Noodles? Why are we here?" Marlena turns her fork over in her fingers.

"I thought about things. The deal the cops offered — even if the charges against Glotto stuck they'd eventually slide right off." Noodles's voice is weak but defiant. "And I'd be running my whole life, no matter how short that turned out to be. A man like you, Glotto, has fancy notions. Fancy things. Fancy connections. You got your friends in high places, all right. And you know what else you got, Glotto? Enemies. In low places." Noodle's lip curls.

Two goons move toward Glotto. One of them points a gun at Glotto's head.

"Let's call this a change in management." Noodles picks up Dasher's plate. He inches over to Glotto and thrusts his hand in the pasta, fishing out his two fingers.

Sauce drips down his sleeve like blood.

Noodles grabs Glotto by the skin on the back of his head and shoves his severed fingers into Glotto's mouth. "Bon appétit, you son of a bitch." Noodles hold's Glotto's mouth shut with both hands.

Glotto struggles for air, flails, but Noodles clamps down harder until Glotto's body goes limp. His death a fitting end for a man who thought he was untouchable.

The game has changed, and now it's their turn to make the rules.

CHAPTER 18
Deadly Decay

VICKIE

I push Stop on *The Great Detectives* cassette. Glotto might have been taken out decades ago, but the neighborhood's got new threats and secrets. A delivery van pulls up on the opposite side of the street in front of the green plywood fence around the abandoned community garden.

Two stocky guys unlock rickety metal doors that lie flush with the sidewalk, the kind that echo when a passerby walks over it.

They unload a van carrying twenty-pound bags of fertilizer. I give them a few seconds, then sneak across the street, lift the big metal doors, and descend down the steps after them.

Each step feels like a gamble, the metal grating shaking under my weight. The air's colder, like it's seeping out from another world.

The basement's lit by three bulbs, spitting at the walls with hiccups of light. Shelves are lined with gardening supplies—fertilizer, shovels, and strange chemicals. The place is a jumble of chaos and order, the shelves meticulously organized but overstuffed.

I hear the delivery guys twenty yards in the distance. Hiding behind a wooden pallet stacked with five-gallon buckets, I wait and listen. Their footsteps pass by me and up the stairs in a rhythm of retreat.

My stomach wrenches at the clang of the outside lock.

The ceiling is low, pressing down. The clammy walls tighten around me in a chokehold. I'm trapped.

There's got to be a back exit. Every building in a city always has at least two exits in case of fire.

I quick step to the back wall, run my fingers along the damp stone, and follow it until I find a vertical seam in the shape of a door and a rusty metal box, the size of a shoebox, bolted to the wall.

I creak open the cover of the box, revealing a round space with a familiar design two inches in diameter. The same design as the gear thingie I found in the gold watch. I rummage in my backpack, take out the metal disk, and stick it into the space. It fits.

The truth crashes over me. The gear is more than metal; it's a key to a hidden history. The characters, the stories, the secret gear—this isn't just a case; it's a legacy, and I'm standing at its heart.

The stone wall slides open with a grinding noise. The vault room is real, not just a story whispered on *The Great Detectives* tapes.

I step inside. The space is the size of a small New York studio apartment.

Shovels and wheelbarrows rest against the far wall, twenty feet away, and six metal tubs line the wall on my left.

Then I see it: a trail of red.

I follow the drag marks to one of the tubs.

Guts. Blood. Bone.

A tidal wave of revulsion crashes into me. Bodies half-wrapped in sheets, swirling in chemicals. A nearby shelf holds labeled barrels of lye and containers of acid.

The dead body in front of the diner a few blocks away and Niko's watch with a compartment holding a key to a basement graveyard. Puzzle pieces slip in place. The garden above isn't just a patch of green; it's a cemetery, a dumping ground for whatever goo is left from these bodies after they've been acid washed, Niko's loose ends.

I need to get out, to breathe air that's not full of death.

I whip around, but my feet root to the spot.

Frank, one of Niko's chumps, blocks my exit, his left hand bandaged just above the knuckles. Same place I'd nicked the burglar with the broken vase.

Frank was the guy who broke into our apartment. Was he looking for the round gear-like key? Was he looking for me? Am I gonna end up taking a chemical bath in a tub?

"We've got to stop meeting like this." Frank's glossy eyes make him look even more creepy. "You've got something that doesn't belong to you. Hand it over."

I grab a brown bottle from a shelf, open it, and sling it at Frank. Acid. The liquid hisses as it hits. Frank claws at his jacket. I bolt, my feet pounding against the concrete floor. The stairs to the street groan under my weight, each step a countdown to freedom.

I don't scream; I don't have time. Survival is my only focus. I throw open the metal door Frank left unlocked and make my way to Sal's Diner just a few blocks away.

Inside I find Sal, Ma, Geraldine, Vina, Marge, and a couple of other customers. My breath comes in ragged gasps, each inhale a struggle. Sweat drips down my back. I lock the front glass door.

Ma is at the coffee maker. "Vickie, what are you—"

"Call the police. And get everybody out of the back." My hands and voice shake, but my focus is keeping people safe. Frank's not far behind me. I don't have long.

Ma's eyes are pools of confusion. "Vickie."

"Frank's the guy that broke into our apartment." I try to keep my voice steady so I don't panic Ma, but urgent enough to get everyone moving.

"Frank? Niko's cousin?" The color leaks out of Ma's face.

Frank stands outside, pulling on the glass door, then knocking, louder and louder. He holds a crowbar in his hand.

Vina calls 911, mumbling the diner's address.

Geraldine gathers the customers. "Sorry, everyone, kitchen fire. Grab your belongings and follow me."

"But there's no smoke," says one wise-guy customer.

Geraldine ignores him and shoos the customers through the back. Her gestures are firm and non-negotiable.

Frank smashes the glass, enough to stick his hand through and unlock it.

Sal comes out from the kitchen with a meat cleaver.

Niko has joined him. "Don't worry, Sal. I'll pay for the door. I just need to talk to Vickie." Niko's voice is smooth as silk, his eyes cold.

The diner's a battlefield waiting to erupt. Sal stands like a fortress, cleaver in hand. Ma is a statue.

Niko's wearing the gold watch Frank took from my room. "I don't want anyone to get hurt." The sound of police sirens, a lifeline, but also a ticking clock grow in volume. "Who called the cops? Now this is getting messy." Niko's voice is tight with anger.

"Niko. What's going on?" Ma clutches the edge of a table.

Niko's eyes are slits squeezing out the last of his charm. "Vickie took something that doesn't belong to her."

I clutch the shoulder straps of the backpack tight. "I found a watch with a kind of key inside. It unlocks a cellar vault under the garden across the street."

Niko shakes his head. "This kid can really spin some stories."

I pan the room with my focus. "There are dead bodies down there."

The sirens are louder, closer.

"Niko, we need to wrap this up. Cops are coming." Frank's voice is urgent.

"I'm really in a spot here, caught between my family's reputation and you, Rosemary. Here's what we're going to do. Rosemary and Vickie, you're coming with me. We'll go somewhere we can talk." Niko's not asking, he's ordering.

Ma looks fragile and small.

"You're not taking them anywhere." Sal acts like a human shield in front of me and Ma.

The room holds its breath, a collective pause in the chaos.

Niko pulls a gun and shoots Sal in the leg.

The shot's a deafening roar that shakes the room. Sal's leg buckles; a cry of pain rips from his throat. Blood spills onto the floor. The cleaver clatters on the tile.

Ma gasps; her hands fly to her mouth.

Sal's face twists in agony, a grimace of raw pain. Blood stains his pant leg. Ma rushes to his side, her hands fluttering in helpless panic.

"Sorry, Sal. That one was a warning. Next shot you won't recover from so quick." Niko waves his gun at Sal. "Frank, pull the car around back."

Frank leaves through the front door.

My mind sputters, calculating escape routes, strategies, anything to get us out. I can't let them take us; I need to think, to act.

"Out the back, both of you." Niko marches me and Ma through the kitchen, to the exit into the alley. At least Geraldine and the others are gone, safe from Niko's reach.

Ma opens the back exit that leads to the alley, and I follow her out.

But when Niko goes through the door, Marge whacks him in the head with a fire extinguisher. Niko crumples to the pavement, unconscious.

"The fire's out." Marge's voice is as even as her swing.

Ma and I hold hands; hers trembles. I give it a squeeze.

We're going to get through this. We're not victims. We're survivors.

CHAPTER 19
Love. Always. Trusts.

TWO WEEKS LATER

Ma's sprawled on the couch, her arm draped over her eyes. Her skin's got vodka sweat pouring out. I pick up an empty bottle from the floor, feel the cold glass in my palm. The apartment's a mess. Just like Ma's life the last two weeks.

"Drinking. Again, Ma?" I give the bottle a shake. Niko's in jail, but the stink of him is rotting Ma from the inside out.

Ma shifts and groans. "Just had a nip. To help me forget." Her lies roll off her tongue like a greased-up meatball down a hill.

I walk over to the trash to toss the bottle, and the cosmetology school flyer is balled up on top of the garbage. Ma's dreams crumpled up and thrown away. I fish it out and smooth it on the counter, running my fingers over the creases.

"Sal called." I dump the bottle into the trash. "He's holding your job for you."

Ma slumps and sinks, swallowed by the sofa. "I just don't feel up to it yet."

Frustration creeps into my compassion. "I'm meeting Uncle Aldo at the diner today to check on everyone. Wanna come? I'm sure they would like to see you."

Ma shakes her head. "I need more time." Her voice is low.

I roll my eyes and scan the cluttered room. "Did the mail come?"

"You expecting something?"

"No, just want to keep track of the bills." I flip through the pile of envelopes on the TV stand. I spot an official-looking envelope and tear it open. My eyes stretch.

"What is it?"

"A mistake. Says I got a scholarship to some private fancy school But I didn't apply for anything like that." I hand her the letter.

She sits up, and reads. "The St. Hilda's School for Girls. A full scholarship. Niko said he was going to put in a word."

"I don't want anything from him." I tear the letter in half.

"Vickie. Please. It's the only good thing that's come our way in a while." Her eyes are like leaky faucets, ready to drip any second.

"I don't—"

"Think about it. For me. It would make me feel better."

I swallow my anger and look for some tape.

Me and Uncle Aldo sit at the counter at Sal's. Marge is in her usual booth. Geraldine and Sal are behind the counter. Sal's on crutches.

"Place looks great, Sal." I eye the replacement door and spotless counter. He's pulled the diner back together tighter than a double-knotted shoelace during the shuttle run.

"Broken glass and a shot-up knee are easy to fix." Sal straightens his crutches under his pits.

"And some things just take time." Geraldine towels off a wet spot on the counter. "How's your ma, Vickie?"

"The same. I keep telling her Sal's holding her job. But thinking about coming back to work just makes her feel worse." I fidget with sal and pepper shakers.

"I know the feeling." Geraldine cuts her joking eyes toward Sal.

Uncle Aldo swivels his neck. "Where's Vina?"

"On a cruise outta Florida. Left two days ago for the Caribbean." Geraldine stacks plates with a soft clink.

"She's one step closer to owning a boat," I say. "Good for her. At least someone's dreams are afloat." Vina's cruise seems like a magic trick, appearing outta nowhere. But it's more like taking her dreams in her own hands and deciding to spend some of the money she's been saving on the dream she's been delaying.

"Dreams are like that. Having a sliver of that cheesecake now makes her look forward to having a bigger slice of dessert later." Geraldine smiles, hand on her hip.

Sal's lazy lean becomes part of the counter. "And I'm sinking my teeth into my dream. Finally going to retire."

Uncle Aldo gives his coffee a stir. "What's going to happen to the diner?"

"New owner." His eyes are a gentle push toward Geraldine.

"Sal helped me get a loan from the bank." Geraldine beams like she just won the lottery. In a way, she did. And so did Vina. Except they're making their own dreams come true.

"Just what you wanted." I nod in her direction.

"And I can't wait to talk trash about the new owner behind her back," Geraldine adds with a wink.

"And today's it for me. Last day in Queens." Marge hands her signed credit card receipt to Geraldine and sits on the stool next to me.

Geraldine offers Marge a peppermint and takes one for herself. "I'm sad to see you go. Think you'll be back to the diner ever?"

"No. I think I needed to close things out." Marge's eyes are distant, like her own words hit her harder than expected. "It was good for me to remember."

"Did everything work out the way you wanted with packing things up?" Geraldine spears the receipt onto a pointed piece of metal on top of several others.

"Yes, it took a while, but I didn't give up." Marge stands, heads toward the door, but stops and looks over her shoulder, throwing her words back like a farewell note. "Love. Always. Trusts."

Marge exits through the brand new door.

Beside me, on the stool where Marge sat, is a book, *The Great Detectives*. "Marge forgot her book." I pick it up.

Through the glass, Marge wraps a scarf around her head and climbs into the back seat of a car. She shuts the door and the car pulls away from the curb.

I open the front cover of the book. There's an inscription:

Vickie, sometimes a girl has to take things in her own hands. Sometimes that's her fists. Sometimes her outstretched palms. Sometimes it's by gripping a pen. This girl is passing the baton. -M. Dasher

There's a silver pen tucked inside the pages. "Geraldine, what's the name on Marge's credit card receipt?"

"Marlena. Marlena Dasher." Me and Uncle Aldo lock eyes.

CHAPTER 20
The Wedding Bouquet

1949

MARLENA

Marlena holds a wedding bouquet tight. Dasher picked the blooms from the trees lining the street outside The Blue Grotto. The white-blossomed Linden leaves are sharp-toothed and heart-shaped, with a point at the tip. Seems appropriate.

Her veil flutters in the summer breeze against her gray wool business suit. She runs down the courthouse steps, gripping Dasher's hand. Her heart pounds, not from exertion, but from the thrill of this new beginning.

The concrete stairs tap a final goodbye to her old life. Each footfall a move away from the past.

At the bottom of the steps, the engine of a 1949 Cadillac rumbles, a throaty promise of power. Noodles sits in the back; his suit likely costs more than the vehicle.

"Looking spiffy," Marlena rights the veil on her head with a playful smile.

"I spruce up good." Noodles wiggles his tie. "Had to come and hand-deliver my wedding gift."

Dasher eyes him. "It's not ticking, is it?"

Noodles grins and throws a set of keys. "My aunt's apartment. It's yours."

Marlena catches the key ring. "I don't think we'll be staying in Queens."

Noodles's gift is generous, but her plans are set. The city might be a haven for Noodles, but not for Dasher and her—not anymore. The apartment's a relic of the life they're leaving behind.

"For when you visit, then. Take them. Trust me, I'm rich now. Got more Argentinian cash than I know what to do with, courtesy of that secret vault. And best part is, Feds can't take the money, 'cause I got immunity. Oh, and check this out." Noodles flashes a gold watch, the metal glinting in the sunlight.

"Classy," Marlena says. The watch is nice, but it doesn't hide the reality of Noodles's situation. A man with more money than sense is still just—a man with more money than sense. But he's not her problem anymore.

"I bought it to distract from my missing fingers. And I always wanted something I could hand down to a son one day."

Dasher puts his arm around Marlena.

Noodles's eyes wax wistful. "Maybe I'll engrave it. It's even got a secret compartment. I know just what I'll put there. Anyways. Good luck. Oh and—it goes without saying, if our paths do cross again, I can't guarantee I won't shoot you."

Dasher's smirk crackles like a whip, snapping between them. "You took the words right out of my mouth."

Marlena leans in and kisses Noodles on the cheek. "A kiss for old times' sake."

Noodles laughs. "You know if things don't work out with—"

Dasher hits the car roof with his hand. "Drive."

The car speeds off, leaving a cloud of city dust in its wake. Marlena and Dasher walk to a waiting 1941 Buick Roadmaster convertible and climb in the front seat.

Marlena takes off her veil, tucks it in her purse, and wraps a scarf around her head. "Where to, Detective Dasher?"

"Somewhere warm, Mrs. Dasher." His arm slides around her shoulders.

"I'm already there." Marlena snuggles close. His warmth is a comfort, a reassurance that no matter the challenges ahead, they'll face them together.

"Now that puts a smile on my face." Dasher's grin stretches wide enough to touch the edges of the world.

They drive down Linden Avenue, the future stretched out before them, an open road, full of promise and peril. Marlena's heart flutters with a mix of anticipation and relief. The road ahead is unwritten, but it's theirs to travel together.

VICKIE

The nameplate on the priest's desk at St. Hilda's School for Girls reads "Father Greg Losër." He's got charisma and good looks, like Niko, except the Father apparently uses his charm for God.

I sit on the opposite side of a desk big enough to land a plane on, sizing up the man behind it. My reflection in the shiny surface is distorted like a funhouse mirror.

We didn't win the lottery, but it's not every day you get handed a golden ticket to a top-notch school. Ma begged me to take the scholarship. Niko wrangled it through his sister Gina. My anger at Niko washed away when I saw a flash of hope in Ma's eyes again. Here I am.

"Welcome to St. Hilda's School for Girls." Father Greg's husky voice is calming.

I glance at the nameplate again and smirk. "Nice to meet you, Father—I'm sorry. I know you can't help it. You didn't pick your name, Father Loser."

His lips press into a line so tight it could slice cheese. "It's French. Pronounced loose-air."

I suck in my cheeks to keep my laugh down. "Loose air? You mean like a fart? I don't think saying it that way is any better."

"Call me Father Greg. How about you? Shall I call you Victoria or Vickie?" His face is stiff.

I drape an arm over the back of my chair. "I guess you can call me whatever you want. You run the place. But if you call me Victoria I might not answer. Says Vickie on my birth certificate. My family is pretty simple."

"If there's anything you need, just let me know." Father Greg throws a small but genuine smile my way.

"I do have a few suggestions." I take out the pen Marge gave me and a dime-store notebook, part of the back-to-school supplies Uncle Aldo bought.

"We'll take all suggestions into consideration, Vickie." He shuffles some papers and folds his arms on his desk.

"You really got to do something about that toilet paper. No wonder the nuns are always scowling." I dip my chin.

He coughs, a punctuation mark ending the awkward moment. "Noted."

A smile crawls across my face. "You know what? I think this is going to be the beginning of a beautiful friendship, Father."

"We can only hope and pray." He tugs at his collar.

I consider his words. Hoping. Praying. The two of us exchange dueling stares. "No thanks. I'd rather be my own lottery."

TRIAL TWO

DARK HIVE

CHAPTER 21
Out for Blood

1969

Charlotte's bedroom is a riot of colors and posters, her twin bed draped with a groovy paisley comforter. She flips through the worn pages of a *Tiger Beat* magazine. "Daydream Believer" spins on her record player, a sleek RCA Victor with its polished wood finish. The needle glides over vinyl, producing a crackling, magical sound.

She glances at poster of dreamy Davy Jones, then stands and twirls, her skirt swishing against her knees. She sings along with the chorus, bopping and swaying to the music.

"Oh, Davy," she whispers, "if only you knew how good we'd be together." She pauses by her vanity, glimpsing the clock: 8:00 p.m. "Jeff's late. Again."

She checks her reflection in the white, antique mirror. Bottles of Love's Baby Soft perfume and a tangle of hair products clutter the dresser. She reapplies her Calypso Pink lipstick, fluffs her hair with a teasing comb, and undoes the top button of her angora sweater. She lifts her boobs with both hands, presses her lips together, sighs, then rebuttons. Then she pulls tissue after tissue from her bra, tossing them into the trash.

The downstairs phone rings. She races into the hall; her Mary Janes slide on the plush, avocado-green carpet.

Down the stairs, into the living room, she skids around the dark green sectional, hits her knee on the teak coffee table, and nearly careens into the color TV console. Another ring, and she grabs the receiver. "Jeff."

No answer, only heavy breathing.

Her face droops, like her smile is being wrung out of her face. "Not funny. I told you my parents will be home at eleven. Where are you?"

More breathing, slow and dense.

"Real mature." She fiddles with the top button of her sweater. "I have a surprise for you. I'm wearing that sweater you like." Her voice dips into a singsong temptress tone.

Long inhales and exhales seep through the line.

She slams the receiver down. A sly smile splays across her face; she shakes her head.

A light from her dad's office catches her attention. She meanders to the office and pushes open the door. Inside, Dad's mahogany desk is cluttered with papers, a Rolodex, and an old Smith Corona typewriter. The phone receiver dangles off the desk. She picks it up, places it back on the cradle.

A rustle in the corner.

Charlotte jumps.

Mittens, her cat, meows.

"Mittens, you're not supposed to be in here." She shoos the cat out.

She swipes a bottle of Jack Daniels from the small bar cart in her father's office and walks into the pass-through kitchen.

Crunch. Broken glass crackles under her shoes.

"What the hell?"

The curtain on the half window of the back door blows in; the window's broken.

She stumbles, grabs the counter placing the bottle on it. The kitchen is untouched except for the missing knife from the block. She turns. A wall of menace blocks her path, a man, towering and unmovable, wearing a melted and mangled rubber mask with razor teeth, the missing knife in his hand. The blade glints in the dim light, long and sharp.

"Oh my God. No. No. No." Charlotte's breath comes in shallow gasps. She bolts through the hall, her vision tunneling to the front door. A car with blinding lights shines through the sheer curtains. "Jeff."

She fumbles with the knob, her sweat-slick fingers slipping. She whimpers, raw, desperate. Finally, she wrenches the door open, trips down the concrete steps.

She runs to the car parked in the driveway, the headlights a beacon of safety. Jeff's car—the engine putters, the radio plays "What Are We Going to Do?" by The Monkees.

"Help me." She pounds on the hood.

The driver's door is open, but Jeff isn't there. A wet red streak leads from the car door to the garden.

She hesitates, but then follows the blood trail. Her fingers brush against the rough bark of a tree. She parts prickly bushes and gasps.

Jeff lies there, covered in blood, eyes open and lifeless.

She stumbles back to the car, and collapses into the driver's seat. The keys are in the ignition. She slams the door, and puts the car in reverse, her foot heavy on the pedal. Trash cans clatter. She speeds backward, checking the rearview mirror. No one's following her.

Trees stretch overhead like skeletal fingers and she accelerates. The headlights carve a path through the darkness. The odometer shows she's gone one mile. Two. Three. She flicks off the radio. "I've got to . . ." A wheeze of deep, labored breathing. She checks the rearview mirror.

The man in the mask sits up in the back seat.

She screams.

The car swerves, crashes into a tree. The impact throws her forward; her head slams into the steering wheel.

The twisted metal of the car groans.

Charlotte's fingers twitch.

The light fades; her world goes black.

NESSA

Twelve-year-old Nessa's eyes flick from the Farmington drive-in movie screen to her older sister, Kristie, and her boyfriend, Chips, in the front seat. "What kind of ending was that anyway?"

The end credits for *Out for Blood* roll, red letters slashing across the screen over creepy music. The metal drive-in movie speaker hangs from the window, crackling with static, making the music muffled. The old speaker's battered casing, scratched and dented, is proof it's been here since forever.

Nessa sits in the middle of the back seat. "So, Charlotte's car runs off the road with a killer in the back seat. Then what?"

No use. Kristie can't answer with Chips's tongue down her throat.

Nessa leans back, tries to disappear; the itchy seat cover sticks to her legs in the July heat. She and Kristie used to have fun together. They're only five years apart, but turns out a five-year-old and ten-year-old have a lot more fun together than a twelve-year-old and seventeen-year-old. Nessa misses the old days of hopscotch, Pick Up Sticks and Candy Land. Now all Kristie's interested in is bobbing for Chips's Adam's apple.

Nessa rolls the windows down; the cool night air mixed with the scent of snack-shack popcorn and hot dogs rushes up her nose. She raps her fingers on the armrest and glances at the cars parked around her. There's probably twenty or thirty of them, everyone either watching the credits roll or making out. The gravel lot is surrounded by the bleak woods beyond, like the setting of every bad horror movie, where bad things happen to stupid, horny teenagers.

Chips slips his hand under Kristie's shirt and she pulls away. "Oh my God, Chips."

Nessa leans forward between the two seats. "Yeah. Oh my God." Nessa lets out a sigh, as heavy as a schoolyard grudge. "What did you think of the plot, Kristie? Chips? Terrible ending."

Chips casts a smirk in Nessa's direction. "The ending's called a cliffhanger. So they can make another one. Don't you know anything, Spaz?" He grabs a cigarette and lights it, splashing an orange glow across his cheeks.

"I know a lot more than you, Peabrain. And why do they call you Chips and not Chip?" Nessa lunges further between them, twists the car radio knob in frustration, searching for a station, then plops back. "Daydream Believer" plays.

"If I was a chip there wouldn't be enough of me. I'm Chips. I'm a whole party. A party in a bag." Chips wraps an arm around Kristie.

"Chips." Kristie purrs, her fingers twirling one of her long curls.

Chips kisses Kristie on the neck. "I'm a little salty. A little sweet."

Kristie pushes him away, squirming. "We can't. Stop."

"Everybody wants more. Don't you want more?" Chips pulls her closer.

Kristie sneaks a look back at Nessa. "My sister's here, Chips."

Nessa kicks Chips's seat. "Yeah. And I'm hungry."

Chips thrusts back against his seat. "Why'd she have to come?"

Kristie smooths her hair, checking her reflection in the visor mirror. "It's the only way my dad would let me come out with you."

"Bummer, man." Chips opens the door. "A real bummer." He scrambles out, then slams the door.

Kristie gets out and follows him. Nessa struggles her way out of the back. "Hey. You're not leaving me here. You don't even know what I want. Wait up."

Standing near the snack shack are a group of teen boys in leather jackets. She knows all his bully friends. Chips greets them with elaborate handshakes.

"What's up, Badger. Squid. Tiny, my man." Chip curls Kristie into him like she's a dumbbell in PE class.

"Chips. Far out." Badger, the tallest of the group, grins. "Looking good, Kristie."

Chips's eyes sharpen to slits; his fingers dig into Kristie's shoulder. "Keep your eyeballs to yourself. She's mine."

Nessa feels a surge of heat rush to her face. "Since when did my sister become a pet?" She gives Chips the stink-eye. "And your friends are creeps, Chips. Don't any of them have real, normal names?"

Kristie steps up to the counter. "What do you want, Nessa?"

"Yeah, *Nessa*. Such a real, normal name," Chips shouts over his shoulder, huddled with his friends.

Nessa rolls her eyes like marbles in a board game. "Hot dog and malted milk. And Red Hots." She digs into her pocket for change; the coins clink. "That's all Dad gave me."

Skips, a nerdy guy wearing a paper hat, takes Kristie's order. He's got a stutter. That's how he got his name. Apparently every high school boy has a nickname with a story. "Hi, K-K-Kristie."

Kristie smiles; her fingers brush the tiny pearl cross around her neck. "Hi. I didn't know you worked here?"

"Yeah. I-I-I like your necklace." Skips's eyes linger on the cross.

"Thanks." Kristie touches the necklace again.

"Haven't seen you at m-m-m-mass. Father Timothy says—"

"Yeah. Haven't been in the mood lately." Kristie takes her hand off the cross and drops her arm by her side.

Chips barges over, annoyed. "Oh no. This guy. We got Skips, fellas."

"That's n-n-not my na-a-a-me." The tiny muscles in Skips's face twitch.

Chips bangs on the counter. "Can we get someone else to take our order, or we'll be here all night?"

Kristie puts her hand on Chips's arm. "I'll take care of it."

"Get whatever you want, babe. My pops gave me two bucks." Chips pulls out the money.

"And it's burning a hole in your pocket." Kristie's laugh falters, like a skipped note in a song, like she's trying too hard."

"That's not all that's burning a hole in my pocket." Chips winks at her.

Nessa crosses her arms, building a wall to counter the sleaze. "Disgusting."

Chips puts his arm around Kristie and kisses her hard, showing off in front of his friends.

Catcalls and whistles erupt.

Kristie shuffles in place. Her face flushes red.

"What's wrong?" Chips asks.

"Nessa's right. I'm not a pet." Kristie's glance toward Nessa is a quiet shout for support.

Nessa flashes a defiant grin. "You heard her."

"You're my girl. What's got you upset all of a sudden?" Chips motions to Skips. The nicknames are a ridiculous Dr. Seuss rhyme. "You care what this guy th-th-th-thinks?"

"Leave her alone." Skips squares his shoulders.

"Or what? What are you going to do about it?" Chips grabs a ketchup squirt bottle and shoots Skips in the face. Ketchup drips down his cheek and onto his white uniform.

The boys' laughter bursts in a chorus of snickers and snorts.

"Hey, want some fries with that?" Badger's unkind words scurry out.

Chips returns to his friends, greeted with back slaps and laughs.

Kristie hands Skips napkins from the dispenser.

His subtle, surprised flinch at her touch says more than words can. "Why are you w-w-w-with him?" Skips's mouth strains with each word. "You're too g-g-g-ood for—"

"Kristie, get your sweet ass over here." Chips crumples her spirit like a piece of notebook paper.

The boys' laughter lurches loudly, landing like punches.

Nessa, fed up, takes a step toward the gathering of boys. "You're all a bunch of idiots. Soggy Chips and the Milk Dud gang."

Nessa folds her arms in a huff. She scans the secluded parking lot of the drive-in theater, where turned-on teenagers gather in huddles. For a lazy serial killer, this place would be a buffet of easy, clueless prey.

Back at the car, Chips, Kristie, and Nessa balance their snacks in their arms. Nessa climbs in the back seat. Kristie and Chips put their snacks in the front, slam the door closed, but don't get in. Instead they grab a blanket from the trunk.

Nessa leans out the window. Kristie's been looking forward to this double feature for a month: *Out for Blood* and *The Creature from Lake Tremble*. "The movie starts in twenty minutes."

"I only need ten." Chips tosses his dirty words at Nessa.

Nessa watches and listens to their conversation through the open window.

"What was up with you at the snack shack?" Chips's tone is demanding.

Kristie looks everywhere but at him. An urge surges in Nessa's chest to crush Chips's face into crumbs.

"Don't worry, I'll let you make it up to me." Chips grabs Kristie's hand.

"I'll be back before the movie starts." Kristie's body wilts the farther she gets from the car.

"You wanted to see this movie," Nessa calls after them.

Chips and Kristie disappear into the woods.

Nessa sinks into the back seat, staring out the window, trying not to think about Kristie.

The drive-in's gravel lot is a messy mix of cars—beat-up pickups, faded station wagons, and a couple of sleek Mustangs gleaming like they just rolled off a magazine page. Headlights flicker, bouncing off chipped paint and rusted bumpers.

Beyond the lot, the woods crowd in, a wall of shadows. Twisted tree branches reach up like bony fingers, making creepy shapes in the sky.

Nessa lets out a frustrated sigh. What does Kristie see in a jerk like Chips?

She shakes out a handful of Red Hots, pops them into her mouth, and chews them slowly. The Red Hots burn her tongue, a fiery sting that spreads to her gums. The cinnamon heat makes her eyes water, a welcome distraction from her gnawing worry about Kristie.

She crunches down hard, the candy shattering into spicy shards that cling to her teeth. The sugar coats her mouth, sickly sweet mixed with the spice. Like a dare she can't back down from, she swallows, feeling the candies' rough edges scrape down her throat, leaving a trail of heat that flares in her chest.

The screen broadcasts previews of upcoming movies, the sound spitting from the silver speaker attached to the car window. Nessa unwraps the foil from her hot dog, the warm, steamy scent of grilled meat hitting her nose. The hot dog is smothered in mustard, bright yellow against the charred skin. She takes a big bite; the soft bun squishes in her hands, ketchup spilling over her fingers.

An advertisement flashes, announcing *The Creature from Lake Tremble* will begin in two minutes. "Kristie's going to miss the beginning." She gets out of the car and stomps into the woods to find Kristie.

Hundreds of yards of curves and turns, shadows morphing into monsters, Nessa's mind conjures shapes that dart between the trunks—faceless figures lurking. She imagines masked killers like the one in the last movie, *Out for Blood*. The murderers slipping between the trees.

"Kristie?" Her voice sounds small in her ears.

She enters a clearing.

Kristie's on the blanket, lying on her side. No Chips. Relief washes over Nessa, even as her legs hesitate. "Kristie? The movie's starting. I heard there's a jump scare in the beginning." Nessa's breath stutters. She puts her hand on Kristie's shoulder and Kristie rolls over under the weight. But her eyes are open. Frozen. Staring. Kristie's shirt gapes in the front; a dark smear of blood stains the blanket under her blonde hair.

No. No. No. Nessa's mind screams to wake up, to undo what she's seeing. She jerks her hand back, bile rising in her throat, her muscles tensing and recoiling from the awful truth.

She flounders, her knees weak, the reality punching her in the gut. She can't breathe, can't think, can't comprehend this horror. And it's not a movie.

Kristie isn't moving, isn't going to get up.

The world spins, darkening at the edges. Nessa presses her back into a tree, its rough bark digging through her T-shirt, into her skin, and panic writhes in her chest.

A hand clamps over her mouth.

"Shhhh." Chips's slimy breath is in her ear, Nessa thrashes out, elbowing him in the ribs. He tightens his grip on her and her mouth. She writhes, trying to yank free; her nails claw at his arm.

Chips loosens his hold enough for her to spin and face him.

"You killed her." Tears prick at the corners of her eyes, but she blinks them away.

"No." Chips shakes his head; his voice trembles.

Her pulse pounds, pressing, pushing. She gauges the distance out of the clearing and lunges for a stick, holding it in front of her.

Chips's hands shake. There's blood on his yellow letterman jacket and his shirt is soaked with it.

Chips's breath barks and bristles in desperate gasps. His pale face is slick with sweat. His lips tremble. His whole body jerks with each of his shallow breaths.

"There's blood all over you. And Kristie's half-naked. You killed her." Nessa's voice wavers, a mix of fury and disbelief. Her mind reels. Kristie's vulnerable and lifeless body is a frozen photo burning through her.

"We were making out. Someone stabbed me." Chip puts his hand over his neck, oozing blood. "I passed out. When I came to—I tried to help Kristie. Nessa. Listen to me. Whoever did this is still out here."

Chips sways. His legs struggle to prop him up.

From the woods, a twig snaps and jerks Nessa's nerves tight.

"Stay here." Chips disappears into the forest.

1. SAVAGE

Her fingers clamp tighter around the stick. She doesn't trust Chips, doesn't know if he's Kristie's killer or a victim too.

Every exhale is shaky and shallow. She walks back to Kristie, kneels, and covers her with the other half of the blanket.

A scuffling noise, sharp and frantic, to her right, like two people struggling, fighting.

Her heart hammers hard, each hit heavy and hollow.

The sounds from the woods shift. A grunt, and a thud, then nothing.

She pivots and scans the dark woods, her fear mounting. "I've got a weapon." Nessa holds her stick like a gun. She edges forward from the safety of the clearing into the forest, each step slow and deliberate.

Branches snag her clothes. She trips over something, and falls. On the ground, beside her, Chips. Dead. Horror frozen on his face.

Nessa wails into the restless woods.

CHAPTER 22
The Final Countdown

1999

VICKIE

Father Greg's office at The St. Hilda's School for Girls smells like stale books and old ideas. I sit in a creaky wooden chair, fidgeting with the hem of my silly short skirt. Only agreed to wear it if I could keep my sweatpants on underneath.

Looks like I'm ending my first year at this joint the way I started, in the hot seat for being me.

The crucifix on the wall seems extra judgy this morning, and so does Sister Irene standing on my right, holding her Bible in front of her like a shield. Sister Gina on my left is the only one in the room backing me up.

Father Greg taps his pen, his eyes fixed on me like I'm a riddle. With each page of my file he flips, his sighs grow louder. "You've been brought to my office sixteen times this year. What do you have to say for yourself?"

"Seventeen." I pick up a porcelain Mother Mary, turn it over, then clunk it down. "This is number seventeen."

"I stand corrected." Father Greg flits his eyes from Sister Irene to Sister Gina, then back to me. I'm in a trinity of trouble.

"On the last day of classes for the school year." Sister Irene repositions her glasses, the chain dangling limp like her neck skin.

"And it's only a half-day. We were so close." Sister Gina places her hand on my back, a gentle encouragement.

Father Greg's gaze pierces through me. He turns the pages of my file, the rustling sound flitting around the room. "Quite an impressive list of offences. Uniform infractions—"

"First, why am I in a skirt that is smaller than a ballerina tutu? I'm not a ballerina." I flick the hem of my skirt.

Sister Irene walks over and straightens the crucifix on the wall, as if to ward off my rebellion. "We compromised. Allowed you to wear your awful sweatpants underneath your skirt."

Father Greg focuses on the file. "The list continues. You ate the communion wafers."

"Any human would get hungry when snack isn't until ten-thirty. It's really a scheduling problem." I squirm, Sister Irene's glare landing like a slap I didn't ask for.

Sister Irene steps forward, placing her Bible on the desk with a thud. "What about the sign she put on Sister Bernadette's back reading, *Needs money*."

I thump the armrest of the chair with my fingers. "Well, it's true. She's always out there ringing bells and passing plates. I was helping her out with her marketing."

"And the whoopee cushion?" Sister Irene's eyes narrow like the gates of heaven shutting tight. "How do you justify that one?"

I snap my spine straight as a ruler. "I'll only take credit for two of those squeaks from the whoopee cushion. The third squeak came from you, Sister Irene. Nothing to be embarrassed about."

Sister Gina stifles a laugh with the back of her hand.

Father Greg looks serious, sets the file aside. "What would you do, Vickie, if you were in my position?"

I shake my leg, the rhythmic movement calming my nerves.

Sister Irene's evil look bores into me. "I don't think she has an answer."

I lean back and brush a piece of lint off my skirt and pretend it's their complaints. "As a matter of fact, I do have an answer. I'd build a school that doesn't cater to just one type of student. Be more flexible with the rules. And also, why am I the only one sitting here? Sarah said really shitty things to me."

Sister Gina raises her eyebrows.

Father Greg pulls down his priest shirt with a tug. "Let's mind our word choice."

An angry heat rises up my neck to my cheeks. "I apologize. Sarah talked a lot of shit about my mother."

"You just rearranged the words and said the same thing." Sister Irene's fist is on the Bible now, like a judge ready to pass sentence.

I lean in closer, my fingers tracing the edge of the desk. "You should've heard the words Sarah used. Very bad words. Like whore. And—"

Father Greg holds up a hand like a traffic cop.

"And she said *bitch*." I whisper the word.

"Whispering doesn't make a word acceptable." Sister Gina tucks her grin behind her hand.

I bounce my stare between the nuns. "And she also made some jokes about my cultural heritage."

"We will look into that." Father Greg stands, looks at his watch.

"There seems to be one code of right and wrong for me, and one for everyone else. Like Sarah." My arms lock in front of me in silent protest against all their holy hypocrisy.

Sister Irene's face is tight and loose at the same time. How does she do that? "You're only thirteen. Who are you to take the matter into your own hands?"

Sister Gina fidgets with her nun sleeves. "It's hard. But you have to learn to turn the other cheek."

"I did turn the other cheek. Both cheeks. I told her to kiss my ass." I nod, nailing my point into place.

Father Greg puts his hands over his face. I look him over. This guy—Father Greg—thinks he's some kind of judge, with his little black robe and holy gavel. But I've seen enough to know that just because someone wears a collar doesn't mean they've got all the answers. I get it, I'm not exactly the poster child for St. Hilda's, but hey, maybe they should've put that on the brochure. "No Vickies allowed." I'm not here to be their perfect student.

He looks at me like I'm some unfixable problem, but the real issue is this place, with its dusty books and dated rules. "If I don't teach Sarah, who's going to? This school? Apparently not. She said some very ungodlike things, Father. I tell you, she's not going to talk that way about me or anyone else. I'm teaching the kids here how to have good values. You're welcome."

Sister Gina clasps her hands in front of her in a pleading pose. "Right now we're talking about you, Vickie. Not Sarah or anyone else."

Father Greg snaps his attention to his watch again. "Sarah's not here right now because she's too upset."

"And she has a black eye." Sister Irene picks up her Bible again, shaking her head.

My grip on the armrests could bend metal. "How about me? She threw rocks at me."

"That's not true. Do you know what God thinks of liars?" Sister Irene's reddening face is a flare of accusations.

"Words are like rocks. Everyone knows that. That's in the Bible. She threw a lot of rocks at me." My shrug deflects their judgment.

Father Greg rubs the back of his neck.

I give him my best angelic face. "God is all-loving. God forgives. Be God-like. Judge not lest ye be judged."

Father Greg whips my file closed. "Actions have consequences. Consequences and forgiveness are two different things. Ultimately it's God who judges."

My forward lean is a challenge. "You mean to tell me God has a big journal of all the stuff I've done. Like you? Like Santa Claus?"

Father Greg's hands are on his thighs. "He chronicles it all."

Sister Gina shimmies her habit. "You've been very patient, Father Greg."

"We all have." Sister Irene does the sign of the cross.

"We have assembly in a few minutes. I'm going to give the matter some thought and prayer." Father Greg stares at the crucifix on the wall.

"Thank you, Father." Sister Gina clutches the rosary beads around her neck, and looks at me with a hint of sympathy.

"I will add you to my prayer list, Vickie," Sister Irene maliciously mutters.

I stand and swivel toward her. "You're on my list too, Sister Irene."

Sister Irene's face twitches and her eyes flash with concern. My list isn't for prayers and she knows it.

CHAPTER 23
Special Drawing

Two hundred and three middle school girls in stiff uniforms fill the auditorium seats, looking like clones. Father Greg, Sister Gina, and Sister Irene stand on the stage up front. The two nuns move like they've had a stick surgically implanted up their habits.

Then there's Sarah, eyeballing me with her one functioning peeper, trying to burn holes in my soul. The other eye's black and swollen, just like I left it. That shiner is a masterpiece. She deserved it for the garbage she spewed about my mother.

Father Greg steps up to the mic. "Before we adjourn for summer break, it's time for the special drawing you've all been waiting for." He flips through his notes.

Goody-two-shoes Cynthia makes the sign of the cross over her heart. She's sweating devotion over this raffle.

Father Greg flips through his notes again, pages fluttering like bored moths. "As you know, Sister Gina's mentor in the faith has organized a very special experience for one lucky girl."

Sister Gina steps toward the mic; her smile clings to her face like wet tissue paper. "Thank you, Father Greg. Sister Agnes of the Sisters of Mercy and Prayer convent in upstate New York has offered a full scholarship for a five-day immersive convent experience."

Cynthia gasps like she's won five bucks from a scratch off. Pathetic.

"The lucky winner will join six other young ladies from across the city for a life-changing experience," Sister Gina drones on. "Sister Agnes was adamant. There are two conditions. One, a drawing would be held for all our middle school girls, so that the scholarship is completely in the hands of the Creator. Two. And this is most important. The recipient must come prepared to have a good time. Much song, and prayer, and companionship awaits. Now, the moment has arrived. Drum roll, please."

The whole room starts tapping their legs like trained seals.

Cynthia closes her eyes, her praying hands probably slick with sweat. "Oh my God. Please, oh please, oh please, let me win."

Over a convent trip? Really?

I send up my own silent prayer. "Oh God. No. No. No. No." Last thing I want is to spend my summer with a bunch of nuns.

Girls lean forward, eyes glued, every breath caught in a prayer. Polished shoes clink against the floor, a ruckus of nerves

Sister Gina reaches into the judgment jar and pulls out a name. "Things are looking up for this young lady. Sarah Marks."

Sarah struts to the front, wearing a smirk that could sour milk. The pews creak with the weight of hopes crashing. Cynthia's face folds in on itself, eyes glossing over with tears. My breath releases like air from a popped balloon. I wiggled out of fate's chokehold.

The crowd applauds.

"But wait." Sister Gina, her voice all syrupy sweet, grabs the doom bucket. "Out of an abundance of generosity, Sister Agnes has offered two scholarship spots to our school. Surprise."

Cynthia beams sunshine through her cloudy face.

I roll my eyes in a mental cartwheel. "You've got to be kidding me." As if one convent queen wasn't enough.

"Drum roll, please." Sister Gina reaches in the bucket and pulls out a second slip of paper. "And the second lucky young lady is — Cynthia Jenkins."

Cynthia squeals, bounces out of her seat. "I don't believe it."

Sister Gina's face glows, a billboard of approval. "I will be accompanying both of you on your trip. Can't let you have all the fun."

Cynthia floats to the front, her smile tearing her face in half with so much electrifying joy she faints, her rosary slips from her hand.

CHAPTER 24
Nun-do

Sunlight streams through the thin curtains, throwing a warm glow on my cluttered Queens bedroom. The small desk is covered with my emergency snack stash from 7-Eleven: Skittles, Starbursts, Sour Patch Kids. I stretch, and eye the calendar next to my vintage *The Great Detectives* poster Uncle Aldo got me. On today's date, in big bold letters: *First day of summer vacation*. I yawn, and slide into my worn slippers.

I stumble out of my bedroom and into the living room which is a mishmash of old furniture. My foot catches on the threadbare rug, the one Ma's been meaning to toss. The floral couch hogs half the room, its faded roses swallowing up whatever's left of the pattern. The TV set sits on a crooked stand, one leg propped up by a phone book from the '80s. Everything's got its own squeak and creak, like the furniture's been practicing for a haunted apartment audition.

Knock. Knock. Knock.

I trudge to the front door, expecting Uncle Aldo. Nope. Sister Gina stands in the hall, and without thinking, I slam the door. Nuns, morning, a terrible combination.

"Vickie! Vickie!" Sister Gina's muffled voice calls through the closed door.

I open the door a crack, peek out. "What do you want?"

"I have great news." Her smile makes me uneasy.

1. SAVAGE

Twenty minutes later, me, Uncle Aldo, Ma, and Sister Gina sit around the small kitchen table, sipping Sanka from mismatched mugs. Uncle Aldo and Ma usually have morning coffee at Nona Bartolucci's, but she's in Atlantic City on a senior center field trip, so he's been coming here.

After a long, awkward silence filled with polite smiles, I decide to punch a hole through the discomfort. "So, what do you get when you cross a Nazi with a nun?"

Uncle Aldo and Ma's stares are electric wires, sparking nerves.

"A nun and a Nazi. What?" Sister Gina speaks up, her voice a mix of curiosity and apprehension.

"A nun," I deadpan. "Get it. Cause they're the same."

Uncle Aldo snickers. Then his expression shifts, all humor stuffed into lockdown. "That's not the kind of joke we tell in mixed company." He picks up his mug, takes a long sip.

"We don't get a lot of nuns visiting," Ma pipes up in a polite putter.

Sister Gina dips her head, her expression soft but unreadable. "I'm not officially a nun yet. I'm in the second phase of my journey. I was an aspirant at Sisters of Mercy and Prayer under Sister Agnes, and now I'm a postulant. A deeper phase of exploration."

She's not even a full nun, but she sure meddles like one. What's she doing here?

Ma settles her elbows on the table. "I looked into being a nun once."

Uncle Aldo raises an eyebrow. "When?"

"Long time ago." Her words come out dipped in old memories.

"First time I'm hearing about this." Uncle Aldo props his chin on his fist.

"You don't know everything about me." Ma's words wiggle out a playful warning.

Sister Gina picks up a spoon. "You were an aspirant?"

"No, the stage before that. A nun was handing out brochures on the corner, and I took one. Looked it over." Ma's hands interlock. She's auditioning for the part of nun all over again.

Uncle Aldo laughs. "Then what?" He grabs a Dunkin Stix from a platter Ma set out. Uncle Aldo brought them. He knows they're our favorite.

"What do you mean, then what? I looked it over." Ma pokes Uncle Aldo with her stare.

Sister Gina's smile flutters around the table, a butterfly that can't find a landing spot.

"I'm glad we're finally meeting." Ma wrings her hands like she's trying to wriggle the right words out of her brain. "Because I want to thank you for helping Vickie get the scholarship to that Catholic school."

"I did it as a favor to my brother. As you know, he's a hard guy to refuse." Sister Gina fiddles with her napkin, crumpling it up like she's squeezing out her nerves.

That's an understatement. Niko's a thug. I'm glad he's out of our lives. Ma's never been the same since she met him.

Sister Gina plants her hand on her heart. "And I've grown fond of Vickie."

I wouldn't say I'm fond of Sister Gina, but of all the nuns, I hate her the least.

Ma's face is twitchy. "How's Niko?"

Uncle Aldo puts down his Dunkin Stix and glares at Ma.

Clouds ripple through Sister Gina's eyes, like a stained glass window catching the wrong kind of light. "Still in prison."

"Where he belongs," Uncle Aldo mutters.

"You're more right than you know. Most of my family's in there. He feels right at home." There's a twinge of sadness in Sister Gina's voice. "But I'm sorry about everything that happened with the two of you, Ms. Bartolucci. And I'm sorry for the trouble he brought to everyone in your family."

"Believe it or not, Niko wasn't my worst relationship." Ma chuckles like a depressed clown. "Anyway, what brings you here, Sister?"

"I have some good news. And some bad news." Sister Gina wipes up a coffee ring with her paper napkin.

Ma grabs the sides of her chair. "Go ahead. We're listening."

"The Sisters of Mercy and Prayer have awarded a scholarship to their summer retreat for two of our girls."

I already know who's going to nun camp, so why's Sister Gina acting like it's some big reveal?

Sister Gina clutches both sides of her mug, like she's drawing comforting warmth into her bones. "It's a rare opportunity for the girls to immerse themselves in nature and fellowship for five days in upstate New York."

Ma brushes a crumb off the table. "Oh. Sounds nice."

Sister Gina takes a deep breath like she's stalling. "On the condition that the participants are chosen randomly."

"Yeah, Cynthia and that snitch-face Sarah were picked." My fingers curl into knots.

"Which brings me to the bad news. Little Cynthia, God bless her, has the mumps. So we drew again and—congratulations, Vickie. You've been chosen as Cynthia's replacement. God truly works in mysterious ways." Sister Gina has just become my least favorite nun.

My whole body coils, ready to strike. "I'm not going to nun camp."

Her focus whirls around the table. "But this is a blessing, truly. As you're all aware, it's been a bumpy year for Vickie at St. Hilda's. In light of this transformational opportunity, I've convinced Father Greg to delay any decisions about the renewal of Vickie's scholarship until we return from the retreat."

"So, you're saying she might get kicked out of school?" Ma takes my hand. I'm not sure if she needs reassurance or she's holding me back from clapping for joy.

Sister Gina releases a sigh, burdened and tired, like it's dragging half her soul out with it. "I'm hopeful it won't come to that."

My teeth lock up, grinding against every irritating word that's just been said. "I really appreciate your sunny attitude and your hopeful nature. But I have to tell you, if I go to this nun jamboree, things will end badly."

"Have more faith in yourself." Sister Gina sips her coffee.

"You misunderstand. Things will end badly for all of you." My tone darkens and I shake Ma's hand off.

Ma looks at Uncle Aldo, signaling for help.

"I think getting away, in nature, could be good." Uncle Aldo's supposed to be on my side.

Ma's head wobbles, a mix of doubt and unease. "I don't like the idea of her being so far from home."

Uncle Aldo pats Ma's hand. He's starting to piss me off. "She's a phone call away."

"Actually, there are no phones. She'll be secluded, but in good hands." Sister Gina should just be quiet because I'm not going.

"Sorry. I'm a city girl. And Ma needs me." I relax into my chair. "Who's going to make sure you're eating like you're supposed to, Ma? Or sort the bills? Or make your coffee?"

Uncle Aldo chuckles. "It's Sanka. Instant. Just add water."

"It's the proportions." My words come out rough as a chipped cup.

Ma fidgets with her shirtsleeve, looks at Uncle Aldo, and he returns a reassuring head nod. "I'll figure it out," Ma says. "I'm not helpless. What do you think I did before you came along? I'll be fine." Ma picks now to become an independent woman.

"This could be good for you, Vickie." Uncle Aldo knocks the tabletop with two fist taps. "I'll look in on your ma a little extra. I'm practically here every day anyway."

"I mean if her scholarship depends on it. Then we do what we gotta do." Ma folds, her gaze dropping to the table, every ounce of fight gone.

I throw my hands up. "Wait a minute here. I have a say in this. I'm not getting on some bus and taken to the Adirondacks so you can practice nun-doo on me."

Sister Gina gives her head a puzzled tilt. "Nun-doo?"

My stare clamps down on her. "Nun voodoo."

"Can you explain what this has to do with her tuition next year exactly?" Maybe Ma's not convinced, or maybe she's trying to have Sister Gina convince me.

Sister Gina spreads her hands out, palms up. "There will be no next year if Vickie doesn't go on this trip. It's a real opportunity for her."

Ma adds cream to her coffee. "Explain what she'll be doing. Maybe that'll drum up some excitement."

Sister Gina levels a look at me. "Time in nature, as I said. And she's going to learn to be silent. There's a lot to be learned in silence."

"Bartoluccis really don't do that. It's not our thing." Ma's not kidding with that one.

"That's what I'm getting at. No insult intended." Sister Gina's voice shifts, balancing the line between kindness and insistence. "It's something she's not going to learn here. Vickie needs to make some changes if she's going to remain at school. Some time reflecting in quiet would be helpful." Sister Gina rubs both palms on her skirt.

"Vix. It's only five days, and it would kill me if you lost your scholarship." Ma offers a soothing threat—warm as a lullaby, but sharp as the tip of a spear, shoving me into five days of false salvation. "Sounds like an opportunity. And people like us don't get a lot of those."

Something about Ma's voice and I know I'm doomed. Five days surrounded by a swarm of nuns, and smothered in sickening sweet, thick, oooey, gooey, good-deed-doers.

DAY ONE

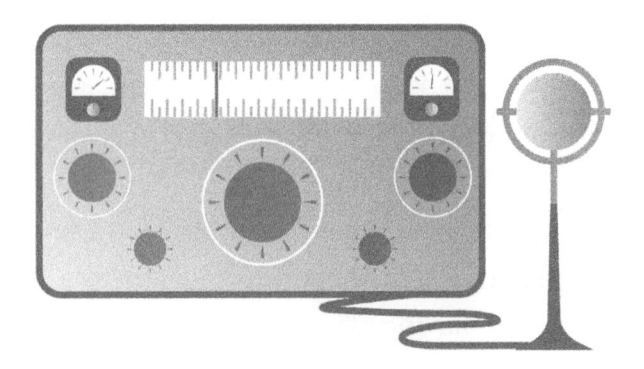

CHAPTER 25
Road to Nowhere

I stare out the window of Uncle Aldo's beat-up police car, wrestling the knot of dread tightening in my gut. Outside, the familiar streets of Queens blur into a haze of gray buildings and graffiti, on our way to the meeting spot for nun camp, the parking lot behind the 7-Eleven.

The cracked leather steering wheel creaks under Uncle Aldo's grip. "You made the right decision."

"Let's just get it over with." I tug at the hem of my skirt, sweatpants underneath.

"Maybe it won't be as bad as you think." He drums his fingers on the wheel.

I turn my head and give him my over-it look. "I'm about to sit on a bus for six hours with a bunch of goody-goodies and nuns strumming ukuleles."

Uncle Aldo lets out a dry laugh, his eyes crinkling at the edges. "Change is good. I lived in Queens my whole life, and when you see the things I have, it gets to you. Just promise me, no fighting. For five days. Not so much to ask, is it?" He locks eyes with me, his face softening with concern.

We pull up to the meeting spot. I spy seven girls being herded by two nuns onto an older clunker VW bus. Some girls are in crisp uniforms, others in mismatched outfits. My insides buck and bend, rebelling against the reality. "Come on, Uncle Aldo. Please don't make me go." I cling to the door handle.

"Have fun, kid." Uncle Aldo gives me a nudge; his hand lingers on my shoulder.

I grab my backpack, sling it over my shoulder, and haul myself to the bus. I climb on, scanning for a familiar face, other than Sister Gina. I don't recognize the other two nuns with her. The only empty seat is beside Sarah. I plop down next to her.

Sister Gina introduces the two other nuns, Sister Myrtha who's the driver, and Sister Sylvan. I mouth the words "help me" through the bus window to Uncle Aldo. He just laughs and waves.

Sarah's face twists; she's twirling her rosary. "You don't belong here." She flips her hair.

"That's the first intelligent thing I've ever heard you say." I pull out a plastic baggie of peanut butter and Ritz crackers Nona Bartolucci smeared and stuck together herself.

"This trip is for people of faith." Sarah laces venom in every word.

"I have faith. In myself." I bite into a Ritz and let the crumbs scatter over both of us.

"Disgusting." Sarah brushes away crumbs. "You probably don't even pray."

"All the time. God, please let Sarah keep talking so I can have the satisfaction of blacking her other eye." I clench my fist and hold it up to her nose.

Sarah huffs and turns to the window. "Whatever."

My mind flips through snapshots of home and Ma, a slideshow of all the mistakes. She hasn't been the same since things went south with Sister Gina's brother, Niko. She doesn't trust herself to make basic decisions, and her drinking doesn't help. Best thing that ever happened to us was when the cops took Niko away. Would've been better if Ma never met him. Then she wouldn't be drinking, I wouldn't be at St. Hilda's, and I wouldn't be on a bus headed to nun prison, trying to keep a scholarship I don't want.

1. SAVAGE

I close my eyes to catch a nap, but squint one eye open when I feel prying eyes on me.

"Hi. I'm Janine." A nerdy girl across the aisle leans close.

"Good for you." I close both eyes again.

"Did you know they raise bees at the convent?" Janine's voice buzzes with excitement.

I pinch the bridge of my nose and make a silent wish for peace and quiet, my eyes open. "I don't care."

"A lot of people hate bees 'cause they sting. But did you know after a honeybee stings, it dies?" Janine nudges her glasses.

The four-hour bus ride is filled with bee facts and dumb singing.

"Did you know they found a 1000-year-old jar of honey in an Egyptian tomb that was still edible? Honey never expires. Bet you didn't know the honeybee queen only eats royal jelly. A honeybee drone spends his whole life to produce one teaspoon of honey. Bet you never thought of that." Janine's voice grates.

Sister Sylvan, a walking cadaver, plays a ukulele and the entire bus, with the exception of me, sings "This Little Light of Mine" over and over and over.

The bus crosses a rickety wooden bridge, and we pull onto the rolling hills of the Sisters of Mercy and Prayer convent. A mix of dread and defeat sinks into my toes. The only thing worse than this journey is the destination.

CHAPTER 26
Beneath the Habit

SISTER GINA

Sister Gina inhales the scent of floral incense and fresh-baked bread in the dormitories of the Sisters of Mercy and Prayer convent. The sunlight filters through stained-glass windows, a bath of color on the polished floors. This place, with all its stillness, is Gina's refuge—a world apart from the noise and chaos of her family in Queens. There's comfort in the way life in the convent moves at its own pace, unhurried and steady.

Seven young girls scamper from the bus to their assigned rooms, clutching their belongings in duffle bags and rolling suitcases. Vickie trails behind. Gina, with her satchel slung over one shoulder, walks alongside Sister Agnes. The weight of her bag tugs, but it's nothing compared to the burdens Gina carried the first time she showed up at the convent.

Sister Agnes's face was the first Gina saw, when Pops dropped her off just after her seventeenth birthday. The Argentenians had already tried to kill Pops several times. When they threatened to kidnap Gina, Pops guarded her like a bulldog over a bone. He buried her in the last place he thought they'd look, a convent.

Sister Agnes shifts Gina's habit with a practiced hand. "Has it really been two years since you were here? I can't tell you the joy seeing you brings to me, seeing you shepherd these young hearts. What a blessing."

They walk down the long corridor of the dormitory. Gina finds solace in the familiar touch of their interlocking arms. "It's trying at times."

Sister Agnes hugs her clipboard to her chest. "We can do all things—"

"Through Him who gives us strength." It's a phrase Gina's said a thousand times, but has never lost meaning. There's strength in these walls, in the quiet determination that binds the inhabitants together in a shared faith. "I often think back to the kindness and patience you showed me here."

They unlock arms. Sister Agnes twists to face Gina. "It was my honor to walk with you on your journey during that tumultuous period."

"It was the first time in my life I didn't feel judged." Gina peeks out the window at the convent's garden. It's a peaceful sight, but she knows that peace is something you have to work for—it doesn't just happen.

Sister Agnes follows Gina's stare. "Love with no conditions is the gift we must give because we have been given so much through our Lord."

Gina grimaces and puts her face in her hands. "Love. It's so hard, Sister."

"Love is easy. Natural. It's the pinching off of love that causes pain." Sister Agnes's words are poignant. Even though she's only in her mid-forties, her wise words and wisps of gray hair make her seem older.

Sister Agnes points to a door at the end of the corridor. "Your room is down the hall from Father Michael's office. I pulled some strings. That side of the building has the best view. The garden. The hives."

"Sounds lovely." The convent is a living rosary of peace and penance for Gina.

Sister Agnes and Gina continue down the hallway. "Father Michael spends the day with us once a week, heads back to his parish before bedtime. He hears confessions, teaches."

"How fortunate. I don't believe I ever met him." Gina's look is like a detective's flashlight, probing the corners. She's only worked closely with a handful of priests during her brief period of exploration.

"He's new to us. Just assigned." Sister Agnes checks off a couple of to-dos on her clipboard.

"Will we meet him?" Gina hopes he's the kind of person who can connect with the girls, like Father Greg at St. Hilda's.

"Yes, he's insisted on meeting the girls—"

Rapid-fire footsteps sound behind them and Sarah bolts past, tears streaking her cheeks.

"Sarah? What's wrong?" Concern knots in Gina's chest, but Sarah is already in the restroom just ahead. Gina hoped pairing Vickie and Sarah as roommates might help them overcome their differences.

Vickie peeks out from her room and ducks back in.

"Vickie Bartolucci." The name cracks out of Gina's mouth like a whip.

"I'll leave you to it. We'll talk later." Sister Agnes pats Gina's arm in a gesture of support. "Girls, let us assemble downstairs for our welcome tour in five minutes." Sister Agnes's voice billows down the hall and through the open bedroom doors. Sister Agnes leaves by way of the stairs to their right. Vickie saunters out of the room she's been assigned to share with Sarah.

"Vickie. Any idea why Sarah is in tears?" Gina crosses her arms.

Vickie's shoulders hunch, her eyes pinned to the floor.

The casual defiance claws at Gina's calm, but she knows better than to show it. "We've talked about violence."

"I didn't hit her—with my fists. I hit her with critical thinking. Turns out her faith couldn't take it." Vickie taps her foot on the shiny floor.

Gina holds her own thumbs in each hand for comfort. She remembers how Sister Agnes never gave up on her. "Grab your stuff. You're rooming with me."

"Anything's better than rooming with a snitch. But I gotta warn you, I snore." Vickie runs her fingers along the wall, tracing the cool stone like she's feeling her way through her thoughts, her laundry bag of belongings slung over her shoulder.

"Fair enough. And before you get too excited, I have to warn you. I fart in my sleep." Gina's voice is deadpan.

"Nuns fart?" Vickie's tone is disbelieving.

"Like a drum set," Gina says with a sly smile.

CHAPTER 27
Storm Warnings

VICKIE

Time for a mandatory tour of the Sisters of Mercy and Prayer convent. Me and the other inmates gather in the great room downstairs. The nuns stand in formation, wedding-reception style, and we walk by them.

Sister Gina stands in limbo between us and them like she's straddling the nun world and the world where the rest of us live. Right now she's looking at me like she's trying to figure out if I'm here to pray or set the place on fire.

The great room is supported by a bare-bones skeleton of dark wood beams and gray stone. The museum-hard chairs are uncomfortable and useless. I don't have to use the toilet to know this is a one-ply joint. There's a giant rug in the middle of the room, puked on with faded flowers.

And don't get me started on the seven other girls in this parade of horrors. It seems like I'm the only one not drinking the cheery, cherry kooky-aid.

Sarah's big blue eyes soak up the goody-goody. She's sticky-taped to Sister Sylvan. And if I hear one more piece of trivia from Janine I'm going to baptize her in the nearest, deepest fountain.

Sister Agnes steps forward, her stout hands gripping her clipboard. "I'm Sister Agnes and want to officially welcome you to the Sisters of Mercy and Prayer. We're pleased to have Sister Gina back with us here."

Sister Gina bobs her head in angelic agreement.

Sister Agnes gears up for more info talk. "You'll find each member of our community offers their own gift to the collective. You've already met your bus companions, Sister Sylvan and Sister Myrtha."

Sister Agnes wriggles out a smile toward Sister Myrtha. "Sister Myrtha delights us with her unique perspective and encyclopedic knowledge on virtually every topic."

Sister Myrtha is not as sunshine-y as the others. I sense, under her bushy eyebrows lurks a dark side. I like her.

Sister Agnes waves to Sister Sylvan. "Sister Sylvan is our head hive keeper."

Sister Sylvan is straight out of a horror flick—the kind where the sweet old lady turns out to be the killer. She's ancient, with a hunched back and twisted hands, likely from arthritis. She's hugging a worn-out prayer book so tight I'm surprised it hasn't turned to dust. Her face is all wrinkles, like a dried-up apple, and her eyes are watery, but sharp. I don't let the frail act fool me—she's probably the toughest one here.

"Thank you for your kind words, Sister Agnes." Sister Sylvan scans our faces. "This one looks like nun material." She fixes her watery gaze in my direction. Likely searching for Sarah, who's standing next to me.

Sarah lights up like a Christmas tree, cradling the prayer book they distributed to us with a teddy-bear hug. "I'm honored, Sister Sylvan."

"Not you. That one." Sister Sylvan points her old claw at me and examines me like I'm some kind of freak-show exhibit.

"Take that back." My prayer book hangs limp in my palm.

Sister Gina's hand clamps on my arm like she's stopping a prison fight. "Vickie, she meant it as a compliment."

This place has me coiled tight. The smell of stinky incense is thick, like someone's trying to choke me with old prayers. And the stone walls are as friendly as a prison cell at Ryker's Island.

"Let us begin our tour," Sister Agnes says, all business.

We march through the great room and down the hall.

"Our cafeteria is on your right. And here's something you'll find especially interesting." Sister Agnes shoves open a door, and the room inside is dim and cramped. "Pardon the intrusion, Sister Frances."

Sister Frances is hunched over a two-way radio, fiddling with dials. She's young, sister Gina's age, but her nervous energy gives off tween vibes. She's got short, curly hair peeking out from under her nun hat, and her eyes are wide, like she's constantly surprised.

Sister Agnes turns to the huddle of eager faces. I'm in the back, not so eager. "We don't have phones, but occasionally we need to connect to the outside world. Sister Frances helps us keep our finger on the pulse of civilization. Any updates?"

Sister Frances looks up. "Hello and welcome. Updates? Unsurprisingly, on the world front, civilization is as uncivilized as ever. As for local news, I'm afraid our radio is in critical condition." Static crackles out of the speaker and she twists the dials.

"And there's a once-in-a-century storm coming our way," Sister Myrtha, the queen of gloom, adds.

Sister Agnes tucks a stray strand of graying hair under her nun veil, not even fazed. "Good to know."

"Perhaps we should postpone our deliveries." Sister Sylvan polishes the end of her walking cane with her wrinkly palm like she's trying to rub a genie out of it.

Sister Myrtha pulls a pencil from behind her ear and scribbles on her clipboard. "Seventy-five percent of weather-related vehicle crashes occur on wet pavement and forty-seven percent happen during rainfall." The pencil scratches away, filling the silence.

"Thank you for your perspective, Sister Myrtha. We've got commitments. And Mother Superior already loaded the bus." Sister Agnes turns to us. "We carry our honey across the state to our largest vendor once a month. Today's the day."

Sister Agnes leads us out to the gravel parking lot, where the bus we arrived in is now filled with nuns and honey. The engine coughs to life. "And they're off."

The nuns wave from the bus windows.

Dark clouds roll across the sky.

Sister Sylvan raises her hand in a blessing. "May God lift you and smooth your path."

"Yeah, that's called hydroplaning." Sister Myrtha is funny in an unfunny way. "The water pressure raises your vehicle so it slides on a thin layer of liquid. Very disorienting and potentially deadly."

I'm the only one who chuckles.

An excited roller-coaster yelp comes from the bus, and one of the nuns juts her crucifix out from the window and shakes it. "God is with us."

"Let's hope your umbrellas are with you too." Sister Myrtha holds out her hand, testing the air for moisture.

Sister Agnes's expression shifts from worry to authority. "Let's continue on, girls."

CHAPTER 28
Nuns and Nectar

Sisters Agnes, Myrtha, and Sister Gina lead me and the seven do-gooder wannabes cross the parking lot. Sister Sylvan scoots ahead as fast as her cane and forward momentum can take her down the green rolling hill on the other side of the gravel parking lot. I wouldn't want to go against Sister Sylvan in a foot race, at least not downhill.

Sister Agnes points with her clipboard like she's showing off an exhibit. "From here, you see our gardens, our hives, and our cemetery."

I kick a loose stone on the path, which skitters across the gravel. "Guess they've gotta dump the dead nuns somewhere." The graveyard is exactly what you'd expect—tombstones stacked like they're waiting for inspection, white crosses perched on top, all wrapped up in a stone wall like some exclusive club for the holy dead.

Sister Agnes catches my comment, but her face remains soft and welcoming. "We are in for a treat. Sister Sylvan has agreed to show you how honey is harvested. Meet her down by the hive house."

Sister Sylvan's already at the bottom of the hill in front of a small stone house, with flower gardens on each side.

Sister Gina interlocks arms with Sister Agnes. "Aren't you joining us?"

Sister Agnes shakes her head, pulling a small silver cylinder from her sleeve. "No hive house for me. I'm allergic to beestings, and I'm down to my last EpiPen until the caravan stops at the pharmacy."

1. SAVAGE

I eye the EpiPen. "You must hate bees."

"I have a deep respect for them. A love, in its own way. You know my favorite thing about bees? Bees know where home is and always return." Sister Agnes tucks the EpiPen back into her sleeve, her voice softer now.

Sister Gina smiles, arms still hooked into Sister Agnes.

"Bees don't return when exposed to systemic insecticides." Sister Myrtha's voice is as dry as last year's prom flowers. "Disorients them, and they spend the rest of their short lives wandering, never to find home again."

I elbow Sister Gina. "That Sister Myrtha's a real buzzkill."

She grins at my pun.

A strained smile slips sideways on Sister Agnes's face, soft yet steely. "Sister Myrtha is a real asset on trivia night. As I said. We all have our gifts." Sister Agnes angles toward Sister Gina. "I hope you'll join me for a catch-up chat before lunch."

Sister Gina lays her head on Sister Agnes's shoulder. "Yes, looking forward to it."

Sister Agnes pats Sister Gina's arm and they detach. "As am I."

The hive house is like something out of a twisted fairy tale—stone walls, no windows, surrounded by flowers that look too perfect to be real. The whole place hums with the sound of bees. Creepy.

Inside the hive house smells sweet, almost sickly, like the whole place is drowning in honey. Sister Sylvan and Sister Myrtha, dressed in beekeeper garb, look like they belong in a sci-fi movie, not a convent.

The girls keep their distance—some stand twenty feet away, their faces etched with a mix of fear and fascination. I feel a sting of envy. They seem to fit in here, all wide-eyed and eager, like they actually want to be part of this saint mausoleum.

Sister Sylvan removes the top of a hive while Sister Myrtha squirts smoke from a canister thingie. The bees swarm, and I think about how easy it would be for them to overtake us, like some kind of nature revenge plot against their keepers.

"We just need a little honey. You don't have to be so bitey about it. Ow." Sister Sylvan winces, flexing her fingers. "I keep requesting a more administrative role. Maybe next summer."

Sister Myrtha walks a tray over to show us girls honeycomb dripping with golden liquid. "We must keep in mind, bees are like nuns. A dying breed."

"The hive is indeed a lot like the convent." Sister Sylvan takes the tray from Sister Myrtha and places it back with care. "And the nuns at Sisters of Mercy and Prayer work together much like our bee friends. There's a mother superior, the queen. Ours is aboard the van right now, but you will meet her when she returns. And they survive on an elixir that never expires. For bees, their sustenance is honey. For us, it's our faith."

Sister Gina examines the hive closer. "Beautifully said, Sister."

Janine raises her hand. "Did you know royal jelly is fed to all bee larvae initially, but only the queen bee eats it throughout her whole life?"

Sister Myrtha returns the smoke canister to a shelf. "Did you know that's why the queen lives five years, but the worker bees only live six weeks?"

Janine's cheeks flush. "Did you know bees can remember and recognize human faces, especially aggressors?"

Sister Sylvan chuckles, fussing with her gloves. "Sister Myrtha's got a rival in the bee trivia department. Maybe we can set up a match, winner gets to care for the best hive."

Sister Myrtha edges her eyebrow upward. "Did you know male bees, drones, are born from unfertilized eggs and have no father, but they do have a grandfather?"

Janine blinks twice, the gears visibly turning in her head. "I didn't know that. Wow."

How did I get stuck in the middle of a bee-nerd convention?

Sister Sylvan closes the hive. "All right, girls, back to your rooms for contemplation. We will sample our harvest after lunch."

"I'll see you after my talk with Sister Agnes." Sister Gina's voice is gentle as she addresses me.

I give a lazy shrug. "What am I supposed to contemplate?"

Sister Gina's eyes are kind but firm. "That's for you to discover."

I put a hand over my grumbling stomach. "I can't think when I'm hungry."

"I won't be long." Sister Gina heads back to the convent. And I walk back to the main building, by the garden. It's that kind of postcard pretty that makes you suspicious, like the world's trying too hard to look harmless. I've seen enough to know that the nicest things usually have the ugliest truths tucked inside. Nothing pretty comes without a cost.

CHAPTER 29
Fractured Faith

The wood frame of the window seat in Sister Gina's room digs into my back like it's got a personal vendetta. I munch on communion wafers. Every crunch a small rebellion against the suffocating quiet; no NYC horn honks or sirens or yelling neighbors. Silent torture.

Sister Gina trudges in, looking like someone forgot to water her — her usual bloom stepped on.

I toss a wafer into the air and catch it in my mouth. "You're not going to say anything? I'm eating communion wafers. From the supply closet." I hold up the bag and dare her to care.

She sits on the twin bed, her hands trembling. "I need a moment." Her voice cracks like a cheap vase tossed off a ledge.

I pause mid-crunch. "You look terrible." Wafer crumbs fall in my lap, but I don't bother brushing them off.

"Not now." She waves me away like a fly. Her eyes are so hollow, I almost feel bad for her. Almost.

I scoop out the remaining wafers and toss the empty bag to the side, where it lands with a crinkle. "How was your time with Sister Agnes?"

Instead of answering, she digs into her habit and pulls out a cigarette. The flick of the lighter is loud in the still room, and the flame dances silhouettes across the worn walls. She cracks a window open, letting in a blast of fresh air.

"I didn't know nuns smoke." I pop another wafer into my mouth, crunching down.

"Yes, Vickie. We smoke. We fart. We scream. We cry. It's almost like we're human." The cigarette shakes between her fingers. She takes a deep drag.

"Geez. What bee flew up your ass?" I recline against the unforgiving window frame. My focus digs in, tearing apart every attempt she makes to keep it together.

"Sorry." She exhales smoke. The room feels smaller with each puff she blows out. "I should've never brought you here."

That one stings. "I didn't ask you to. It's not like I want to be here," I fire back. My sweatshirt feels like it's shrinking, tightening around me with every word.

"That's not what I meant." She stubs out the cigarette in a water glass between our two beds. "It's this place. It's not what I thought it was."

Before I can ask what she means, raised voices vibrate through the hall—sharp, angry, and getting closer. I jump up, head for the door.

"Vickie, wait," Sister Gina calls, but I'm in the corridor.

A woman screams. At the top of the staircase, a priest stands—Father Michael, I'm guessing. He's tall, salt-and-pepper hair, red-faced and fuming. Two flights down, Sister Agnes is sprawled on the floor, abandoned like a puppet whose strings got yanked.

Sister Frances, the young, nervous one, rushes down from the landing. "Sister Agnes!" She looks at Father Michael with wide, fearful eyes.

Sister Sylvan appears from the kitchen. Every muscle of her face is locked in place. "What is the meaning of this?"

Sister Frances helps Sister Agnes to her feet.

"Father Michael?" Sister Sylvan prompts, flinging a questioning glance from the bottom of the stairs.

"I must've slipped. I'm fine." Sister Agnes's voice is steady, but her eyes yell pain. A silent message passes between Father Michael and her.

"Father Michael and I were having a spirited discussion and I lost my focus."

"Is that nun code for a screaming match?" I let the quiet words trickle out, loud enough for Sister Gina to whip her head around in response.

"If you'll excuse me." Sister Agnes bolts, tears streaming down her face, not from the fall, but a deeper cut.

CHAPTER 30
Reverent Rain

Lunchtime. All the nun-tivities I've done have worked up an appetite in me. A giant pot of something that could be stew sits on an airport runway of a table. Steam curls to heaven. There's a platter of bread, each slice so dense it could double as a doorstop, a bowl of mashed potatoes, and another bowl of green stuff. I grab a plate and load up.

Sister Gina pats my hand. The nuns and the other girls have their heads bowed. Marcy, a tiny girl, a year younger than the rest of us, giggles at my eagerness.

Sister Sylvan clears her throat. "Gracious Lord, we gather at this table as one family, blessed by Your bounty. May this meal nourish our bodies as Your love nourishes our spirits. We give thanks for the hands that prepared it and the hearts that share it. Guide us in humility, service, and gratitude, as we partake of these gifts. In Your holy name, we pray. Amen." The chorus of "Amen" bounces off the walls, synchronized like they've been rehearsing for a Broadway revival.

Father Michael sits at the head of the table.

Sister Gina butters her bread with slow, deliberate strokes, eyes down, like she's got something heavy on her mind.

I notice Sister Agnes is missing. The way she said, "I must've slipped. I'm fine," didn't sit right with me. It's a sin to lie, but what about not telling the whole truth? That's a gray area the nuns probably debate over tea.

No one at the table is talking. Polite smiles and dainty bites. I'm not used to a quiet meal. Trying to talk at a full-throttle Bartolucci family gathering is like jumping into double dutch—good luck timing when to enter.

"Want to hear a joke?" I poke at the quiet like it's a dead body—just checking to see if it'll move.

Sister Frances beams. "I love jokes."

Just as I'm winding up for my joke, Sister Gina's butter knife lands with a clang, like a judge's gavel—no fun allowed. "No, Vickie." Her focus pans across the other nuns. "How is Sister Agnes?"

"Resting in her room." Sister Frances shoves a big forkful of peas into her mouth.

Rain pounds against the windows, as if trying to drown out the now uneasy silence.

"Looks like we came inside just in time." Sister Sylvan folds her hands in her lap. "Everyone be sure to save room for dessert. We have a special treat planned in the parlor."

I shovel mashed potatoes into my mouth. Delicious. I keep my eye on an empty chair in the middle of the cluster of nuns, likely Sister Agnes's usual seat.

The parlor is a mix of cozy and creepy. The kind of place either perfect for a cup of tea or a ghost story, depending on the lighting. The wallpaper is faded flowers. Two wingback chairs face the fireplace. A collection of statues—saints and angels—stare down from the shelves with eyes that seem too lifelike.

In the middle of the room is a round, polished table covered with a lace cloth that looks like it's been hand-crocheted by someone with way too much time on their hands. Bread, three pots of honey, and a fancy tea set with twelve cups sit on the table.

The girls gather around.

"Who's ready to sample our honey?" Sister Gina picks up a knife and spreads honey on a piece of bread. "How wonderful. The fruits of our labor." She savors the bite.

"Actually, it's fruit of the bees' labor." Janine's accurate words are loud enough for all to hear.

"We are blessed." Sister Sylvan passes tiny plates around to each girl.

"And we must persevere." Sister Myrtha could suck the joy off a smiley-face sticker.

Sister Sylvan lifts a jar of honey, holding it up like it's a jewel. "Brought to you by our heavenly Father and the bounty of his tiniest servants."

"Grab your plates and be sure you sample each variety of honey." Sister Frances arranges the bread slices in neat rows next to the vats of honey, her eyes sparkling with excitement.

I scoop a spoonful of honey; the golden liquid drips slowly onto my bread, each drop a promise of something sweeter. My mouth waters, and I take a big bite, savoring the taste of flowers that bursts on my tongue.

Sister Frances tastes her honey with a satisfied nod. "Very floral."

Sister Myrtha spreads honey on a slice of bread from the second of the four containers with military precision and samples. "A muscular taste." She smacks her lips together.

Sister Frances tastes from the same jar. "I'm not getting that at all. Floral and feminine to me." She sets her knife down with a light clink.

"I must be blunt." Sister Myrtha wipes her hands on her napkin.

"I suppose you must." Sister Sylvan hands out wet napkins for our sticky hands.

Sister Myrtha wipes her hands on a napkin. "The lighter honey I find off-putting. Inferior. I believe it's from your hives Sister Sylvan."

Sister Sylvan's focus flicks to each girl, assessing.

Sarah, the snitch, has her eyes on Sister Sylvan's approval. "The honey is divine. Thank you for bringing it to us, Sisters."

A slow smile unfurls on Sister Sylvan's face, blooming with the kind of grace you see in slow-motion flower videos. "How sweet you are." She offers Sarah another piece of bread.

Sarah curtsies. If this honey wasn't so good, I'd puke it up. What a kiss up.

Father Michael pours himself some tea; the cup clatters against the saucer. "I appreciate how industrious bees are."

"I appreciate all of you for the same reason. Many hands." Sister Frances refills her cup.

Sister Myrtha gives her tea a stir. "I love that the bee is willing to die for the hive. The selflessness. Much like Christ."

"Yes. Indeed." Sister Gina rubs crumbs off her fingers onto her plate.

I swirl the honey on my plate, watching it pool, thick and slow. Sweet, but with a bitter aftertaste — kinda like this whole scene.

The honey's good, but it's not enough to sugarcoat whatever's crawling underneath this place. Feels like a trap dressed up as a treat.

CHAPTER 31
The Hive's Light

I stand by the window in the room I'm sharing with Sister Gina, and I stare out at a storm, tired from my day. Lightning slices over the hive house.

After lunch Sister Sylvan made us all play gardener, teaching us about mulching. A fancy name for spreading wood chips around plants. My fingers still smell like rot. At least we got to stay in the greenhouse out of the rain.

Then came part two of beekeeping at the hive house with Sister Myrtha, who enjoyed watching us squirm in those bee-hazmat suits.

And I'd rather gargle nails than make another candle with the sister whose name I can't remember. I've never seen anyone so excited about melting honeycomb.

After that, we were supposed to make soap. It's like no one's ever heard of Walgreens. But since Sister Agnes was a no-show, Sister Gina took over, explaining how to mix lye and fat.

Thunder rumbles, shaking the window.

A shape skulks outside through the rain. Father Michael? What's he doing near the hive house in this weather?

The door to my bedroom groans open, and quick footsteps thud against the wooden floor. Sister Gina.

"Step away from the window." Her voice strikes through the room.

She paces to her writing desk. "It's lightning. Not safe."

"Someone's outside." I press my face to the glass

"Vickie, step away." Worry is clear in her tone.

A misty veil spreads across the glass with each breath I take. "I think it's Father Michael. What's he up to?"

Sister Gina slips beside me. "Let's mind our own business." She yanks the curtains closed.

We cluster for dinner. The dining hall feels colder, like the rumbling storm outside has seeped in.

Sister Myrtha folds and unfolds the napkin in her lap. "Sister Agnes is usually so punctual." The empty seat among the nuns seems to thunder along with the storm.

Sister Sylvan's hands lie flat, fingers splayed as if bracing for whatever's next. There's a twitch in her wrist, a small betrayal of nerves. She stares straight ahead, unblinking. "Perhaps Sister Agnes is still in her room recovering. She took quite a tumble."

Sister Frances's brow furrows with deep Grand Canyon creases. "I went to check on her after lunch. She wasn't in her room."

Sister Myrtha slurps water from her glass. "I do hope she's all right. Blood can clot the brain up to twenty-four hours after a fall."

Father Michael cuts into his chicken cutlet; the knife scrapes against the plate. "I'm sure she will join us shortly."

The storm's wild outside, but I can't shake the feeling that it's calmer out there than in here. Sister Agnes missing dinner is one thing, but the way Father Michael's playing cool like it's all fine is fishier than the chowder. He was arguing with her a few hours ago.

Thunder booms; dishes stacked by the window rattle.

Sister Sylvan's expression is tight. "I noticed the light is on in the hive house."

"Me too." I check Father Michael for a reaction.

Sister Gina serves me a warning look.

Father Michael sets his glass down with a soft clink. "I'll turn it off after dinner."

Sister Gina places her napkin on the table with precise care. "I'm happy to take care of that, Father."

Sister Gina's got that twitchy look, and I don't buy for a second it's just about the light.

Sister Sylvan's gaze locks on to Sister Gina's. "You'll need a key. I'd give you mine, but it's been finicky. Luckily, Father Michael has the spare. May she borrow it?"

"Of course." He hands over the key.

Sister Myrtha stands and intercepts the key exchange with an outstretched hand. "Sister Gina, I find storms calming; both you and Father Michael are our guests, I'll turn off the light."

Sister Sylvan's face washes with surprise. "That's thoughtful, Sister Myrtha." Then her gaze flits to the door and her fingers twist together. "The van should've been back by now."

Father Michael leans back in his chair. "I'm afraid you're stuck with me until the van returns. Likely until the storm is over."

Sister Myrtha slides the key into her habit. "It's possible the bridge is out again."

"Oh dear." Sister Sylvan shakes her head and pours gravy over her rice. "Our sisters are getting more of an adventure than they bargained for."

It's not just about a light left on. I can see it in the way they dance around each other—there's a game here, one I'm stuck on the outside of.

CHAPTER 32
Candles in the Wind

After dinner, me, the girls, Sister Sylvan, Sister Frances, and Sister Gina are corralled in the parlor.

Sister Sylvan stands under a massive crucifix that looms on the wall and has likely been soaking up prayers for centuries. "Since Father Michael is with us a while longer than expected, he's generously agreed to answer some questions."

The girls take out the prayer books and pens. They turn to the blank pages, poised to take notes. I stay put, arms by my side. I lost my propaganda book—on purpose.

Sister Frances smiles and passes me an extra prayer book and pen.

"Thanks." I let my frustration hiss out like a slow leak in a busted tire.

We're scattered around the room like jack rocks, some sitting, some standing. Father Michael steps behind a lectern to the right of Sister Sylvan and tweaks his priest collar. He makes eye contact with each of us. "Ladies. How about we start with questions about the word of God. I know it can be confus—"

My hand shoots up before he can finish.

"—ing." He props on the lectern. "Yes, young lady. Please say your name for me. I'd really like to get to know each of you."

I'm standing behind Janine's chair, holding its rough edges. "Vickie. Vickie Bartolucci."

He flops open an oversized, fancy Bible like a dead body. "You have a question about scripture?"

"Yes. So, everything in the Bible is supposed to be true, right? Take it at face value?" I set my loaner prayer book on a nearby table and fold my arms.

"Exactly." His fingers flex and release, an excited dance.

"Jesus said he's a vine. And he says he's a gate. So, how can he be a vine and a gate?"

Awkward snickers crackle in the room.

I ask because I want to see if he can back up his claims—or if he's just spitballing like most people. It's a test; push a little, see what breaks. The ideas that stay strong might be worth considering.

"It's figurative." He shuffles through the pages of his Bible, his fingers brushing over the golden edges.

I yank the thread, letting it unravel. "What does figurative mean—to you?"

"Figurative means a statement not intended to be taken literally." He glances to the crucifix like it might back him up.

"So, we *can't* take the Bible at face value?"

Janine stops scribbling and watches Father Michael. Sarah's mouth hangs open. The whole room waits.

"Some discernment is needed." He reaches for his glass of water and takes a swig. "Why don't we discuss something a little more relatable, like life. The world we're in. I remember when I was your age, everything seemed so big. Any quest—"

My hand slices up again.

"You have another question?"

I blow hair out of my eyes. "Yes. It's me. Vickie Bartolucci. If God is so forgiving, why are there courts and prisons?" I scratch the back of my hand, waiting for his next response.

"Excellent questions. She's one of your students, isn't she, Sister

Gina?" He takes another, longer sip of water. "When we do something wrong, there are Earthly consequences. But make no mistake, we must be in this world but not of this world. Only God can judge us."

My hand is ready to shoot up again, but he holds up his palm. "How about this: I want you to get to know me as well. It's important you feel you can approach any priest and be open. And so, I would like to model openness for you. Ask me anything about my personal life. Nothing is off limits—"

My sweatshirt sleeve slides down my arm, I'm raising it so high.

"Anyone? Anyone else?" He gulps the rest of his water.

Sister Frances refills his glass with a nearby pitcher.

No one moves.

He nods at me, resigned.

My chin's up and my chest is out. "Vickie Bart—"

"Yes, I know."

"What wrong stuff did you do when you were my age? You get in any fights?" More laughs gurgle from the group. My ears perk, ready for juicy details.

"I told the occasional lie, stole a candy bar or two, got into lots of fights. Though I did more running than fighting. Why don't I tell you the story of when I knew I wanted to be a priest?" He surveys Sister Sylvan, whose head bobs in approval.

My initial interest drains through my toes.

"A bunch of bullies, big guys, chased me and I hid in a church. It was beautiful inside. Stained glass. Candles down front. I lit a candle. I had never done that before. That's when I saw him."

Janine, wide-eyed, pauses from her furious note-taking. "Jesus?"

"No. A man who had done the unspeakable. Taken someone else's life. He was in there hiding. We connect in a clash of stares. 'Who are you running from?' I ask."

"The police." I earn a few more laughs with my comment.

"Probably. But I'll never forget his answer—he said he was running from himself. And I knew right away what he meant. Didn't matter that everyone out there was judging him for what he did. What mattered is that he was judging himself. And he came into the church for relief from that. He wanted God to judge him so he could stop the self-inflicted torment. And the most surprising thing happened. He found forgiveness."

Sister Sylvan puts her hand over her heart. "Beautiful."

I doodle on a page of my book. I don't even think before the words fly out; the question just shoots out like a bullet. "So, being a priest or a nun is like hiding out. So you don't have to deal with your problems."

Sister Gina's face washes with emotion—not anger, but something else.

Sister Sylvan's fingers interlock, each one wrapped around the other in a tight bind. "It is the noblest of pursuits. Not a running from, but a calling to. And the vows we take are the most honorable. Chastity, poverty, obedience." Her voice is steady, like she's reciting something she's said a thousand times.

I color in my doodle with gusto. "Well, I'm already doing two out of three."

Sister Sylvan grabs Sister Gina's hand and gives it a pat. "Girls come to us for all sorts of reasons. We invite them to stay for a while." They exchange the kind of look a proud grandmother and granddaughter might. "We walk with them. Whatever their journey, their pain, ours is not to judge, only love. Our hope for all of you is the same thing we hope for ourselves. That during your stay you can take some time to stop and wonder. Humanity longs to delight again."

Sister Gina's whole body relaxes. "You must unlock your heart to receive beauty."

"Amen." Sister Sylvan releases Sister Gina's hand.

Sister Myrtha bursts into the room, wet with rain, her umbrella dripping. "Father Michael. Sister Sylvan. Sister Gina. Come quick."

Sister Gina turns to Sister Frances. "Will you watch the girls? Perhaps lead them in contemplation."

They rush out, leaving Sister Frances, who feels more like one of us. "How about cookies and hot cocoa? They help *me* contemplate," she says.

Squeals of delight erupt when she pulls out the treats, and I use the cover of the commotion to slip out of the room.

CHAPTER 33
Sealed Fate

I crouch behind a bush near the hive house door with a side view of the inside. I grabbed a rain jacket with a hood, but my shoes are an inch underwater. Father Michael, Sister Gina, Sister Sylvan, and Sister Myrtha congregate. There's this creepy quiet, the kind that makes you feel small, like a bug that survived a near-miss squash.

The hive house is a mess of gardening gear, rusty shovels and spades leaning against the stone walls like a bunch of worn-out soldiers. A long, battered table sits in the middle, cluttered with gloves, seed packets, and pots of dirt. Shelves line the walls, crammed with jars of honey, dusty candles, and old gardening books that haven't seen a hand in decades.

I shift so my view's not blocked. Sister Agnes's body is laid out on the floor. My stomach twists like I just got sucker-punched. No way it's real. I try to look away, but my eyes are locked in place. Sister Agnes — dead.

My hands shake. I dig my nails into my knees to hold myself steady.

Sister Myrtha swats away a stray bee. "The door was locked from the outside. When I entered, I found her like this." Every wave of her hand feels like she's fighting more than just insects — batting back emotions.

Father Michael's down on one knee, touching Sister Agnes's pale, swollen neck. "From the feel of her, she's been dead for a few hours."

My thoughts are all over the place, crashing into each other. I'm shivering and wet. I should leave. But I can't. Not yet. There's a tightness in my chest, like my heart's stuck in a vice, and it's not letting go.

Sister Gina's fingers wrap around her rosary like it's an anchor in a swirling current. She's a tough nun-to-be, but today she looks like she might crack right down the middle. Sister Agnes was her mentor, her lifeline, her friend.

Father Michael covers Sister Agnes's body with a tarp he grabs from a shelf. "We'll need a coroner."

"And to notify the authorities about the accident." Sister Sylvan fidgets with her veil.

"If it was an accident." Sister Myrtha's voice is sharper than the corner of the table she's leaning on.

Sister Sylvan takes a step closer to the body. "Of course it was an accident."

Sister Myrtha matches Sister Sylvan's step forward. "Everyone knows about her bee allergies. The last time she was stung, she swoll up just like this before her shot kicked in."

"Why didn't she use her EpiPen?" Sister Gina speaks for the first time.

Sister Myrtha's eyes roam the room. "No sign of the pen. Odd. She never left the convent without it."

She didn't have her EpiPen? Sister Agnes wouldn't forget something like that.

Sister Sylvan's hands won't stop moving, this time fidgeting with her apron. "Why on Earth was she in the hive house?"

"We need to radio Mother Superior." Sister Myrtha's face is covered with worry.

"And Sister Agnes's family." Sister Sylvan dabs her eyes with a pressed handkerchief, then returns it to the pocket of her habit.

"I'm afraid we were the only family she had left." Sister Gina's voice breaks.

Father Michael stands, brushing off his knees. "Well, I don't wish to be insensitive, but there's nothing we can do for her now. And since the van hasn't returned, that means the bridge is definitely out. The coroner won't be able to get to us until tomorrow."

Sister Sylvan steps to the side for Father Michael to pass through on his way to the door. I crouch lower, every muscle tensed like a spring ready to snap.

"Father Michael." Sister Sylvan stops him with her words. "Might you lead us in a prayer?"

"Of course." Father Michael and the rest close into a tight circle around Sister Agnes. "Eternal rest grant unto our beloved and faithful Sister Agnes, O Lord, and let perpetual light shine upon her. May her soul, and the souls of all the faithful departed, through the mercy of God, rest in peace. Amen."

A chorus of amens is followed by signs of the cross.

Father Michael opens his eyes. "We have other concerns as well. Eight of them."

"The girls." Sister Gina doesn't have to say more.

Father Michael nods, his back to me, just a few feet away. "Under the circumstances, as soon as the van returns—"

"I understand, Father." Sister Gina hugs the prayer book to her chest. "I'll help get the girls pack and ensure they're ready to leave tomorrow, so we can head out as soon as the bridge is repaired."

Sister Myrtha rests her palm on Sister Gina's back, fingers spread. "I'll ask Sister Frances to radio for the coroner first, so he might make preparations."

Sister Sylvan rearranges some of the clutter on the table. "I think it's best if we shield the girls from the news of Sister Agnes's passing for as long as we can."

Sister Gina stares so hard at the door, I think she might have seen me.

"Sister Myrtha, are you sure the door was locked from the outside?"

"Yes. Positive." Sister Myrtha's voice is firm.

If the door was locked from the outside, someone wanted to be certain Sister Agnes couldn't get out. That's no accident. And if the murderer's still on the grounds, I'm going to find them.

CHAPTER 34
Wet Footprints

I brush my teeth in the bathroom of the room I share with Sister Gina.
Footsteps.

Sister Gina stands at the bathroom door, arms crossed, her face shadowed by the glow of a floor lamp. "How was contemplation?"

"Great. I had some good thoughts. Really getting the hang of it." I spit into the sink. The minty taste lingers. I grab a towel, dab at my face. I head into the bedroom, my shoes squishing.

Sister Gina knows I wasn't where I was supposed to be. She always knows. She's not just nun smart. She's street smart, from my neighborhood.

"You stayed in the convent the entire time?" Her eyes flick to the floor. My wet footprints glisten.

"Where else would I go?" My heart slams around in my chest. My alibi's as thin as this towel. What's my play? Keep it cool, or confess?

I walk to my bed.

Squish. Squish. Squish.

I sit down, peel off the wet shoes and damp socks. "All right. So I might've followed you to the hive house. And I'm sorry about Sister Agnes."

"Me too. It's a loss for all of us. Let's keep it between us for now." She picks up the towel I tossed aside, throws it to me for my wet feet, then turns back to face me. "Hopefully, we can return home before the authorities arrive and avoid upsetting the rest of the girls."

"What do you think happened?" I rub my feet dry with a towel.

"Bee sting. An accident." She straightens the pillows on her bed. Her movements are quick, too quick, like she's distracting herself from telling me the truth.

"Mixing up salt and sugar is an accident. Being locked inside a hive house that you won't go near because you're allergic to bees, and not taking an EpiPen, sounds more like—"

"Like what?" Her hand grips the bedpost like she wants to rip it off and wield it like a club.

"We both saw Father Michael leaving the hive house earlier this evening—in the rain. And why hasn't he mentioned he was there?" I push into her space.

"It's not our business. It's best we don't get involved."

"Sister Agnes is dead, and we're just supposed to look the other way?" There's more going on here, and she knows it. "And what did Sister Agnes say to you earlier today that had you so upset?"

Sister Gina's face tightens.

A knock. Sister Frances steps inside. "Hello, Vickie. Sister Gina, may I speak with you for a moment?" Sister Frances's eyes are not as twinkly as usual, they're kind of darty.

"Of course." Sister Gina walks toward Sister Frances with a quick glance back at me. There's a storm cloud of unspoken words between us.

"When I attempted to radio regarding that matter—"

"It's okay. Vickie knows." Sister Gina doesn't bother to explain how I know.

"I see." Sister Frances's eyebrows twist.

"Go on," Sister Gina prompts.

"The radio isn't working." Sister Frances's eyes are popped open wide.

"Could it be the storm?" There's worry in the wrinkles on Sister Gina's forehead.

"That's what I thought, but the radio's missing a transistor." Sister Frances's voice is low, like she's afraid someone might overhear. "Radio parts don't just unscrew and walk away."

I cross my arms and ping pong my glance between the two nuns. "They do if they have help. From a murderer."

DAY TWO

CHAPTER 35
The Last Amen

SISTER GINA

Gina eyes the morning light spilling into the convent sunroom and casting a patchwork of pale streaks across the worn cafe table. The air carries the scent of rain-soaked dirt, clinging to the room from the open window. The storm has passed, but it left behind unease and Sister Agnes's body.

Sitting with Sister Frances and Vickie, Gina is rigid in her chair, on edge. She glances at Vickie who lounges back in her chair with an air that screams defiance.

"Don't you have packing to do?" Gina asks.

Vickie shrugs. "My luggage is a laundry bag. How long did you expect it to take?"

Vickie's got the kind of attitude that could turn a saint into a sociopath. She reminds Gina of herself when she was that age.

Gina turns to Sister Frances. "Any progress with the radio?"

Sister Frances swivels her head like a heavy pendulum. "Can't find a spare part or a workaround. We need the missing transistor."

"At least the rain's stopped. Hopefully, the bridge will be passable, and the van will return soon." Gina keeps her voice as smooth as a marble statue, but inside she's on shaky ground. She balances mourning Sister

Agnes's death with remaining strong for the eight young girls under her guidance.

"Then what?" Vickie's eyes have the intensity of a hawk zeroing in on prey.

"We go home." Gina attempts a smile, and makes her words sound hopeful, confident. But for Gina, she's not sure where home is. She never felt at home with her family in Queens. The convent was where no bad thing could get to her. Not anymore.

"Are you going to pretend there's not something odd going on here? I think we should tell Sister Frances." The challenge in Vickie's voice is as sharp as broken glass, and Vickie's daring Gina to step on it.

Sister Frances folds her hand and offers a receptive smile.

Vickie clears her throat. "We saw Father Michael locking the hive house a few hours before we found Sister Agnes. And we all heard Sister Agnes and Father Michael arguing before he sent her flying down the stairs." The words tumble out like of her mouth like a pitching machine in a batting cage.

Gina forces herself to keep calm. Keep in control. "We don't know that he pushed her. If that's what you're getting at."

The color drains from Sister Frances's face. Her hands grip her teacup like it's the only thing anchoring her. "There's something I need to tell you." Her voice trembles. "I assist Sister Agnes with the accounting for the convent. A few months ago, I noticed some discrepancies. Small ones, but when I dug deeper I found thousands of dollars were missing—$27,000 to be exact. Proceeds from convent deliveries never made it to our bank account." Sister Frances's gaze bounces back and forth, trapped in a seesaw of uncertainty. "Sister Agnes and Father Michael were in charge of deposits. When I told Sister Agnes, she said she'd speak to Father Michael."

Gina's thoughts are a tangled knot she can't seem to loosen. "Did she speak to him?"

Sister Frances sips from her teacup. "I only mentioned it to Sister Agnes a few days ago. Father Michael is only here once a week. So maybe she did? And I fear that may have been the subject of the argument you overheard. I feel awful that my accounting suspicions might've caused Sister Agnes's death."

Gina's resolve to find answers hardens, the weight of responsibility pressing down on her like a thousand unanswered prayers. This isn't a small issue. This information is a motive for murder. "Where are the accounting books stored?"

Sister Frances's body tightens. "Father Michael's office."

Gina rotates her teacup in the saucer, then locks eyes with Sister Frances. "I'd like to see them."

Sister Frances looks over her shoulder. "Are you saying we should ask him if we can—"

"I've always been one to ask for forgiveness, not permission. Perhaps that's a flaw that will serve us here." Gina's tone takes on a new edge.

Sister Frances goes pale again. "You mean break into his office."

"Technically it's not his office. It's the convent's." If there's dirt to be found, it's buried somewhere in that room.

"I couldn't do that. I've taken an oath of obedience to authority."

Gina settles a reassuring hand on Sister Frances's arm. "Okay. Then you check Sister Agnes's room. Maybe she left something behind. Be sure to look everywhere. I'll take the office. I haven't taken an oath of obedience to any order yet. I'll dig through the dirt, and when I find something, heaven help whoever's responsible."

Sister Frances stands, her movements stiff, as if she's bracing herself for what's to come.

A sudden realization strikes Gina—Vickie isn't in her seat. "Where's Vickie?" Gina pushes back from the table, the legs of her chair scraping across the floor. "Oh no." Her words carry the full weight of dread she feels. Vickie on her own is like a match in a room full of gasoline.

CHAPTER 36
Off Limits

VICKIE

I slip inside Father Michael's office and my heart does a cha-cha in my chest. The room is medium-sized, wrapped in wood paneling. A wall of books, a desk, a couple of leather chairs—neat and tidy.

I creep to the desk and give the top side drawer a yank. Locked. My gaze drifts to the ginormous portrait of Jesus on the wall. "Sorry, Jesus. You might want to look away." I nab a paperclip from a desk dispenser. A few twists, and *click*, I pull open the drawer. Inside, past a stack of papers and a bible, I spot an EpiPen and a tiny square with wires shooting out one end. Has to be the radio's missing transistor.

Footsteps. "Crap." I look up at the portrait." I mean darn. Sorry again, Jesus."

Gotta stay sharp, keep my wits unholstered.

I shove the papers back over my found evidence, dive under the desk, the cold floor biting into my knees. The floorboards in the hall creak, and I hold my breath. The door opens. Steps get close, then an upside-down face pops into view from behind the desk.

I'd know that snitch face anywhere.

Sarah.

She rights herself, then crouches. "Found you."

I crawl out, brushing dust off my sweatpants.

"What's all the sneaking around about?" Her eyes are so full of nosiness, they might float off her face.

"I'm not telling *you*." I glance at the open drawer, and hope she doesn't see it.

But, her head pivots to the drawer; she reaches inside, and her fingers toy with the papers. "What were you looking for?"

I push her arm out of the drawer, snatch the EpiPen and transistor, slipping them into my pocket. "None of your business."

Sarah picks up the bent paperclip I used, twirling it between her fingers, a smirk on her lips. "You picked the drawer lock?"

I give a no-big-deal shrug. "Maybe."

"Impressive. So what did you find?" She pulls out the Bible from the drawer. "Who locks a Bible in a desk drawer?"

"You don't. Unless it's valuable, or . . ." I clutch the Bible. "Something is inside." I open it; the pages are hollowed out and stuffed with cash. "Whoa." The cash, the EpiPen, the transistor—they're all pieces of a murder plot.

"How much money is there?" Sarah's slowing me down with her questions.

"Twenty-seven grand." I don't have to count. The amount Sister Frances said was missing. I scoop up the cash-filled book and make a dash to the exit. Sarah's glued to me like fly paper.

Footsteps.

The door opens, and Father Michael steps inside. "What's going on here?"

I clutch the Bible to my chest. I don't think—I stomp on Father Michael's foot, hard.

He stumbles backward.

"Run, Sarah." I push her to the door.

Sarah bolts.

Father Michael yanks me.

I knee him in the stomach.

He doubles over and wobbles.

I dart past him. The corridor warps into a dizzying tunnel. Sarah and I sprint to the room I share with Sister Gina. Every second feels like a tightrope walk over a canyon. One wrong move, and everything plummets.

We burst into the room; Sister Gina and Sister Frances look up.

"Hide us." Me and Sarah dive into the closet.

The closet's cramped. A coat hook jabs at my back, a silent bully in the dark. The air is stale with the scent of musty fabric and old wood polish. I'm squeezed between a winter coat and a stack of mothball-scented blankets.

A loud knock on the door.

"Father Michael?" Sister Gina's tone is casual.

"Sisters. Sorry for the intrusion." Father Michael's voice is calm, too calm.

I peep through a slit between the closet door and the frame. Sarah's elbow nudges my side, and I bite my lip to keep from yelping. My knees press into rough, splintered floorboards that dig at my skin. Sarah's breath is hot and fast, hitting my cheek in the tight space. Dust tickles my nose, but I clamp a hand over my mouth to stifle any sneeze.

Sister Gina rests a relaxed hand on the desk chair. "Not an intrusion at all. Would you like to join us for a morning prayer?"

"Another time. I have to attend to a matter involving two of our young girls. I thought they might be in here."

His gaze scans the room, lingers on the closet. My chest thuds like a bass drum in a metal band.

Sister Gina stands up straighter. "We've been in the room for a half hour or so. Anything we can do?"

"No, sisters. Thank you." His gaze shifts away, but I swear I feel his suspicion. The door closes behind him.

Me and Sarah climb out of the closet, breathless.

"Vickie." Sister Gina's tone is sharp, and I can tell she's holding back. But time's ticking; we'll be hauled away in the van soon. Who's to say what will happen to the evidence we've got once we leave.

"Before you say anything, I know what I did was wrong. I shouldn't have gone into Father Michael's office. But look." I dump the Bible full of cash on the bed and sit.

I add the EpiPen, and the transistor. "These things were in Father Michael's locked desk drawer. He killed Sister Agnes." I spurt the words, a geyser, well past time to blow.

"My Lord." Sister Frances gasps, crossing herself.

Sister Gina snatches the transistor and hands it to Sister Frances. "Radio the police."

Sister Frances turns the transistor over in her hand. "But the bridge?"

"Let them figure out how to get to us. Just call them. Vickie and I will distract Father Michael." Sister Gina's voice is steady, but there's steel beneath it.

Sister Gina grabs her shawl, draping it over her shoulders like armor.

"What about me?" Sarah's voice is small.

Sister Gina's hand rests on Sarah's shoulder. "You keep everyone else occupied."

My eyes land on a shoebox on the bed, labeled: *For Sister Gina*. "What's that?"

Sister Frances's fingers trace the lid, her voice soft. "I found it under Sister Agnes's bed. Nothing but photos, a book, and some newspaper clippings."

Sister Gina's at the door. "Let's go."

Me, Sarah, and Sister Gina join the girls huddling in the parlor, their luggage in a neat row. Even though the van hasn't returned, they're ready to jet.

Sarah staggers to the middle of the room, her hand gnawing her stomach like she's about to faint. She collapses. Everyone rushes over, concerned.

Sarah moans. "Oh no, I think I caught the mumps from Cynthia."

Sister Sylvan rests a hand on Sarah's forehead. "Oh dear."

Father Michael stomps down the staircase.

Sister Gina's expression is neutral, but I know her better. She makes a beeline for Father Michael. "May I speak with you? I noticed something peculiar in the hive house earlier. I think it's best if I show you before I tell anyone else." She glances at me, my signal to trail behind her.

CHAPTER 37
Karma

Father Michael unlocks the hive house. He leaves the keys dangling. I'm crouched behind an old tree, twenty feet away.

Sister Gina follows Father Michael inside, but I catch a glimpse of her face. She's got this composed nun thing down to an art, but now, she reminds me more of her brother, Niko, with the calculated charm of a hit man.

Every muscle in my body is coiled tight. As soon as I get the signal from Sister Gina, I'll make sure Father Michael's karma clocks in.

Sister Gina's talking to him, pointing at something in the corner of the hive house. Whatever she's saying has him fidgety. I can't hear. But I want to. I really want to.

I duck-walk over to a bush where I can hear their voices and get a better view through the open door.

Father Michael stands shoulder to shoulder with Sister Gina at the entrance. He dabs his forehead with his handkerchief. "I don't think we should disturb anything. What did you notice?"

"Down by the body." She coaxes him deeper into the room, and he kneels by dead Sister Agnes.

Sister Gina backs up and hovers by the door. Everything's going according to plan. Then, Sister Gina grabs the knife used to cut the honeycomb, holds it behind her back.

"What's she doing?" The words slip from my lips in a rushed hush.

Her gaze is locked on Father Michael like she's possessed. "There were only two people that know about the murder, Sister Agnes and you."

Confusion blankets his face. "Murder?"

"But, now I know, too." Sister Gina still holds the knife behind her back.

"Don't do it. Don't do it. Stick to the plan." My lips mutter-whisper like a rapid-fire prayer. I imagine there's an epic battle inside her. The instinct she inherited from her mafia family at odds with her new spiritual self.

"I know what you did, Father Michael. Sister Agnes told me everything. And soon everyone will know." Sister Gina looks over her shoulder and our gazes connect. I don't recognize the expression on her face. Her eyes are empty now, like the windows of an abandoned house.

Then her usual light returns; she steps outside and drops the knife in a flower bed by the door.

I scurry fast, help her slam the door shut with a satisfying thud, and twist the key in the lock. *Click.* That's the sound of justice. I hope Father Michael enjoys his little time-out.

Sister Gina could've done this by herself, but I was here in case things went wrong. And something almost did go wrong. The number of bodies almost doubled in the hive house. Judging by her shaking hands, Sister Gina knows how close she came to ending Father Michael's life.

I press myself against the exterior of the hive house, my heart pounding.

Sister Gina was right. The cops found a way to get to us. Two arrived on horseback. They took our statements and now are at the hive house.

The convent buzzes with whispers. The nuns and girls watch from the windows, faces full of confusion and fear. They've got questions, but the answers bite hard.

1. SAVAGE

The cops shuffle Father Michael out of the hive house. The stone building doubled as a classroom, crime scene, morgue, and prison all in the span of forty-eight hours.

Father Michael's in handcuffs, his head hanging like a man who just realized he's out of chances.

Sister Gina stands next to me with every emotion locked behind a fortress wall. But I can't shed the feeling this all seemed too easy.

I catch Sarah's look across the parking lot, but there's no victory party. I nod, and she nods back. No longer enemies, but not quite friends. Father Michael's face as they load him into the cop car is something I won't forget. He looks like he's been sucker-punched, and I'm glad. He thought he could hide behind his collar.

A cop car pulls up, which means the bridge is working. Soon the van full of nuns will arrive, my holy ticket to freedom.

CHAPTER 38
Last Wishes

I return to the room I share with Sister Gina to do one last check for stray stuff. Sister Gina's perched on the end of her bed, alone. I need to talk to her without anyone else around. "Father Michael didn't do it."

"What?" Sister Gina looks up with tired eyes.

I join her on the bed. "He didn't do it."

Sister Gina's hand rests on the dusty box Sister Agnes left her. "It's hard to believe that a priest would kill someone. Priests are human too. Trust me, he's guilty."

I turn toward her. "The whole thing is too clean, too neat. He was the only one with a key to the hive house, besides Sister Sylvan, who was glued to us all day."

"Exactly. And we both saw him lock the hive house." Her chin quivers like she's holding back.

"That's my point. Too convenient." I stand and pace the small space. "It's all wrapped in a box with a big bow, and I don't buy it."

Sister Gina picks up a glass of water on the nightstand and takes a sip. "You don't trust your own eyes?"

"All I saw was him leaving the hive house. But what if he didn't know Sister Agnes was in there when he turned the lock?" My speedy thoughts spur me to stand.

"The hive house was a wreck, and Sister Agnes was in plain view. You saw her, Vickie." She follows my pacing with her stare.

"What if she was alive when he locked the door?" I lean against the wall and cross my arms.

Sister Gina wipes away a tear. "You're saying Sister Agnes was hiding? In the hive house? Why would she do that?"

"Sister Agnes was allergic to bees. Only one EpiPen left, and she made sure everyone knew it." I walk to the window, and fixate on the hive house. "The last place she'd want to be is the hive house. But I can't figure out what Father Michael was doing there in the middle of a storm?" I scratch my head, hoping to joggle answers out. "We saw them arguing that day. Saw Sister Agnes take a tumble—very public. Maybe she sent Father Michael a note to meet in the most private place she could think of to finish their conversation."

She rises like a soldier called to duty. "What are you saying? That Sister Agnes called a meeting with Father Michael and when he didn't see her there, he locked her inside? Unintentionally? You're saying Sister Agnes planned this?" Her hands straighten the bedding that's already straight.

"Technically, it's not murder or suicide if you just let the bees be bees. If someone who takes their vows seriously wanted to die guilt and sin free, her conscience could blame the insects." My mind's vibrating with possible motives. I expect Sister Gina to tell me I'm nuts, but she doesn't.

"But someone took the transistor from the radio, her EpiPen, and the cash. How did all that end up in Father Michael's office?" Her hands churn like a mill grinding over something unseen.

"Exactly. Sister Agnes didn't just want to die; she wanted Father Michael to take the fall." I step closer to Sister Gina.

Sister Gina grabs her water glass and drinks again. "So a nun who wants to die guilt free frames someone else? Doesn't sound very nun-like."

"Yeah, that part doesn't sit right. Unless she felt justified. She had time to plant the transistor, the EpiPen, and the cash. But why?" I point to the shoebox on the bed. "The box she gave you. Nuns don't hold on to stuff, but she clung to press clippings, photos, and that yearbook. And why did she give them to you?"

Sister Gina rubs the dusty box. 'I'm sorry, Vickie."

"For what?" I sit on the bed.

"Getting you involved in this." She moves to the window like a ghost haunting her own life. "I didn't know when I brought you here what Sister Agnes had planned. But after she told me—"

"That day you came back looking like you'd gone ten rounds with a bad dream?" I ask.

"Yes. After she told me. I had to help. And when I tell you what she said, it'll all make sense." Sister Gina's eyes mist. She walks back to the bed, sits, and opens the box.

CHAPTER 39
The Weight of the Cross

FATHER MICHAEL

Father Michael stands in the stark fluorescent light of the prison intake area; the cold tile floor presses up through the thin soles of his shoes. A guard, her face impassive and indifferent, hands him an envelope. "Place all personal belongings in here. You'll get them back when you're released."

He removes his clerical collar and the necklace he wears underneath—a delicate pearl cross. It's been with him for so long, it's like part of his skin, fused with the layers of guilt and penance he carries. The metal, warmed by his flesh, brushes against his palm; a final touch and he places it in the envelope.

Strange that something so small can hold the weight of a thousand Hail Marys. The cross isn't just a symbol of his faith—it's a reminder of the blood on his hands, the promises he's broken, the lives he's destroyed.

"Please take good care of it." His voice cracks, splintering like glass under too much pressure.

The guard nods, her expression softening. "Of course, Father."

"M-m-m-means a lot to me." A familiar tightness in his throat, the old stutter clawing its way back, a beast he hadn't battled in decades. "Funny. I haven't stuttered in y-y-y-years."

The tangled words in his mouth are a bitter reminder of who he used to be—Skips, the stuttering kid from the side of town where dreams rust and hope collects dust, the kid everyone made fun of. Everyone except Kristie.

His mind, a vulture, circles over the carcass of his memories. The image of the drive-in theater flickers like an old movie reel spinning.

1969

Skips is behind the counter at the snack shack, fumbling with popcorn bags and soda cups. "K-K-Kristie." His gaze intersects with the girl in front of him. Long hair and an easy smile, the kind of person who seems untouchable in her perfection.

"Hi." The tilt of her head spills warmth, friendliness. "I didn't know you worked here."

"Yeah, I do. I l-l-l-like your necklace." His eyes drop to the tiny pearl cross. Simple. Beautiful. Pure. Like her.

Kristie's finger traces the cross. "Thanks."

A half hour later, behind the snack shack, Skips tosses a trash bag in the dumpster. He notices Kristie walking into the woods with Chips. Her steps are unsure, like a song played out of tune, drawing Skips's focus.

He should ignore the scene, but what if Kristie needs his help. Instead of going into the snack shack, he hurries to the back of the drive-in lot and into the woods.

He hears whispers and finds Chips and Kristie on a blanket. Chips is on top, his hands roaming where they shouldn't.

She pushes at him."Let's get back." She turns her head to avoid his insistent kisses.

Chips doesn't stop.

"The movie's starting." Kristie's tone is pinched, and urgent.

"And I'm just getting started too." Chips oozes entitlement for whatever he wants, whenever he wants.

"Come on. Stop." Kristie's hands press against his chest.

"Relax. I'll be quick." Chips's tone is dismissive.

"Get off of me." Kristie's voice quivers, sharp and brittle, and something within Skips shatters like thin ice. He steps from behind the trees, his hand squeezing the large pocket knife he always carries—a gift from his father when Skips left for a two-week camping trip with the Scouts. "Get off her." The forceful steadiness in his voice surprises him. He knows he would never be able to take Chips in a fight, even with his knife. He knows he can't give Chips time to turn around or stand. He plunges the knife into Chips's neck. The blade sinks deep, and blood spurts in a gruesome arc.

Chips's hands fly to his throat, but it's no use, his blood pours. He tries to stand, then collapses back onto the blanket. Passing out. Skips watches as Chips's eyes widen in shock, pupils dilating like ink spreading across paper. His hands claw at the wound, blood gushing between his fingers, staining the blanket beneath him. Chips's eyes flutter, unfocused, rolling back into his head as his legs give out. His body convulses once, a violent spasm, before going limp, the life draining from him in stuttering gasps.

Kristie scrambles to her feet. "Oh my God." Kristie's scream pierces the night, shrill and jagged, ripping through the silence like a siren. She lunges forward, hands trembling as she tries to press the blanket against Chips's throat, the fabric soaking through instantly with crimson. Tears streak down her cheeks, her breaths coming in panicked bursts. "Get away from me, Skips." Her voice isn't full of gratitude or relief, but revulsion.

Skips closes the knife, shoves it into his pocket. "It's n-n-not like that." His words fall flat, useless against the reality of what he's done.

Kristie stumbles back, nearly tripping over the uneven ground as she scrambles to put distance between herself and Skips. "I've got to get help." Her hands are stained with blood, shaking uncontrollably, and she clutches her chest like she's trying to hold her heart together. "He'll die," she gasps, backing away, her voice high and splintered with fear. Her eyes are wide, glossy with tears, darting.

Kristie tries to run, but he grabs her arm, his grip tight. He's panicked to explain he was protecting her purity. She struggles, wrenches her arm away, yanking it free from Skips's grip with a strength born of terror. Kristie stumbles, her shoes sliding in the wet leaves "Let go of me, you freak." Kristie's words strike at Skips's core. Skips's hand catches the delicate chain around her neck. It snaps; the pearl cross falls into his palm.

Kristie falls backward and her head strikes a rock with a sickening thud.

Skips bends down and puts his hand under her head. She's motionless. Blood seeps into her hair and onto his fingers. Tears flood down his face, an unstoppable river of regret and disbelief.

Footsteps.

"Kristie?" Nessa's voice.

The weight of what he's done crushes him; he stands and runs, the pearl cross clenched in his trembling fingers.

Skips doesn't look back; he sprints, the world around him a blur. The pearl cross digs into his palm, sharp and unforgiving, a painful reminder of everything that's gone wrong.

1999

"Father?" The female guard's voice offers comfort, but demands compliance. She hands him an orange prison uniform. The security door buzzes open. "This way." She motions him ahead.

The door clangs shut behind him, shaking his soul. The click of his shoes on the tile floor marks the rhythm of his silent prayer — *Our Father, who art in heaven* . . . The words somersault through his mind, a feverish chant to drown out the memories of Kristie's face, her blood, her eyes fluttering closed like the final act of a passion play.

He walks, and thinks of the parable of the prodigal son. But in his version, the son doesn't return home to a feast. Instead, he's dragged back in chains, his sins laid bare for all to see, with no fatted calf waiting, only human judgment.

The stutter is back for a reason. It is God's way, reminding him he could never outrun his past. Skips had never truly left—he was just buried under the collar, waiting for a moment of weakness to resurface.

CHAPTER 40
Fractured Faith

VICKIE

Me and Sister Gina sit side by side on her creaky old bed. The box between us spills its guts—yellowed press clippings about a girl named Kristie's murder, a yearbook open to a grainy black-and-white pic of Father Michael, and a few other dusty relics.

Sister Gina's fingers glide over the clippings. "I'm sorry I've put you in this position." Gina's voice is thin. Her eyes play hopscotch between Father Michael's high school mugshot and Kristie's newspaper photo, as if Sister Gina's connecting dots only she can see.

I snatch a loose clipping, just to hold something. "Yeah, well, I'm here. So."

"When Father Michael was assigned to Sisters of Mercy and Prayer, Sister Agnes recognized him right away. And of course, he recognized her." Gina keeps talking like she's gotta get it out or it'll eat her alive. She fumbles with the clippings. "When she went to his office to present him with a card, filled with well wishes from all the sisters at the convent, that's when she saw the cross around his neck. And here's what happened."

THREE WEEKS EARLIER
Sister Agnes

Sister Agnes peers through the slightly cracked-open door and inches it wider. Father Michael stands in his office in an undershirt, and the pearl cross necklace lays on his chest.

Agnes swings the door and steps in. "Where'd you get that necklace?"

Father Michael jumps. "Nessa."

"It's Sister Agnes now, Father. And Kristie never took it off." She clenches her fists to stop her fingers from shaking. "The police searched everywhere and never found it. They said whoever killed her probably kept it as a trophy."

Father Michael walks over to the window and stares out. She watches him, her mind spinning. Could this be real? Could Father Michael be the monster behind her sister's death?

Agnes's throat tightens, her heart a twisted knot. The past she's run from now crashes down, cold and unforgiving. She wants to scream, but her voice feels trapped under years of silence. The convent was supposed to be her refuge, not another layer of hell. Her fingers dig into the door frame. She's spent years praying for answers, and now that they're here, she's not sure she can bear them.

Agnes wants to be wrong. Wants Father Michael to have a reasonable explanation. "Did you find the cross in the woods?" She takes a few steps inside.

He hangs his head. "It was an accident."

"What was an accident?" She grabs the corner of the desk for support. Black spots form in front of her eyes.

"I was protecting Kristie. Chips would've defiled her. You know what he was like." Father Michael turns to Agnes. His voice trembles on the edge of justification, laced with a desperate need to be understood. "You know how he was, Nessa. He was going to hurt her." He clenches his jaw, the muscles twitching under his skin. "I was trying to save her when

I stabbed Chips. But Kristie didn't understand. The way she looked at me." Father Michael's fingers tap a frantic rhythm on the desk, betraying his outward calm. He forces a steady breath, but his chest still heaves. "She looked at me like I was the monster, not Chips. Like I'd betrayed everything she'd ever thought I was. I grabbed her arm to try and explain, to help her see. She wrenched free, stumbled, fell, and hit her head."

Agnes feels her heartbeat pounding in her ears, drowning out his words. All these years she'd thought she'd buried her grief, but now it's back, raw and blistering. The room tilts, her vision blurring as the reality hits—this man, this priest, has been carrying her sister's death like a ghost chained to his side. The tears she's held back for years threaten to spill, but she forces them down. She can't break now, not in front of him. "When I found Kristie's body, Chips grabbed me in the woods. I thought he was the killer, until we heard a sound in the woods. You. He left me and you killed him. You killed Kristie and Chips."

"When I heard you calling for Kristie I hid. I had to make sure you found her and got help in case she might be alive. I didn't care if Chips lived or died. God forgive me. But, Chips must have regained consciousness." Father Michael slumps into the desk chair, the weight of his confession pushing him down. "Chips found me in the woods, watching. He confronted me. I was still holding Kristie's necklace. He went biserk, punched me. And for the first time in my life I stood up for myself. I fought back."

"You killed him." A single tear slips down her cheek, burning like a drop of acid, each inch it travels another piece of her resolve crumbling.

"If I could take it back, I would. But I was protecting Kristie and defending myself."

"Why didn't you go to the police?" She sits, numb, the room closing in around her.

"I confessed my crimes, just not to the police. To our Lord. And he forgave me. I've spent my life in penance, sewing seeds of good deeds.

What good could I do locked away?" Father Michael's focus flickers to the cross on the wall, a faint tremor running through his fingers as he speaks.

Agnes pushes herself up from the chair, every movement slow and deliberate, like she's dragging herself out of a pit she never meant to fall into. She's not just standing—she's gathering the pieces of her shattered faith. "If you won't go to the police, I will."

Father Michael pushes up and circles around the desk, his motions smooth but strained, like he's rehearsing his next moves carefully. "You know as well as I, matters like this are best handled within the church."

Agnes inches backward, each step tentative. She's desperate to put distance between them, to find air that isn't tainted by his confessions. "You're right. I'll go to the archbishop."

He matches her steps. "He has heard my confession and shares my perspective."

All hope is sucked out of the room.

Agnes sprints into the hallway, her sobs choke in her throat. and her vision clouds with tears.

VICKIE

I sit cross-legged on the bed, flicking through the clippings like it's some kind of twisted family photo album.

Sister Gina closes the yearbook. "Sister Agnes knew the church would protect Father Michael, splash the situation with a fresh coat of holy water on it and call it a day. And she didn't have any hard evidence. The confession only she heard and that necklace only she saw him wear—like some kind of twisted talisman."

I rearrange the clippings. "So Sister Agnes decided to frame Father Michael for her own death. To avenge her sister's death." Sister Gina nods, slow, like she's weighing each word she might speak. "I guess Sister Agnes felt that at least Father Michael would pay in some way."

"Doesn't sound very nun-like." I stack the clippings like a deck of cards, mimicking Sister Gina's words back to her.

"Nuns are human too. Sinners who have to decide each day where to draw the line around our humanity." Sister Gina scoops up a couple of the articles and drops them onto my pile. "That's why Sister Agnes trusted me to help. I was supposed to be the one to witness the argument and see Father Michael entering the hive house. Then I would find the items she planted in his office. Of course, you beat me to both those things. I guess she knew because of my family and their criminal activities, I'm familiar with blurry lines."

I lock eyes with her, two boxers before the bell rings. "Now what?"

"That's the question." Sister Gina gets up and walks to the desk. She sticks her finger into the wax of a lit candle, holds her finger up to the air, watching it harden, then peels it off.

I drop the clippings into the box. "We can't let Father Michael go to prison for a crime he didn't commit, even if he deserves it."

Sister Gina closes her eyes, her breath shaky. "I'm a horrible nun." It slips out like she's been holding it in too long.

"Yes. Yes, you are. The worst." My words are sharp, but there's a flicker of softness. "But you're kind. And you're a loyal friend to Sister Agnes. And you're human."

Human. The word hangs.

She swallows, her eyes glassy. "Yeah. Human." She turns back to the desk. "It's not fair of me to ask, but can you give me a couple days? Before you say anything."

I nod, but my head's buzzing. We've stepped into something way bigger than us, and there's no easy way out.

Sister Gina releases a breath, and for a second, the heaviness seems to lift from her shoulders. But only a second.

Silence replaces our secret sharing.

My gaze drifts to the crucifix on the wall. I can almost hear it whispering, like it's reminding Sister Gina of what she's supposed to stand for, what she's about to lose.

CHAPTER 41
Sins and Sanctuary

FATHER MICHAEL

Father Michael sits on the metal bunk of his prison cell, the hard coils under the mattress digging into his thighs.

The cell door clangs open, and a prisoner enters, well groomed, big smile.

"Yo, you coming, Niko?" a gruff voice calls to the man with the charming smile.

Niko. The name's familiar. Michael heard Agnes mention it. Sister Gina's brother?

"Just a minute. This won't take long." Niko's voice glides like a knife through silk. He cracks his knuckles, the sound sharp, echoing in the small space. "I hear you have unfinished business with my sister."

Michael knows what's next. He braces. There's a quiet acceptance in his stillness, a resignation to the violence.

The impact hits like a sudden jolt, jaw searing with pain. His vision splits, scattering light and darkness in chaotic bursts. The cold, unforgiving floor rushes up to meet him, stealing breath and thought.

Kicks to his stomach follow, but Michael's mind skips back to another beating he ran from as a teen. One month after Chips's and Kristie's funerals, Chips's friends resumed their endless torture. His vision blurs and the present recedes.

1969

Skips's soles slap the ground like a desperate drumbeat. Badger, Squid, and Tiny are tight behind him in a chase. They love cornering him, pushing him, punching him. But this time, Skips sees an escape—a chapel, the door ajar, a sliver of sanctuary. He slips inside, slams the door. The peace is a stark contrast to the chaos he's left outside.

The chapel's empty, save for the flickering candles that line the altar at the front, splintering off the stained glass. Wooden pews stand in solemn rows, their surfaces worn and scarred. Skips inches forward. He reaches for a match, and spies his reflection in the mirror above the candles. His face is lined with the strain of the unspeakable deeds he's committed, and his eyes are hollow pools burdened with guilt.

"Who are you running from?" The question bleeds from his lips to his reflection.

"Myself," he answers.

And he understands. It doesn't matter what the world thinks, what judgments others cast. The real torment comes from within, from the endless self-condemnation gnawing at him. He looks up at the huge wooden crucifix dominating the wall above the altar. He craves God's judgment, so he can stop judging himself.

Salty droplets streak his skin, shining in the dim, holy light, his soul crying out for the forgiveness he doesn't think he deserves. Then something inside him shifts. A flicker of hope in his dark despair. He falls to his knees and vows to dedicate his life to making up for the night he ended three lives—Chips's, Kristie's, and his own. *And in that dark moment, Skips steps into the light.*

CHAPTER 42
A Fresh Start

TWO DAYS LATER
1999

VICKIE

I'm slouched on the sofa. Ma's in the bedroom getting dressed for the day. Uncle Aldo's standing by the window, his silhouette cut against the gray Queens skyline. He hands me the newspaper without a word; he crooks his neck to make sure Ma's not entering. The headline blares back at me: "Priest Confesses to Murder in 30-Year-Old Cold Case — Convent Scandal Uncovered." My brain pieces together what this means. It's like the universe decided to throw me another curveball, and this one's coming in hot.

Uncle Aldo folds the newspaper, stuffs it inside his jacket. "I think it's best we don't tell your mother. She'll just worry. As far as she knows, the retreat was rained out, so you came back early along with everyone else."

Ma floats into the living room, all smiles. She hands Uncle Aldo a cup of coffee.

He sips from the cup. "Best cup of coffee I've ever had."

Ma's pride percolates. "It's only Sanka. But see, Vix? I didn't fall apart while you were gone. I can do stuff like make coffee." She tweaks the buttons on her shirt, preening like she's dressed for the red carpet. Then she turns to Uncle Aldo, eyebrows arched. "So, what did you want to tell us?"

"Have a seat." He gestures to the sofa. Ma sits, her hand gripping the armrest. "It's nothing bad, is it?" Her fingers trace the floral pattern on the fabric.

He fiddles with his watch. "I'm getting closer to retirement. And I've been thinking for a while of making some changes."

The sofa cushion squeaks under me. My nails dig into the edge of the cushion. "What kind of changes?"

"I've been applying to jobs, and I've decided to accept a new position." He swirls the coffee in his cup.

Ma's eyes light up, and she sets her mug on the table, the coaster wobbling under it. "That's great."

"In Maine." He sets his cup down with a soft clink.

The word slams into me like a fist. "Maine?"

"You're leaving us?" Ma's voice cracks, her grip tightening on the armrest.

"Leave my favorite little sister? And my favorite niece? No way. Do you know how boring my life would be without the two of you?" He chuckles.

"I don't understand, then." Ma twists the bottom of her shirt.

"I'd like you to come with me." Uncle Aldo's gaze bounces between us.

"To Maine?" The words taste as foreign as they feel.

"Yes. Yes. Why not, Vix? "Ma's all in, not even hesitating. She's fizzing like a soda shaken one too many times. "A fresh start for us. It could be good."

"But we love the city." The thought of leaving everything behind—everything that makes us who we are—makes my stomach churn. Nona Barolucci always talks about how terrible leaving her home in Italy during the war was. Now I get it.

A knock on the door snaps the tension in half.

Ma shoots me an manic look. "Who could that be? So much excitement in one day."

"I'll get it." And I beat her to the door. I pull it open. Sister Gina stands there in civilian clothes, which is like seeing a guppy out of water. "Sister Gina. You're—naked."

"It's just Gina now. I hope I'm not intruding." She peeks inside the room, craning her head toward Ma and Uncle Aldo. "Wondered if I could speak to Vickie in private."

"Oh sure. Aldo and I will be in the back. Give you some privacy. Can we get you anything, Sister Gina? I mean, Gina. A coffee?" Ma's still chipper with the prospects of a new life.

"No, thank you." Gina steps inside.

Ma flashes a wide smile, taking Uncle Aldo in the back bedroom.

A knot tightens in my chest. "I saw the newspaper." I close the door.

"Sometimes friends—or brothers—in low places come in handy." Gina pulls a folded letter from her purse. "I wanted to come by and thank you." She lets out a shaky breath, her eyes not quite meeting mine. "I've been thinking about what you said. A lot of things you said. But specifically about nuns hiding out. You're right—I've been hiding from my family and my past, and that's not the right reason to make a lifelong commitment to the Church. So, for better or worse, I'm going to face my crazy relatives. I mean, if *you* can do it—"

I laugh, a release valve letting go of all we've been through together.

"And then who knows. Maybe I'll return to the order or, well, I'm just not sure." Gina fidgets with the letter.

"You'll figure it out." I put my hand on her shoulder.

"But enough about me. I've got some good news for you, Vickie—your scholarship has been renewed." Gina hands me the envelope.

"Thank you." The letter feels heavier than it should, like it's packed with all the possibilities I didn't think I'd ever have again. And don't really want.

"Don't thank me. Sarah had her dad contacted Father Greg on your behalf. Her dad donates a lot of cash to the school." Gina winks.

I tap the letter against my leg. "Turns out I won't need the scholarship. That school was never a good fit for me. If we're being honest. I think we both know that." I tear the letter in half and place it on the coffee table.

Gina's lips twitch, like she's holding back a flood of words. "I understand. I guess it wasn't for me either. So, what's next?"

"I think we're moving. To Maine." The words taste less bitter, but I'm not sure what has changed.

"How do you feel about that?" Gina's tone says she really wants to hear the answer.

"A new beginning could be good for Ma. And good for me too." This is what we need—a good rain to wash away all the footprints.

"I like the sound of that. See you around, Vickie." Gina hugs me. Awkward at first, but then not so bad.

"See you around, Sis—Gina."

For the first time in a while, I feel like maybe—just maybe—things are going to be okay.

ONE MONTH LATER

Uncle Aldo and Ma sit in the front seat and I'm in the back of his beat-up police car. He pulls the U-Haul into a suburban Maine neighborhood, the kind that looks like a postcard until you realize you're actually living in it. The houses are small, neat, and a little too perfect.

A black Mercedes, too fancy for the neighborhood, pulls away from the curb.

"I've never lived in a house before. It's that one right there?" Ma bounces in her seat. She points to a small house with a white picket fence that screams *normal*.

"Yeah. Compared to Queens, rent's dirt cheap." Uncle Aldo turns off the engine with a satisfied grunt.

I peer out the window, trying to shake off the uneasy feeling that's settled in my gut.

Our house is tinier than the rest on the block, but is well-kept. But next door is a mess—overgrown lawn, paint peeling like a bad sunburn, and an old man standing in the yard, glaring at us like we're trespassing. The whole scene yells trouble.

Ma catches the look on my face as I narrow my eyes at the neighbor's yard. "What's wrong, Vickie?"

Unease crawls up my spine like a spider. "Something's not right about that house."

"The one next to ours?" Ma crooks her neck to get a better look.

I look at Ma, then Uncle Aldo. "I think we live next door to a serial killer."

Ma's gaze drifts back to our house. "But look. We have shrubs."

"Yeah, they're nice, Ma." I pat her shoulder from the back seat. "We're home."

TRIAL THREE

DARK FENCES

CHAPTER 43
Dead Wishes

Maine
1987
MAURY

The officer must be mistaken.

"Both of them? Dead?" The words slip from Maury's aging throat. Wrong names. Wrong house. Wrong everything. Yes, that's it. A mistake.

His name is Smiley. Officer Kenneth Smiley. Salt-and-pepper hair, a bit of a belly. Kind eyes. There's irony in the name. Maury's sure that his is just one more door of the many Smiley has knocked on in his police career to deliver similar devastating news.

But this is Maury's house, Maury's daughter, Maury's son-in-law that Officer Smiley's talking about.

And tonight is a rare moment out for the couple—Nadia and Benjamin's fifth wedding anniversary. A night out that Maury encouraged. "Take some time for yourselves," he'd said. The echo of his advice turns his stomach.

He's unsure how long he fixates on the officer's badge, anchoring himself to the small metal star, turning the horrific words over in his mind.

Head-on collision.

A college kid.

Slippery roads.

Lost control.

Only one thought breaks through — Hugo's only three.

"I can't sleep, Pop-Pop." Hugo shuffles and half-trips down the hallway over his footed pajamas.

Maury accepts Officer Smiley's calling card, shaking his hand. "Thank you, Officer." He closes the door, his thoughts a tornado swirl of Smiley's words and a now-murky future.

Life changes in an instant.

Maury squeezes his eyelids in silent prayer and turns, managing a quivering smile that dies before it's fully formed.

"What's wrong?" Hugo sleepy-slurs his words. A stuffed animal dangles from his right hand.

"Nothing for you to worry about tonight. Let's get you some warm milk. That always helps me. The morning will be here before you know it."

Tomorrow Hugo will wake in a new world that will demand he grow up faster than any child should. Maury can't stop that from happening, but he can delay it for a few more hours.

One more night of pleasant dreams.

1988

Cake, candles, presents. In the past, Maury had no taste for birthdays. Not for himself, not for his late wife, not for his daughter, Nadia.

A birthday was just another ordinary day.

Until a chilly summer evening one year ago, when a knock at the door extinguished his last chance to celebrate with Nadia.

Maury wishes he could replay every one of her birthdays, not sparing any Disney princess dress, Sour Patch kid, or frivolous extravagance. But the road to hell is paved with dead wishes. So much death the past few years.

1. SAVAGE

Best to focus on making new memories. New wishes.

Today is an extraordinary occasion. A once-in-a-lifetime moment. Today Maury celebrates life. Flickering candles, sugary frosting with sprinkles, gifts in gaudy wrapping are all glorious necessities. Today, Hugo, his grandson, turns four.

Maury studies Hugo's small frame perched on a worn leather footstool in the living room. The boy's eyes twinkle beneath the brim of his navy-blue and red baseball cap. How is that possible after everything that's happened? Maury would do anything to keep that twinkle.

Hugo's hands, like tiny starfish, stroke the eight-week-old terrier-poodle squirming in his lap—a new heartbeat in this old house. A red bow bops from one side of the puppy's neck to the other. Hugo tightens his excited grip on the pup. The wiggling bundle of life wrapped in a fur coat yelps.

"Careful," Maury's voice scratches through, offering soothing guidance. "Got to be gentle. A little love goes a long, long way. Remember that." Maury demonstrates, guiding Hugo's fingers until the pup's whirlwind of energy eases into a contented rumble.

"Happy birthday." Maury's words catch. He wishes they carried more than sentiment. Wishes they could shield Hugo from every scrape and bruise, the kind you see and the kind you don't. Wishes they could exempt Hugo from the disappointments on the other side of childhood.

But Maury knows better than to eliminate every hard knock.

Tee-ball, bike riding, swimming, climbing trees, and now caring for a living thing. Risk-taking builds confidence. Little Hugo has no problem with adventure. It's Maury who holds his breath with every stretched limit. One close call after another.

Still, caring for Hugo is saving Maury's life, a daily reason to keep going and not give up.

"Happy birthday, Pop-Pop," Hugo chirps, mirroring the puppy's joy.

A chuckle erupts from deep in Maury's belly. "It's not my birthday, it's yours. But thank you."

"You're welcome." Hugo's eyes don't leave the puppy.

"Have you thought of what you'll name him?"

"Candy." Hugo's little chest swells, his answer immediate and certain.

The boy's joy spills into Maury. "Candy? Why Candy?"

"Because I love all kinds of candy. And I love my puppy dog. And I love you." Hugo's logic is a straight line, a child's reasoning pure and clear.

"That makes me happy. I love you, too. More than you know. Now, how about some cake?"

Hugo's eyes light up like sparklers. "Can I blow out the candles?"

"Of course. But don't forget to make a wish first."

Hugo puffs up, squeezing his eyes tight, looking ready to explode. "I want Candy to live with me forever."

Maury's heart constricts. Nothing's forever. He remembers his own greatest fear—will he live long enough to raise Hugo?

He pushes back the dark thought before it invades his face and spoils the moment. "Wait to blow out the candles to make your wish. And you're supposed to keep it secret."

Hugo's face scrunches. "Why?"

A superstitious truth as delicate as spider silk passes through Maury's mind. "Because if you don't, it may not come true."

Candy runs in circles around Hugo. "Can I take Candy outside to play?"

Maury weighs the request. He doesn't like leaving Hugo alone, but it's a nice night. And Maury could use the time to prepare the surprise. "Yes."

Hugo beams.

"But don't forget the leash. And stay on the porch."

In a flash, Hugo is at the door, leash secured to Candy's collar.

"We'll have your birthday cake outside. OK?"

The screen door slams and echoes through the room.

Seizing the moment, Maury springs into action with a speed that causes him to grab his back for extra support. He hurries from the living room into the kitchen. The chocolate cake is already on the counter, topped

7. SAVAGE

with four white candles. Maury crooks his head back around the doorway to ensure he is still alone, then removes the glass dome covering the cake.

He opens the kitchen junk drawer, the perfect hiding spot for Hugo's birthday treasures. Hugo's expecting the cake, but not *Sonic the Hedgehog* characters. Maury places Metal Sonic, front and center. Then, Knuckles to the left, and Charmy Bee on the right. A warm smile slips from his chest to his lips. A year ago, he was sailing into the sunset of his golden years. Now, look at him, starting over, and with a preschooler.

Maury gazes through the tiny window above the sink and admires the sun dipping low, its last light bleeding into the horizon. The world is turning that shade of blue that's not quite dark yet, not quite dawn, as if color is holding its breath, waiting for night to fall.

Movement captures his attention. The evening breeze rolls clouds through the sky. A blue jay lands on the top of a birdhouse that hangs outside the window. A white phone-service van on the shoulder of the road, two houses down, rolls into park as graceful as a swan on the asphalt river.

Jubilant sounds tickle his ears. Hugo's giggles and Candy's panting are loud enough to permeate the kitchen walls all the way from the porch.

Somehow, his life is beautiful again. When did that happen?

Maury rummages for a lighter in the junk drawer. The phone rings. He shuffles over a few steps and picks up the receiver. "Hello?"

"I'm calling about your car's extended warranty."

"What?"

"I'm calling about your car's—"

"Not now. It's my grandson's birthday. And I don't have a warranty. Or a car."

"It won't take—"

"I have to go. Goodbye." Maury hangs up the phone and returns to the junk drawer, picking up the lighter on the counter.

The first is the hardest to light.

One, two, three strikes of the lighter before the wick catches fire.

He pauses, watching the dance of the flame. Fire. Heat. Life.

Maury lights the last three candles in one swoop, then drops his arms. Hugo will be pleased.

Lifting the cake, he walks from the kitchen through the living room, cupping his hand to guard the candles against the stirring air.

Candy's joyful bark is now a whine. The puppy scratches at the door.

"Candy! Please. Patience is a virtue."

Maury wedding marches through the living room, one step at a time, careful to keep the candles lit. Through the screen door, the brisk evening air whispers a reminder he's seventy-two and this porch, these bones, have seen many seasons. He pushes the screen door open with his back, both to hide the surprise and prevent Candy from running inside, then turns, all smiles for the big reveal. "Happy Birthday."

He scans the front porch.

The front yard.

No Hugo.

Candy scampers up and down the steps, his leash trailing behind.

"Where's Hugo?"

Maury pivots. Careful of the dripping candles, he searches the porch again. "Hugo?" He stumbles on a squeaky toy, almost dropping the birthday treat, then places the cake on the neon-green end table Hugo helped him paint last month.

Ah, I know this game. His pulse settles into a normal rhythm. "Come out, come out, wherever you are!"

Maury listens. Ear pressed into the air as if it is a wall. "Guess Candy and I will have to eat the cake all by ourselves?"

Silence.

"Hugo?" Maury walks down the steps. Water from the sprinklers spritzes his face and boots. Candy scrambles over to him. Maury's heart, a drumbeat slowing down with time, thrums a little faster.

He searches the small front yard, circling the forty-foot oak tree and checking behind each of the tall but manicured shrubs lining the porch.

The sun sinks lower behind the houses and below the tree line across the street.

He wouldn't leave the yard. He knows better. Maury rushes to the sidewalk.

He spies a splash of color on the cracked gray concrete. Hugo's baseball cap. The one his father bought for him when he took him to his first baseball game. Boston Red Sox. Maury picks it up and traces the emblem with his finger. A cap he never takes off.

Maury stares down the street in both directions. No sign of the boy.

A white service van turns the corner, speeding out of sight.

He hugs the cap to his chest. "Hugo?"

The streetlamps flicker on. Almost dark.

Police.

Call the police.

Maury bolts to the porch. He stumbles on the second step and reaches for the banister, steadying himself.

A gust of wind blows through the trees and extinguishes all four candles on the birthday cake in the span of a solitary beat of Maury's shattered heart.

"Not again. I can't lose you too, Hugo."

Life changes in an instant.

CHAPTER 44
Justice is Blind

```
2001
Present Day
```
VICKIE

There's an odor in the Maine Courthouse. Convict sweat. Or fear. Air has a taste, too. Tangy, fizzy. Like potato salad that's been in the sun too long. Makes my stomach twist.

My hair's a tangled mess, combed, but rebelling. Dark strands fall over my eyes. A curtain I don't want to open.

My sweater with a signature V on the lower right pocket fits me tight like a permanent hug. Calms me down. I clench the soft fabric in both of my fists.

I'm first to go up front. The entire room's got their eyes on me. Nothing new. Most everybody in this town is white. Pasty white. Oat milk in your coffee white. I'm fifty percent Italian, fifty percent Korean, so I can't hide. I don't care. I'm one hundred percent Vickie Bartolucci. Nothing they do will change that.

But today, I can't decide if this courtroom's a stage I wanna perform on or a pit I wanna climb out of.

I look around—a full 360. The place is packed tighter than the 7 train during rush hour in Queens, but the cold quiet has my attention.

1. SAVAGE

Something familiar about it. Church. That's what it reminds me of. Even the seats look like pews. The sea of faces all dripping desperation, all looking for somebody to save them from their circumstances, their lives, themselves.

And then. The side door flings open. *Surprise.*

In this chapel, God's a lady, staring down at me from her raised platform. The leather chair moans when the judge takes a seat. Another surprise.

This God's got a big ass.

"All right, Miss Vickie Bartolucci." God speaks and has an accent. Could be from New York. It's been two years since we moved to Maine from Queens. Feels like a life sentence. I gave up trying to fit in a long time ago.

The judges accent is like mine, but it sounds different coming from her—more practiced, more phony, more Maine-like. "This is the second time you've been before this court. I see here—petty theft—again."

I can't help the words that tumble out of my mouth. "Practice makes perfect." Uncle Aldo grabs my arm and leaves his hand there. It's a warning.

"Smile, Vickie." Ma's advice this morning. "It'll take the edge off your words. And call 'em Your Honor. They like that." But my lips don't want to move. My body doesn't always do what my brain says.

Uncle Aldo's grip on my arm tightens. "Vickie."

"I'm joking. Geez. Your Honor." I give her this awkward curtsy. Maybe that will lighten the mood. And my best effort at a smile. My mouth parts over my braces. A gift from a dentist Ma dated for a few weeks.

Her nostrils flare. I instantly regret my choice.

The judge shuffles papers. Dozens of down-and-out lives rest in her manicured hands. She is God. For right now, anyway. "This courtroom is a joke to you?"

"Your Honor, if I may?" Uncle Aldo, always keeping the peace, steps in. Ma's brother. It's not easy growing up with a cop in the family. But today it could work in my favor. It's about time something does.

215

God nods. "Go ahead, Officer Bartolucci."

He clears his throat, shifting on his feet. "I'm just Uncle Aldo today. Listen, she's a good kid. No dad at home. And I'm doing my best to guide her."

The word *dad* punches me in the stomach. Always does. "I don't need a dad. Me and Ma do just fine," I spit out, quicker than I should.

"She's on the right track. Making a lot of progress. If you could cut her a break this one last time. You know what juvie is like. No place for a kid who's trying to get right." His voice is soft, wrapping me in a blanket and presenting me to this woman who appears to have just smelled the inside of a sweaty tennis shoe.

The judge peels me with her beady eyes. I'm no potato. "Ms. Bartolucci, what do you have to say for yourself?"

Silence hangs like one of Cousin Joey's farts.

Her words press down on me. Every rustle, every cough, echoes in my eardrums.

"Ms. Bartolucci, are you still with us?"

Everyone's always talking *at* me. "Yeah, I heard you. I'm not used to people so anxious to hear what I've got to say." Even though I snap at her, for some reason the judge's face relaxes. Guess I struck a chord. I should stop while I'm ahead, but I'm not the type to do what I should. "And you don't know anything about my life."

The judge's voice drips with something I can't place, but it's not pity. "Listen. I grew up in one of the worst neighborhoods in Queens. That's right. I'm a Queens girl myself."

I knew it.

Her accent slips. She loses a little polish. The past is creeping in. You can take the girl out of Queens, but you can't hide Queens for long, even under a long black robe. She leans in. I smell a sob story brewing.

"Went to one of the worst schools. And you know what's worse than having no father? Having *my* father."

There it is.

"You're lucky to have someone in your life who cares about you as much as your uncle does."

This one gets my attention. My lip quivers. Did she see that? I look around. *Get a grip, Vickie.*

"I'm going to give you one last shot. Not because I believe in you. But because I believe that man right there loves you. And love is a powerful thing."

"Thank you, Your Honor." Uncle Aldo's every word is braided with gratitude.

The judge's stare suffocates me. I'm hot all of a sudden. "But, Ms. Bartolucci. Vickie. Remember this. Be the better person. There are a lot of wrong turns you can take in life and plenty of people happy to take them with you. Be the better person. Am I clear?"

"Thank you, Your Honor." Uncle Aldo speaks before my mind can fully register her words.

I'm dizzy. So many emotions at once. If gratitude is one of them, I can't latch on to it. Something else is speaking through me. "Thank you?"

"Vickie. Stop," Uncle Aldo whispers, quick and harsh. His grip on my arm turns iron. "That's enough."

No chance I'm shutting up. I've got to get this out. "If you're finished insulting me" —anger bubbles up from my toes— "I'd like to answer the question. No. No, you're not clear. I don't know how to be the better person. What does that even mean? I'm Vickie Bartolucci. I'm not going to become someone else. I don't know how. You can take me or leave me. Your Honor."

At least I ended on a good note. Ma would be proud I called her *Your Honor.*

CHAPTER 45
Driving Lessons

Car doors shut, seat belts snap. I wait. An Uncle Aldo beat-down is coming. Not with his fists. Worse. With his words.

He turns the ignition, but doesn't budge the gear shift. Doesn't look at me, sits there, his gaze fixed out the windshield.

The pine tree air freshener tied to the rearview mirror spins. I'm grateful for the distraction. Uncle Aldo gets to me in a way other people don't. My feet stick to the floor mat. I pull up one foot, then the other, before putting them back in place. Someone spilled coffee. Probably lots of cups of coffee over many stakeouts. The distant drone of the city surrounds us with brief angry spurts from horns. I'm glad for the noise. Better than silent judgment.

Then Uncle Aldo inhales like he's winding up to take a swing at bat. "What were you thinking?" His grip tightens on the steering wheel. "You can't speak to a judge that way. Especially when she's doing you a favor."

"She's doing you a favor," I shoot back, the cold metal of my seat belt pressing against my collarbone. "She doesn't know me. She doesn't know anything about me." Moving here has been hard. Lonely. But I don't do sob stories.

He exhales hard. His sigh sputters with frustration and disappointment. "And I don't know you either, apparently. You're not acting like the Vickie I'm used to. You keep digging this grave for yourself, and you're not going to be able to get out. Is that what you want?"

He's mad, but there's more. Fear? Worry? Pain? This isn't just about me. This is about Ma too.

"I'm not a magician," he says. "I can't get you off every time. And I can't keep doing this with you. I've got a job. A family."

I lower my gaze, the lump in my throat pulsating. Intermittent smatterings of a radio talk show register. Has that been on this whole time?

Uncle Aldo notices the station and flicks the knob off. His voice is low. "I'm sorry. I didn't mean that."

I swallow hard, pushing the pain down. Judgment hurts more coming from him. "I'm sorry to be such a burden."

"What?" His voice cracks.

"You could be at home with your *real* family."

The heavy bubble of regret around the two of us makes it hard to breathe.

"Stop." His voice trembles. "You and your mother are my family too. You're like a daughter to me. And I'd do anything for both of you. You know that."

"I know."

He puts the car in gear and drives out of the courthouse parking lot.

The hum of the city grows louder. The scent of the pine air freshener mingles with the undercurrent of gasoline.

"I don't get it." His tone is desperate. "You got food. You got clothes. If you need something, just ask me. Why do you take things?"

It's my turn to say something. I let out a dry, nervous chuckle. I don't want to answer, but something deep inside does the speaking. "I do it because I'm good at it. Cousin Tony is good at fixing cars. You're good at your job. Even Ma is good at dating guys."

He snorts. "Quantity and quality in dating are two different things."

"Yeah, well. I want to be good at something."

His grip on the wheel softens. Color returns to his knuckles. "Listen to me. You had it right the first time with what you said in the courtroom. And so did the judge. You're both right. You're good at being Vickie Bartolucci. But now it's time you forget what everyone else is doing and become the best Vickie Bartolucci the world has ever seen."

Something tugs at my lips, not a smile, but relief that the tone of our conversation is shifting. "I'm pretty sure the competition isn't that fierce."

"Don't be a wise guy. Capisce?"

Rolling my eyes, I nod.

"What?" He freezes in place, cupping his hand over his ear.

"Capisce. Geez."

His eyes, lined with age and worry, are too much for me. I look away.

"And there's one more thing," he says.

"You've got to be kidding me?" I fidget with the strings on my sweatpants.

"You need friends. You're in high school now. Fresh start."

"It's summer."

"Well, it wouldn't kill you to talk to a couple kids your age. It's good you help your mother, but you need your own life. You need to get out of that house sometimes. You know what I'm going to do? You're fifteen. I'm going to get you your work papers. You can earn a little cash."

"You're doing me so many favors. Slow down a little." Sarcasm drools from each word.

He grins. "Yeah. A job will give you a real sense of accomplishing something."

CHAPTER 46
Fences and Flyers

I'm wearing my nicest pair of sweats because thanks to Uncle Aldo, today I'm job hunting. I've even got on the dressy jacket from my Queen's Catholic school uniform, which I haven't worn since I was thirteen. Way too big for me back then. Sister Irene said I would *definitely* grow into it. I know she meant it as an insult about my size. I didn't let it bother me. Didn't give her the satisfaction.

Ma is slunk back on the recliner, still in her silk robe and yesterday's makeup, slurping her morning caffeine. Diet Pepsi. How can she drink that crap so early in the morning? Better than what she drank last night. Came home drunk again. Means she had a good date. Her definition? A man who might stick around for a week or two. I lose track of her good-bad-okay-horrible dates. She does, too. Better that way.

She looks up, smiles.

"Sorry I didn't come with you to court yesterday." Ma's voice is shaky. No one else would notice. But I do. I always notice.

"You know I didn't need you to come." I'm used to doing things myself. Figuring things out for both of us. And I don't want her to feel guilty.

She rubs at her heart like her bra is too tight. But she doesn't wear a bra at home. "I didn't want my being at your hearing to go against you."

"Ma, it's fine."

"I get so nervous." Her eyes have that glaze.

"For the last time, Ma, it's fine." I sound too angry. I have to be careful and treat her extra gentle in the morning.

She scooches out of the recliner. "I'm gonna see if I can find my rosary and say some prayers for your job hunting today. I haven't seen those beads since last year when the lotto got so high and we bought those tickets. You remember?" She raises her pitch. It's her way of making me feel better. Distracting me. Her eyebrows almost touch her hairline, until they squeeze some light into her eyes.

I frown. "Yeah. We didn't get a single number."

"Next time will be our lucky day." She pats my arm.

I sling on my backpack filled with enough snacks to get me through the morning and Ma follows to the front door.

I'm outside and she's inside. She smooths my hopeless hair. "You're growing up so fast. But you're still my little girl." Ma pinches my cheek. I hate that.

"I'll be back before you know it." I adjust the collar of my jacket, scrunched under the strap of my backpack.

Over the chest-high fence, I see our neighbor. Ma does too.

"Vix, what's he doing over there? To that tree?"

The crumpled man who lives there, whose name I don't know, is suspicious. I've seen him a few times before. Even close up, his eyes are empty. Lifeless. Like our Queens apartment after all our stuff was loaded into the moving van and we flicked the lights off one final time.

Serial-killer eyes for sure.

Ma says I have a wild imagination, that I exaggerate. But the opposite is true. I don't consider myself the creative type. I'm a realist. I see what's in front of me. A man waiting to murder us in our sleep lives right next door. Less than fifty feet from our house. Less than sixty feet from my bedroom window. Less than seventy feet from the knives in the kitchen drawer.

I squint. The neighbor's stapling something to a pine near the street. He wobbles like a bobblehead doll on the dashboard of a junky car. "Uh-oh. He's teetering."

"That's so sad." Ma breathes out her words.

She angles her head to get a better view. "He always looks lonely."

"Are you surprised? Who'd visit him? Man's creepy."

Ma has the far-off look she gets when something hits too close to home. "I don't think he's got anybody. I don't want to end up like him." Her shoulders slump like a little of her life leaks out with the thought.

I widen my stance, pin her with a glare of solid reassurance. "You don't have to worry. I'm here. I'll always be here."

"You're only fifteen. I can't put that on you for your whole life." The trembling in her lips matches her voice.

"We're family. Who else are you gonna put it on?" It's the tragic truth. But sounds kind of comical when you say it out loud.

The two of us snicker. We laugh a lot together. Makes the hard times sting less. She's probably still a little drunk from last night. But she got up extra early to see me off. That's something.

My body is like a puppet I send out on errands. But my thoughts never leave the house or Ma's side. Some people have to check things before they walk out the door. They call it OCD tendencies. Nona Bartolucci has those tendencies. Sometimes she'll go back and make sure the stove is off three or four times before we could take her to get her hair fixed back in Queens. Doesn't matter if she hasn't turned the stove on in two days. I guess I got the worry gene from her. Except I don't go back and check the appliances. I check on Ma. "Are you sure you don't need anything?"

"Don't you fret about me. I've got plenty to do."

We hug, and I crunch down the gravel driveway.

Ma waves. "Good luck, Vix."

"Don't forget I left a sandwich for you in the fridge. You can have that for lunch." I throw my words to her over my shoulder.

The door clicks shut.

I take a breath and look around.

While me and Ma were saying our goodbyes, my neighbor must've gone inside. Don't see him.

His house looks like the perfect place for a murder. Stands out among the manicured lawns. Neglected yard. Tall, tangled grass begging for a trim. The scent of wood and mold, or maybe a dead body buried under the wild daffodils that bloom each year whether you take care of them or not. I can't shake the chill that dances up my back every time I pass. I pegged him as a closet murderer the day we pulled into the driveway with our U-haul.

He's old. But I think something else is going on over there. Dirty windows with the curtains always closed are a clue. If I walk close enough, I bet I could see the words *"Help me"* written in the grime, likely by one of his long-dead victims.

I stare at the ivy choking the life out of the brickwork. But something about the house calls to me. Secrets to be shared. Watching me, waiting for the right time.

Then I see a white blur doing somersaults in the breeze, until it lands on me. I peel the paper off the right leg of my sweats, the wind still pinning the flyer in place. The face of a young kid is on the front and the word "*Missing*" is stamped above it.

"My grandson." The voice is hollow, and close. I'm so focused on the paper, I don't notice my neighbor at the edge of the woods across the street from his house. This must be what he was stapling to the tree a couple minutes ago. The old man's got piles of papers in his hands. The rustling sound they make reminds me of dry leaves skittering across the street. I try not to gawk, but my eyes have their own ideas. I don't think I've ever heard him speak. Wait. Did he say grandson?

The dead-eyed man stares back. Then, it occurs to me. Maybe the old man was the one murdered in that house.

"How long has your grandson been missing?" The awkward words stumble out. Too late to yank them back.

"A long time." He doesn't look at me—it's like he's talking to the ghost of a memory.

"I was close with my grandfather too. There's a special bond between grandparents and grandkids."

"Yes. He called me Pop-Pop."

"That's what I called Pa Pa Bartolucci too."

"Guess that's what Pa Pa sounds like to his little ears. Candy was just a puppy when he disappeared. Now Candy and I are both a couple of old men."

A nudge against my leg makes me look down. An old, tiny dog. My fingers bury into its fur, coarse and warm.

"Candy. Behave," he half-scolds.

"I've lived next door for two years. Why haven't I ever seen Candy?" My hand strokes through the fluff.

"I keep him inside, safe, with me most of the time. He probably thinks he's human. Hasn't seen another dog since he was a puppy."

"I can help you put up flyers if you want. I'm only job hunting today." I try to sound casual, like I'm not twisting my assumptions about him around in my head.

The neighbor's gaze meets mine. "That's kind of you. I'm being foolish. He's been gone for thirteen years. I stopped putting up signs years ago. But I woke up last week and thought, I should try again. Gives me something to do besides drinking to forget."

I give Candy one last rub. "I'd better get going. By the way, I'm Vickie."

He nods, kinda like a thank you without the words. "Maury."

Doesn't sound like a serial-killer name. But then again, neither does Jeffrey or Ted or Wayne.

"Thank you for stopping. And for listening," he says.

I know I shouldn't, but once I reach the edge of the sidewalk, I turn back to watch him one last time. But he's gone again. Vanished.

"Candy and Maury. Pop-Pop," I say out loud. Then I notice I'm still holding the picture of the missing kid. There's a trash can on the curb. But it seems wrong to throw the flyer away. So I fold it up and put it in my back pocket. I save the piece of paper. I'm not sure why.

CHAPTER 47
Camouflage

I pause, hand on the door of Talmadge's, one of Maine's fanciest department stores, palms sweaty — *stretching myself*. That's what Uncle Aldo calls it.

The sign in the window says *Help Wanted*, but do they want someone like me?

A bell dings a hollow greeting. My sneakers squeal on the pristine floor. It's another universe in here.

I've been on and off the bus all day and doing a lot of walking in between. My lip is sweating and my jacket feels too tight. On the cheerier side, my backpack is lighter because I've made my way through most of the snacks.

The walls breathe out fancy smells that slap you with a hefty price tag. The perfumed air is so thick and syrupy, I half expect bees to be buzzing around the bottles. I cough to get the taste out of the back of my throat.

The store expands into aisles of dreams. I'm a shadow among the clothes racks, drifting through potential futures draped on hangers. No one notices me, no one spots the counterfeit in their midst. No one yet.

I pick up a candle and pretend I might be interested in buying it, camouflaging myself as one of them. Out of habit, I turn over the candle and inspect the bottom for a barcode and an amount. Always check the prices. Even in the Dollar Store, not everything is a dollar anymore. The tag makes my heart palpitate.

I'm as out of place as black-and-white Dorothy in the technicolor land of Oz. Toto, we're definitely not in the Dollar Store any more. A family of four could eat for two days with what they want for this tiny wax stick that doesn't even smell like apple blossoms. Although, I don't really know what apple blossoms smell like.

I spot a second *Help Wanted* sign in the jewelry section. Following the breadcrumbs of the signs, I make my way to the counter. Conscious of how I walk. I can't stop my feet from plopping no matter how much I try to be graceful.

Leaning on the glass counter, my palm sticks from the sweat, but the surface, cool and slick beneath my skin, is refreshing.

A saleslady adjusts a necklace inside the case. For all her rearranging, looks the same to me. She scans me up and down without really seeing me at all. That's a skill. I wonder if I have to be able to do that to work here.

"Yes?" she says with a honey-sweet voice. The artificial kind, laced with corn syrup.

"I'd like to apply for the—"

The woman places an application and pen in front of me, and flutters off to an old white lady with a chihuahua in her purse.

I gulp in some perfumed air and scan the application.

I've filled out a few of these already today. Feels like scratching my name into a lottery ticket, and all I can win is a minimum-wage miracle. But this is the first time I've hesitated before writing my address. I know judgements will be made. I live in a nice enough area, but not this store's type of nice. I tap my pen on the counter and look around.

I spot two girls, floating around the outskirts of the jewelry aisles. One of them has hair that glows like a halo under the store lights, probably full of secrets and receipts from hair salons I can only pronounce if I see them written down. The other's hair is a little duller. The moon to her sun.

1. SAVAGE

These two make me think of the movie *Dumb and Dumber*. But I dub these girls Blonde and Blonder. The kind of blonde color you know is not real and meant to distract.

But I'm not so easily dazzled. These two are street—just the Park Avenue kind.

I glance at the rest of the application and see the words that snatch away any hope — "*attach a résumé.*" I clear my throat—gotta keep it smooth, like the silk scarves on the next aisle. "Pardon me," I say. My voice comes out all greasy, more like a pickpocket's handshake. Nothing silky about it.

The saleslady gives me a look over her shoulder, a half-second peek. "One moment." She's busy with the old lady, who's clutching a wallet so big it reminds me of Nona's manicotti, all stuffed and ready to burst.

I shift my weight, stand my ground. My sneakers squeak against the marble floor, out of place among the click-clack of high heels parading around like they own the place. They probably do. I'm the misfit here—a stray mutt in a land of poodles.

I wait, tapping the counter with my pen, each knock a second ticking away my life. I notice my reflection in one of the small standing mirrors on the wraparound counter. I should've let Ma fix my hair.

Slipping through the aisles, I spot Blonde and Blonder. A chill slides down my shirt, like someone dropped an icicle down my back. Something's off.

"That's the one," says the blonde to the old lady with the dog in her purse, gazing into a mirror, admiring a necklace around her neck.

"You think so?" The old lady's eating up the compliments like fish eggs on a cracker.

"Definitely," says the blonder, platinum one.

"So gorgeous on you," echoes the blonde.

These two princesses are putting on a royal performance.

"Thanks, girls." The old woman's drunk on attention. "I'll take this one," she says to the saleslady.

While everyone's eyes are on the old woman, Blonder slips a shiny trinket into her oversized designer bag. I'm itching to do something, say something to the saleslady, but it's not my show.

I manage a warning cough, something to snap the saleslady out of her trance. But she's too busy calculating her commission. Instead, Blonde and Blonder register what I'm doing and glare. "Excuse me," I say.

"What is it?" The saleslady's face screws up, like I'm the one stealing.

I clamp my mouth shut. She's not worth the energy I'd waste explaining. And she'd never believe me over a pair of snow princesses.

I scrunch up the application, ready to bail, when Blonde and Blonder click-clack so close I'm drowning in the stink of their essential oils and fruity gum.

"Public or private?" Blonde asks, her words sticky and sweet like her scent.

She's playing with the wrong toy. "You talking to me?"

"Who else?" Blonder gives sideways lips in my direction.

I respond without hesitating so they know they don't get to me. "I pee outside."

Their laugh grates my ears. "You're funny," says Blonde. But her eyes are vacant as a liquor store on Sunday.

"Public or private *school*? Not restroom." Blonder is still fishing.

I slap her with a look of warning. "What do you think?"

"Do you shop here a lot?" Blonde prods.

"I'm looking for a job. Do you shoplift here a lot?" I throw back. I'm nobody's punchline.

They give me frozen smiles, the kind that only shift their pouty red lips a millimeter. "So funny," they both say in unison.

"And exotic." Blonde scans me top to bottom like I'm on the clearance rack.

"We come here every afternoon," Blonder says, leaning in close enough for her hair to brush my cheek. Gross.

"You can't beat the prices," they sing together.

"Where are you from?" Blonder pries again.

I'm getting tired of this. "My mother."

"Are you spaghetti and meatballs?" Blonde says. I know the insult. She means Italian.

"Or spicy noodles?" She means Asian. The way she says it makes me scowl.

"I'm TV dinners. Are you burning crosses? Or swastikas?" I spit back.

Their masks crack, for a second. Good.

"Wait. What?" Blonde loses her sweet edge.

"We're not racist," Blonder's quick to say.

"Your questions are." I don't budge.

Right then, the cavalry arrives. A security guard flicks a suspicious look at me, ignoring the blondes. I'm surprised it took him this long to realize I don't belong.

The girls nudge and giggle. "We've got to go," says Blonde, slipping away and not looking back.

"We were just being nice." Blonder pretends her feelings are hurt.

"Yeah, we felt sorry for you," Blonde throws over her shoulder.

They head to the door and I'm not far behind, careful to keep a few yards between us.

The security guard somehow beats us all to the entrance, lurking.

The blondes pass through the security scanners and are back on the street with ease. How's that possible? Something's wrong. They're waiting outside. Watching. Laughing.

Today they're messing with the wrong girl. I came here looking for a job, not a fight, but looks like the fight found me.

I inch to the doors, through the scanners, not taking my eyes off of them. Then alarms shriek.

The guard's on me, asking to check my backpack.

I don't have anything to hide. "Sure."

There's something about the way the blondes look at me, then wave through the glass and scamper off.

Then the guard pulls an expensive necklace from the side pocket of my bag.

"Oh no," slips from my lips, but the words are drowned out by the sound of my heart pounding and the last chance the judge gave me being flushed down the toilet.

CHAPTER 48
Steel and Glass

I'm cradled in Uncle Aldo's police cruiser. My comfy womb. The car meanders down an unfamiliar road, leading me to a new and dangerous world—juvenile hall.

Motionless, hands folded in my lap to stop them from shaking, I'm all concrete and steel on the outside, but inside, my stomach's doing flips.

My skin is tight like I'm about to shed it. But I don't let any of that show. "I didn't steal the necklace." The words trickle out, and hang there, heavy.

Jaw clinched, Uncle Aldo grinds his teeth, the way he does when he's thinking hard or worried.

He releases a long now-what sigh. "Then this is for all the times you did steal." His hands slide around the wheel. "I'm gonna do everything I can to get you out of juvie as fast as possible. Just stay out of trouble until then."

A lump the size of one of my softballs forms in my throat. "I'm sorry," I whisper.

He stares forward with eyes that have seen too much, that know too much—about me. "We'll figure this out." His voice is jittery. I'm not used to uncertainty coming from him. He sounds nervous, and I am too.

The turn signal clicks—we're here.

Juvenile hall looms ahead. Razor-blade-crested chain-link fences surround a cold-looking building.

Uncle Aldo doesn't need to say anything—his tight shoulders say it all. He's about to hand me over to these uniforms. He has to. I'm lucky. Better him than a stranger.

In the parking lot, the car rolls to a stop. He doesn't turn off the engine right away. He sits, hands still on the wheel. Then, like he's peeling himself away from the moment, he kills the engine. The silence is thick, a blanket neither of us wants to crawl out from under.

We get out, and the car doors shut with a finality that thunders in my chest.

His steps are slow. He stops, turns. "Vickie." There's a hint of something raw in how he says my name. "You keep your head down. Stay out of trouble."

I nod, chin up, eyes trained on his.

The front door opens with a buzz and a click. Uncle Aldo doesn't come in. There's a female guard behind a thick pane of bulletproof glass. Her face fluctuates between boredom and contempt, like she's the one locked up.

"Keep it moving." The guard speaks through a steel speaker grill, the words distorted.

I decide not to look back at Uncle Aldo, but change my mind. One more look. Maybe that's what I need to get me through whatever's ahead of me. But it's too late.

The female guard pushes a button and then metal the door clangs closed, shutting out my old life.

After making my way through reception, I move on to a room for processing, still dazed, my heart banging against my ribs, on the verge of busting through.

1. SAVAGE

There's a different guard here. He scans me up and down with his too-close-together eyes. I spy the nameplate on his desk—Rod Wringle. Sounds like an elf from Santa's workshop. Looks like one too. Short for a man, his belly hangs over his belt, like the blubber's trying to escape from a hostage situation.

He thrusts a package into my hands that I almost drop. Wrapped in plastic is an orange jumpsuit, a nightshirt, underwear, rubber shower shoes, and white tennis shoes with no laces.

"Take good care of them." His voice sounds like he's been gargling with gravel. "You won't get another set of fresh clothes until next week. Be in your cell for the night by 8:20. Lights out at 8:30. The door will automatically lock. If you need to go to the bathroom, call out for the guard on your floor and they will take you. You need to be up with your bed made by 6:20. If you do a half-ass job, you'll do it again. You're allowed books and letters and up to five photos. Am I clear?"

His words are just noise. A script he's probably recited a thousand times to a thousand kids who look like me—scared, but too tough to show anyone.

I nod, a jerky movement like a marionette with someone else pulling the strings. "I only brought one photo," I rasp. My throat's a desert. I pat my pocket, reminding myself to take the photo out before I change clothes.

There's no sympathy in Wringle's small eyes. He's doing his job. I'm a box to be ticked.

Changing behind a curtain, the bright-as-a-traffic-cone orange jumpsuit feels like sandpaper. I wonder what Uncle Aldo would say if he saw me now. Would he shake his head, tsking at the waste of my life, or would he look at me with tired eyes that say "I expected better"? Maybe Ma would've given me her glassy look, the one that says, "Just another Tuesday."

I fold my clothes and hand them to Wringle. My photo from home is now in the front pocket of my jumpsuit.

I scan myself from head to toe in a mirror that's probably a two-way.

I felt out of place in the department store, but is this really where I belong?

My cell door latched closed twenty minutes ago and the lights automatically turned off ten minutes later, just like Wringle said. My breaths come out shaky, but who's here to care? Nobody.

There's a stench that sticks to my skin—like sweat and anxiety had a baby who hasn't been bathed since birth.

I inspect once-white walls, speckled with stains. Stories I don't wanna know.

Down the hall, a scream—raw and ragged. Someone's nightmare, out loud for all of us to hear. Moans follow like a chorus warming up for a show nobody wants to see. And there's an inhuman laugh coming from the cell next to me.

I turn the covers back.

My cot's as hard as a slab of stone draped in a thin sheet, which scratches against my palm. The pillow might as well be a sack of cement, but when I lay my head down, it supports me.

In one swoop, I flip up the sheet, using it as a force field of protection, covering everything but my face.

I glance at my one photo on the wall—me, Ma, and Uncle Aldo back in Queens. Ma's got a glint in her eyes that says she's got a plan, before drinking dulled her glow. Uncle Aldo's got a half smirk like he knows something and isn't telling. I look different. Like a kid who still thinks maybe things could turn out all right.

Hopeful smiles have a hard time reaching me now.

I'm not gonna cry. Queens girls don't cry. They fight.

But not yet. There will be plenty of fighting tomorrow.

DAY ONE

CHAPTER 49
Wrinkles

Keep your head down and stay out of trouble. That's what Uncle Aldo said. Tugging tight on each corner, I make the bed sheets all neat, erasing every crease with my hands. Wish life was as easy to fix. But my mistakes are bigger than a six-inch wrinkle and a lot harder to smooth out.

Through the bars of my cell, I check the clock in the hall.

You need to be up and the bed made by 6:20. Officer Wringle's words.

Click-clack, the lock on my door opens, the bars slide, and my gut squeezes.

Now what?

I wait.

Officer Wringle's warning replays in my head. *If you do a half-ass job on the bed, you'll do it again.*

I survey the bed and spy a corner not tucked under the bunk.

Clop-clump. Clop-clump.

Craning my head, I look through the bars again, down the corridor. Officer Wringle's boots scrape across the concrete, stirring up a cloud of grit that makes my skin squeal. My heartbeat revs up like someone is pedaling on my chest. I dart back to my bunk, tuck the corner, and with quick swats, smooth the pilled cotton.

"Inspection." His voice has an edge like he's looking forward to bed checks. He's king of this grimy castle — my miserable new home — and he knows it. I've seen his type at school. The bully. And I've been the bully. My payback?

I assess him like I'm picking teams in PE.

He's giving my sheets so many dirty looks they're going to need to be bleached. "Not acceptable." His voice is a slap, flat and cold.

"What's wrong with it?" I keep my tone steady. But inside I'm a jack-in-the-box with a broken latch. Hard to keep the anxiety pushed down. *Easy, Vickie.*

"I see a wrinkle."

"Where?" I bite back the anger that wants to pop out. I know there are no wrinkles. And he knows I know. This is about power. About control. About dominance.

"There." He's quick, yanking the sheets onto the dirty floor. "Start over."

Only my eyes move, from the floor to his razor-edged gaze.

"You got a problem?" He's taunting me. Officer Rod Wringle may have an elf name, but he's no elf. Elves don't taunt, trolls do. And I've got to let the troll have this win.

I wrench my eyes away and step to the bed, bend to pick up the sheets, and brush off a dust bunny. I sense his gloating glare on my back.

So many dark fantasies crowd my mind. Throwing the sheets in his face. Striding up to him, challenging him toe to toe, nose to nose. Punching him in his doughnut gut.

Keep your head down. Uncle Aldo's words weigh on me.

I don't look at Officer Wringle.

"Thought so." He chuckles, and I seethe.

Swallowing back my protests is like a betrayal of myself.

But I'm in prison.

Prison lesson number one: *The problem's not the handcuffs they put on you, but the ones you have to put on yourself. They leave the marks that last.*

The sun's not even up and already I've got my first self-inflicted mental bruise.

I'm curious what emotional trauma they might be serving up for breakfast.

1. SAVAGE

Bleach. Vomit. Burned bacon. So this is what prison dining is like.

I find an empty seat at a table in the prison cafeteria with more scuffs and scars than my softball. I focus on my tray, ignoring the orange jumpsuit itching my skin like I'm covered in fiberglass.

I throw my body forward to scooch my chair in, but the legs are bolted down. They moan against the floor, sending prickles across my skin. Sounds too much like someone's last breath.

I look around. Across the room, a guy built like the Q100 bus, wide and unstoppable, concentrates on splitting his food into two sections on his plate. And I'm so focused on him, I don't notice *her* until she plops in the seat across from me. Until she blocks my view. Until she speaks. "I'm Denia." Her chirpy voice could make a corpse cringe.

I lift an eyebrow. "Good for you." I attempt to shift my chair away from her, forgetting the legs are stuck in place. "What's up with the chairs? Why are they bolted down?"

She leans in, conspiratorial-like. "In here, anything can be a weapon." Her eyes sweep my face. "What's your name?"

I don't have enough imagination to pretend she's not there so I answer. "I'm Vickie."

"What do you like to do for fun?" Denia's question wheedles through the buzz of the cafeteria.

The room's a freaky carnival. Full of kids too broken to bother with masks. "Oh, doesn't get any better than this." Sarcasm. Not sure if she gets it. "What do—"

"What do—" she repeats my words like an echo.

"What do you—"

"What do you—" Her eyes have a dead twinkle that creeps me out.

"What do you like to do for fun?" I finally get out.

"For fun? I like interrupting you." She laughs, and it's unlike any natural sound. The closest thing might be a goat with a sore throat.

"That's interesting," I manage to say, gritting my teeth against her goat noise. "Quite a laugh you've got—"

"Thank you." She's oblivious. Thinks I was offering a compliment. Or maybe she's smarter than I think. I'm already doubting my instincts and intuition.

There's something in the air here that pulls the rug out from under your swag. Maybe that's lesson number two of prison life: *Never trust anyone. Not even yourself.*

"Yeah. Go get your kicks somewhere else." I flick my fingers, sharp, hoping she'll take the hint.

"You can't get away from me. We're neighbors. You're in the cell next to mine."

That's her inhuman laugh I heard last night. The stuff of nightmares.

She locks her eyes on mine, more serious now, the goat laughter gone. "I came to warn you."

I don't overlook the mark on her arm, a large bruise. The mystery about how she got it is there, beckons, but I choose to mind my own stay-out-of-trouble business.

Arms folded, I ease back on my hard metal seat, muscles tense, ready. "Warn me about what?"

"Him."

I follow her gaze to the mountain of a kid, the one who treats his food like he's solving a Rubik's Cube. He has one of those familiar-looking faces. The eyes. But I've never met him. I'd remember.

"That's Big Leonard," she says.

Annoyance sparks. "I can take care of myself."

"I tried to warn Oliver. But too late now." Her tone turns frosty.

I should cut the conversation off, walk away, but my questions tumble out before I can cork them. "What happened to Oliver?"

"They can't find him. I don't think they're going to find him." I can almost taste the silence after her sentence, the kind that suffocates.

Denia grabs a piece of my toast and bites it. "Oliver thought he and Big Leonard were friends. They both loved playing video games together in the activity room. But I always knew Leonard could snap Ollie like a puppy's neck if he wanted. If he ever got angry. And he's always getting angry. They'll smell their way to Ollie's body if nothing else. Just got to give it a few days to stink. Funny how you always hurt the ones you love. You should be my friend."

I freeze my face in place as best as I can while I process her words. Friends? Not going to happen. "Be your friend? So you can try and hurt me?" I glance at her arm again. Can't help but stare. The bruise is a shout in a quiet room.

"See my tiny little hands? I couldn't hurt a fly." She's a peacock, all spread feathers for show.

I pull my attention back to Leonard, to the weird dance he's doing with his food.

But Denia's got a way of holding my focus like she's latched on and not letting go. Since she's dripping information like a leaky faucet, I'm going to collect as much as I can. "What's Leonard doing to his food?"

"He and Oliver both used to do it. Separate their food. Put half in a napkin for later, I guess. They were so funny together. Opposites. But also the same." There's a twist of pain in her voice, or maybe longing? Regret? Empathy?

But she's on me again. With that glare. "What are you looking at?" I ask.

Her finger stabs at me, poking my shoulder just above my right boob. Quick and unexpected.

"Hey!" I spit out. I'm relieved my reactions are slower in here; otherwise, she would've gotten fists.

Stay out of trouble. Uncle Aldo's simple request is proving harder than I thought.

She jabs me again. Middle of my chest.

"Stop that."

"Ms. Hoity Toity doesn't like to be touched?" She pokes me over and over with her finger.

I grab her hand, twist. Not hard, but enough to send a message to her tiny poke-happy hands.

"Ow. Ow. Ow. Pea-knuckle. Pea-knuckle. Pea-knuckle," she cries out.

I drop her hand like I'm holding fire. "What?"

She's huffing, face twisted. "Pea-knuckle. Means I give up."

My laugh sneaks out, rough and short. "Yeah. Well, I don't give up. So I don't need your pea-knuckle word."

She huffs again like I'm the crazy one. "It's a game. Pea-knuckle is a game."

"Touching people is a game to you?" I cross my arms over my chest, a barrier, a challenge.

And then he appears. Officer Wringle. The Troll.

Denia shrinks, all bravado gone, looking for a hole to disappear down. "I've got to go." She scurries away.

"Watch it." Officer Wringle's voice is a gravel road, rough and unwelcome. He brings his little stick down hard on the table, so hard the floor under my feet shakes.

The twinkle in his eye when I jump is hard to miss. He enjoys seeing my fear.

I hate myself for giving him any reason to be happy.

CHAPTER 50
Lost Dreams

ALDO

The stench hits me the minute I'm in the door of the warden's office. Stale, like a locker room that's seen too many lost dreams. The kind of stink these juvie kids can't even smell yet. Won't be until a twentieth high school reunion that the stench really hits them.

Time. The great dream killer.

The whole place has got a strangling vibe. The walls know too much, but they aren't talking.

I tug at the collar of my uniform. It shrank or I grew. My wife's chicken parm is irresistible and worth the extra pounds and heart attack I'm sure it'll give me one day.

A woman sits all proper-like behind a standard-issue metal desk in the middle of the office. Her uniform is also too tight, but for different reasons. I suspect she likes the fit. Her nails are filed into long red claws. She's every inch a warden, but with something more, something not quite on the level.

"Thanks for making time, Warden." I hover by the door of the small office.

She flicks her hair back, then gestures to a seat across from her. "Call me Tiffany." She peeks at my badge, squinting. "Reynaldo?"

"Officer Bartolucci," I correct her.

"Officer Reynaldo Bartolucci." She cocks her head, a hint of a smile. "Your lucky day. You caught me. I'm heading outta town this evening for two days. Mandatory training. What do you need?" She leans in as close as the desk between us will allow. "How can I help?"

"I understand there's a boy missing—since last night."

"Oh. Yeah. Guess when a kid disappears in a state facility, you fellas don't wait twenty-four hours to see where things land." Her tone's flat like yesterday's cola. "Need a copy of his file?"

"Nah. Got the paperwork right here." The file is full of reports. And photos of his biological parents. The Greens. And foster parents. The Franklins. But one detail sticks in my mind. His age. "He's young. Ten."

Tiffany lets out a sigh full of mint. A weak attempt to cover up her last smoke. "If the law would let them, the state would be hauling these kids in here straight out of the womb."

I shuffle through the pages. "So, you wanna brief me on what you've done to find—" I glance down, finding the name. "Oliver Green?"

"We turned the place upside down. In case someone like you came knocking." She's got that rehearsed tone, like she's reading from an invisible script, but with a touch of steel mixed in. She's warning me off. "Look, I need this job. So yeah, we did our due diligence."

Suspicion's crawling up the back of my uniform. I'm here to find answers. "Is there anything we can do to assist you with the search?"

"If you wanna keep searching, be my guest." Her trailing smirk comes off a little too sharp. "But Officer Reynaldo"—she bats her eyelashes—"between you and me, don't waste your time."

I choose to ignore her flirting. "Why's that?"

She motions me closer, and I shift forward. Her perfume invades my space, some flower trying too hard to be sweet. "'Cause the kid's dead," she whispers, like it's a secret only between us.

I reel back. "How do you figure?"

"Seizures." She tosses the condition out like it's nothing. "Epilepsy. Miss one dose and end of story. Right there in his file. We were late giving him his meds one morning last month. It happens. And he was passed out by lunch. Close one. Like I said, I need this job."

The whole situation stinks worse than the room. "No harm in taking another look-see. Check every nook, every cranny. Under beds. Laundry chutes. He's scrawny. But a body, alive or dead, is hard to miss."

Her eyes roll, tired or fed up, I can't tell. "Been there, done that." My guts churn. A wink comes my way like she's playing a part. "I hear you. Gotta keep up appearances. Still, if you want to find the body, you know, so you can close the case, I'll tell you who probably knows."

She nods at the glass wall. On the other side, in the holding area, a kid's lost in his own head, seated at a table, rocking. He's a big fella. "That one probably knows something. Big Leonard they call him."

"Have you spoken to him?"

"Pointless. If you're over sixteen, the kid won't say a word. Doesn't trust adults. Especially adults in uniform. But have at it."

"Thanks. I'll give it a go."

"Good luck. I'll put it like this. He's calm, like he is now, and then all of a sudden he's in a rage. He's got strength like I've never seen. I've been in law enforcement twelve years now, and I'm telling you, I don't go near him, and I'm no shrinking violet."

"What makes you so sure he knows?"

"He and Ollie spent a lot of time together."

I open the file to the photos while absorbing her comments, and flip back and forth between two. The dark blotches are unmistakable. "These bruises on Oliver. The two recent photos in his file don't match up with the intake pics. He didn't have the marks when he arrived."

She sits back, lips balled tight. "The kid's a klutz. Those seizures don't help. All the thrashing."

Her response is more of a denial than an answer. I close the file folder. "Thanks."

She smirks—like we've made an agreement I don't know about. "Some of what I shared is off the record. Better if this entire conversation never happened. I need this—"

"Job." I finish her sentence. "Got it." I've never liked prisons, especially prisons for kids. Some hard cases in here, but locking them up isn't the answer. "Mind if I look around, now? Chat with some folks?"

"Knock yourself out." She offers her hand.

I grasp her palm, careful of the nails. There's an electric sexual charge in the wink she gives me. But I'm a family man.

I walk out of the office and close the door. The glass on the shared wall with the holding area is mirrored. I can't see her, but I wave, knowing she's watching.

In one corner of the lobby, there's a television mounted high on the wall, encased in a protective plastic shell, tuned to some bland, inoffensive channel.

The low murmur is better than the quiet. Dangerous to leave some of them unsupervised, alone with their thoughts for too long. Still, the taunting glimpses of the outside world from the TV seems cruel.

Cameras are mounted in every corner. No privacy here. No moment of solitude. Hard predicament for anyone. Especially teens.

The walls are bare, except for a few notices in plastic sleeves, reminders of rules and schedules. Even the faded papers look defeated, corners curled.

Three tables with five chairs around each are positioned under the TV.

I approach the hulk of a boy, still rocking back and forth to an invisible tune.

"Is this seat taken?" I ask, pausing. Big Leonard hasn't looked at me yet, hasn't stopped rocking. Like I'm invisible. But the boy also hasn't strangled me. So far, I'm winning.

I go to move the chair back. Bolted. I sit, squeezing into the space and watch for his reaction.

Nothing.

Then, the boy's swaying stops. He meets my eyes with an unfocused stare so intense all the oxygen is vacuumes out of my lungs.

Out of instinct, I put my hand on my weapon. But remember he's a kid.

Big Leonard pounds the table hard with his fists, sending a reverberation through the floor that rattles my chest. The giant boy stands, looming over me.

Our gazes lock, my face a stone slab.

Big Leonard's lip trembles. A volcano on the brink of erupting.

Then he rumbles away.

His footsteps thud on the tiled floor.

"Rain check it is."

CHAPTER 51
Mirage

VICKIE

The aftertaste of prison breakfast lingers in my mouth like I licked a nine-volt battery. I bend over a water fountain in the lobby holding area, slurping up as much as my mouth can hold. I can feel the lead pipes making me dumber with every drop. But that's a problem for later.

Straightening, I wipe my chin with a scratchy sleeve. A familiar figure sits at a table across the room. I blink like he's a desert mirage. Still there.

Uncle Aldo?

He's with Big Leonard. A loud bang and Big Leonard breezes by, grazing my arm.

Unfazed, I smile and walk close to Uncle Aldo. "You're even worse at making friends than I am. What are you doing here?"

"You're not happy to see me?" Uncle Aldo's gaze drills into me with a mix of worry and pride. Maybe because I made it through the night.

"You haven't even given me time to miss you. I saw you, what? Twelve hours ago." My heart sprints. I play cool, but I want to hug him and wake up from this bad dream. "I thought we could only have visitors in the visitation room behind the glass. That's what they said in processing. They make you sign a book and hand over everything in your pockets, too, when you visit."

"Well, I'm a cop. And also, I traded cases so I could be here. So I could check on you. There's a missing boy." The words sit in the air.

"Yeah, Oliver."

Uncle Aldo's eyebrows raise, all curious. "How do you know about him?"

My arms cross like a shield. I don't want him to see how I really feel about this place. "People talk. A lot. In fact, they don't shut up unless you bend their fingers back. It's kind of a 'crazy person' game they play in here."

Uncle Aldo inches in closer, and his Old Spice hugs me. I can tell he wants to hug me for real, but doesn't want to taint me. Hugging a cop isn't going to play well. "What else you hear?" he asks.

A smirk erupts. "What do you want to know?" The corners next to his eyes crinkle. "So is this kid dead?" I ask. Sounds blunt. I'm not good at gift wrapping my words.

"Missing."

"Pfft. Did he walk out the back door? The front door? Crawl in the toilet? There's a fence with razors on it coiled around this place. Where could he go?"

"That's what we're figuring out."

"I would check the laundry, the drain pipes, the crawl spaces in the ceiling. Guess you already checked the cameras?" I'm full of suggestions, always am. Thinking about this kid's situation is taking my mind off my own. The relief feels good.

"You're a natural at this stuff."

Heat rises through my orange collar. I'm not comfortable with compliments. "It's just common sense." I look down, planning to change the subject off of me. "Wherever this kid is, he's likely better off. So take your time finding him, if you know what I mean."

Uncle Aldo's look gets serious, lines deepening around his eyes like dry creek beds. "I'm afraid I can't do that."

I roll my eyes so hard they could wobble right outta here. "Play dumb.

Pretend you're Colombo, that old TV detective, or Cousin Joey."

Uncle Aldo laughs. "Can't do that. This kid's on medicine for seizures. Missing a dose is bad news. And he's missed at least one already."

My sigh sounds like deflating a balloon. "Okay, I'll keep an eye out."

"Just be careful. The kid got some bruises on him. Not sure I buy they were because of seizures."

Uncle Aldo hands me a small notebook and pen like he's passing me the stick in a twisted relay.

"Jot down anything unusual." Our gazes snag. "You doing all right?" His voice is low.

"Sure," I lie.

"I know places like this aren't easy." He sees right through my bullshit. Always has. "But don't worry, I'm going to figure a way to get you out of here. I'm working on a plan." His voice is firm, sure, like he's making a promise.

The desperation's wild in my chest, clawing up my throat. "Why don't you take me with you now? Turn on your lights and sirens, and just go. That's a plan." I pass it off as a joke.

His hand's on my shoulder, grounding me. "You know I can't."

I know, but doesn't stop the wanting, wishing. "I'll be fine," I whisper so low I'm not sure he hears.

"I know," he says. "All right. I'll be around a few more minutes, if you need anything. Going to have a chat with the head security officer. You've got this, Vickie."

I watch him go, feeling like I'm halfway between nowhere and hell. And I've only been outta my cell three hours. Eleven more hours to go until I'm sealed up like a can of vegetables again.

I need a distraction. I finger the notebook and pen.

CHAPTER 52
Weak Prey

ALDO

The walls of the security office stare at me. Fake eyes bulging out of their sockets. The heads of animals mounted, frozen in death. A faint buzz from the overhead lights makes my shoulders tense. The kind of buzz that messes with a guy's thoughts.

Across a desk from me sits Officer Rod Wringle, a man with an intensity that settles uneasy in my stomach. He fishes in a bowl of lemon drops, pops one in his mouth, then tilts the bowl to me. I shake my head. "No thanks."

"I love these things." He sucks loud. "Have we met before?"

"I don't think so." I glance at those stuffed animal heads—warthogs, deer, wild boar—a world away from the concrete and bustle of Queens. Where I grew up. Not much hunting there. After my transfer two years ago, I'm still getting used to Maine. Every city has weirdos. But they are a different breed here.

"Hmmm. I never forget a face," he says.

I ease back in my seat, feeling the cold pleather. "You must be a good shot."

An unsettling glint surfaces in his eyes, like he's got a sneaky secret. Officer Wringle idles forward. "Yeah. But I don't hunt with a gun. I kill them with my hands. And a knife."

There's already a lot that disgusts me about Wringle but I need to hide those feelings. Put him at ease. Build trust. "Maybe I will have a lemon drop. Hard to resist."

I grab one, holding back my grimace at the thought of his grubby fingers fondling each one.

Wringle drums the desk, a rhythmic, relentless beat. "I trap the animals first. Wait 'til they're weak."

"I see."

"What brings you here, Officer Bartolucci? Come to spy on me?"

"Not at all. Couple questions about the missing boy. I don't want to take too much of your time. Sure you're busy."

He relaxes back, satisfaction on his face. "Always happy to make time for fellow law enforcement. You know, I thought about applying — to the force."

My eyes stretch. "What stopped you?"

He raises his shoulders. "I chose security. You boys are always looking down on the security profession. Coming in here like you know everything. Just because you got training. Well, I could tell you some things, only experience can teach you."

He's looking for a fight. I ignore his posturing. "Experience is key. How long have you worked here?"

"Six months." His chest expands, puffing himself up. "But I've done security my whole career. Almost a decade. I'm good at it."

I nod, still priming him for my big request. "What's your favorite part of the job?"

"I like overseeing, being in charge. I keep things safe. Calm. And, I'd be lying if I didn't say I like the power."

These are children he's talking about. My uneasy feeling grows. "And what's the worst part about overseeing — the kids?"

Wringle angles in, the gleam in his pupils sharper. "Well, you can get some really bad apples. Rotten. To the core."

I swallow the bittersweet lemon drop saliva. "Ever been afraid for yourself?"

He chuckles, arrogant. "They can get real crafty. You never know what someone's gonna do. They're locked up, caged like an animal. You know how it is?"

I squirm in my seat—don't want to let on how much this guy's climbing my nerves. "Hmm." I've been a cop for a lot of years. The cases with kids involved are the ones that get to me. "Which of your skills have come in handy the most?"

"I got sharp hearing. So I'd have to say with my reflexes and my hearing, I catch everything. And like I said, I never forget a face. Like yours. I've seen you somewhere before."

"Who knows? It's a small world." Wringle laughs, but there's no joy in the sound. I squeeze a smile from my face, hoping I've warmed him up enough. "Well, I could sit and listen to your insights all day," I lie. I can't wait to get out of his orbit. "So, the missing kid, Oliver—"

"They called him Ollie," Wringle corrects me.

"That's right."

Wringle points at his eyes, then ears, triumphant. "Told ya. I don't miss anything. Scrawny kid. Young. But they can be the worst. They're the ones I have my eye on. You kind of get a sense. Don't you worry. I've got everything under control."

"I don't doubt that. Have to ask these questions. You know, paperwork." Wringle gestures with a hand to keep going. "He's ten. That unusual?"

"Not when you've been doing this as long as I have. You see a lot. All types. Kid was in a foster home. His real parents wanted him back, but they had some mental stuff happening. Kid had only been in foster care for a week when he stabbed the foster father."

"I read that in the file. Still surprises me."

"Told you. A caged animal is dangerous. If they feel cornered, no telling what they might do."

"I thought we were talking about kids."

He waves an indifferent hand. "Animals, kids. Same thing." He means it.

"Got time for another question? Well, more of a request."

"Oh, I'm enjoying this. Yessir. This is fun for me, talking shop. Just two guys, in law enforcement. Shooting the shit."

I get to the point of my visit. "One more thing. I'd like to see the security camera footage from last night."

"Won't be possible. I mean, I'd love to show you. But the cameras haven't worked since before I got here. The state's supposed to send someone to fix them. But I think that's why I was hired, because I'm like a surveillance system."

"I see. Wringle, how does a ten-year-old boy disappear with an officer of your caliber watching over things?" If Vickie were here I wouldn't be able to hold a straight face and neither would she. My bullshit is off the chart and onto the next page.

"I'm telling you, it's orchestrated on the inside. Kid's probably hidden. And one of these other kids knows where. But don't worry," he says, pointing at his eyes, then ears.

I mimic the gesture, pointing at my own eyes and ears. "Well, thanks for chatting."

Wringle grins, all teeth. "No problem."

On the other side of the closed door, my whole body grimaces. I need a shower to get rid of the stench of Wringle's stupid.

CHAPTER 53
Leftovers

VICKIE

My heart beats through my eardrums in the prison yard. My eyelashes catch streams of sweat. My throat burns all the way to my lungs.

"Forty-eight. Forty-nine. Fifty."

Officer Troll pokes us with his little cop stick if we don't count every jumping jack out loud.

"Sit-ups. On the ground. Now." He sputters words like a broken sprinkler.

Make it stop. My silent plea.

Lying on my back, I sell each neck raise like my midsection is crunching. My twenty grunts are enough to pass for sit-ups. Officer Troll's not the sharpest cheese on the platter.

After six laps jogging around the yard, I feel nauseous. Light-headed.

But everything passes. Or ends. If you wait it out long enough. That's not a lesson I learned in prison. Life taught me that.

The Troll finally chirps a whistle, signaling us to stop.

After his second cup of coffee, he subtly squeezes his legs together in a universal pee-pee dance. Nature's calling and he's off to take a leak.

The background blends into a distant murmur. Everyone scatters throughout the space like a choreographed dance number in an off, off, off Broadway musical. But I don't know the steps yet. It's my first rehearsal.

I look for a cue.

I'm not sure what to call the others. What to call us? Prisoners, inmates, students, kids? A few are playing basketball. Denia is playing hopscotch in imaginary squares. Others are flipping a deck of cards over in a push-up challenge. Aces are worth one pushup. Kings, queens and jacks are worth ten. The entire deck is worth three-hundred and forty pushups. This torture game might be the craziest observation I've made since I got here. But the day isn't even fully cooked on one side yet.

I catch my breath, hunched over.

The yard and the holding area are the two places where we have the most freedom to move around unsupervised. According to the schedule, we are held in both places at least twice a day. Lots of wide open space. A plus for us. Gives the guards a break.

Already, I notice the guards are only on top of breaking up fights when the warden is watching. But in the cafeteria and recreation room, there are too many utensils and cables that might be used as weapons. Guards are always posted and watching there whether the warden is around or not.

Big Leonard sits at a table in the shade. What's he doing?

He takes a napkin from his pocket and pulls out food scraps, but doesn't eat them. I crane my head so far, my spying becomes obvious and I just walk over.

Black and tan fur pokes out from under the bench seat.

A smile breaks and I crouch, my hands all over a dog. Labrador, collie, pit bull? She's a mutt like me.

I look up. Big Leonard grins, too.

The power of dogs.

I scratch behind the mutt's ear, feeling the coarseness of the fur. Big Leonard's doing the same. Then he takes a sausage from the napkin, holding it out for me to feed the prison pet. The dog gobbles down the meat treat.

1. SAVAGE

I'm ready to stand, not wanting to stay longer than I'm welcome, but Leonard stops me. "He likes you." His voice is deep and softer than I expected.

"Dogs are a good judge of character. 'Cause how you look isn't a factor," I say.

Big Leonard nods, agreeing.

I take the opportunity to bond further with Big Leonard. "People are always assuming stuff without knowing me. That I speak Korean. I don't. That I'm irresponsible because I'm only fifteen. I'm not. That I'm a bully because of my size. Sometimes I'm a bully. But I feel bad about it after."

A toothy grin erupts on Big Leonard's face. "They think I'm tough because of my size." He looks down and blushes. "I'm not."

The moment is real and earned. I continue petting the dog, careful not to look at Big Leonard too much. Don't want to mess things up now that he's opening up to me. "I'm a pretty good judge of character for a human. I mean I'm not at the dog level, but—I think you're all right. And you seem gentle to me."

His face twists like he's tasting something sour. "Sometimes I'm not gentle."

Uh-oh.

I should stop. But I don't. "What are you in for?"

"I beat people up. But then I feel bad. Sometimes." The fact he can be violent wouldn't have surprised me a few minutes ago, but in light of this interaction, it does.

"You must've done major damage to have ended up in here."

"I don't know my own strength." Big Leonard's reply is almost a whisper.

The vibe between us grows. I don't want to rush things, but I think of the missing kid, Oliver, who might be dead by now. And what if he's not? What if he still has a chance? What if this is my only shot to find out what Big Leonard knows? "If you don't speak up, they're going to think you are responsible for Oliver disappearing."

"He's my friend." His voice is filled with so much earnestness it cracks.

"I believe you. Don't you want to find him?" He stares into my eyes. I keep going. I've made it this far with him. "He was taking medicine. Without it, he could die. I know you don't want that."

He locks me in place with attention so intense he's got me by the throat. "Some things are worse than death."

Every muscle in me pauses. The weighted emphasis he places on the words. What could be worse than death?

"Hey. What have I told you about feeding that dog?" A shout shakes me loose from the shared moment. Officer Troll.

Wringle draws his cop stick, aiming for the poor mutt.

With a roar, Leonard's up, grabs the stick mid-swing.

Officer Wringle struggles, but Leonard's fast. He sends the Troll to the ground.

Big Leonard's victory doesn't last.

The crackle of a taser.

Leonard's body shakes, falls to the ground, and convulses.

Wringle's quick. He cuffs him. Then forces him to his feet, leaving me, the dog, and a yard full of stunned teenagers.

The chain-link fence supports my back, reclining against it.

A half hour has passed.

I watch the facility door for a sign of Big Leonard.

Nothing.

I expect there will be a punishment, but how do you lock a kid up that's already in jail? Leonard would be a hero, defending a helpless animal, anywhere else. But here he's in trouble for what he's done. I scan the yard, then take out the black-and-white pocket notebook.

Fits just right in my palm. I've seen these at the Dollar Store. But this one's special. It came from Uncle Aldo. I use the pen to form letters as neat and small as I can. A fresh notebook makes you want to be better. To think deep thoughts. To write prettier. I usually write big, especially when I'm feeling big emotions. Right now, I'm feeling so much, I'd fill this notebook with two sentences.

Back in Catholic school, Sister Irene would say, "Why does everything about you have to be so big?" Even at thirteen I knew what she meant. Not just my writing. My personality. My eyes. My body. I was different than the skinny white girls, herself included.

What she said didn't bother me the way she wanted. She taught me a lot of useful lessons, but not the ones she meant to teach. I learned mean girls come in all sizes, shapes, and ages. Sometimes, they hide under a headpiece and black robe.

I never want to be mean to people who don't deserve it. I didn't deserve that treatment from the nun.

What did Uncle Aldo say? *Jot down anything unusual you see.*

Too many unusuals to list. My hand is cramping just thinking about it. And it's not even lunch on my first day.

My thoughts.

First Draft.

DAY 1

JUNE 11TH

LET'S START WITH THE MISSING KID. OLIVER. OLLIE. HE'S HERE. PEOPLE DON'T JUST EVAPORATE. SOMEBODY KNOWS WHERE HE IS. OR HAS AN IDEA. HE LIKES VIDEO GAMES. THAT'S WHAT DENIA SAID. HE'S SCRAWNY. ON MEDICATION. IN DANGER. WHATEVER HE'S HIDING FROM, IF HE'S HIDING, MUST BE WORTH RISKING HIS LIFE.

DENIA. SHE COULD BE HARMLESS OR HAVE BODIES HIDDEN

UNDER HER BUNK. SHE'S GOT A BIG BRUISE ON HER ARM. AND SHE DIDN'T DO IT TO HERSELF. SHE HAS TINY HANDS.

BIG LEONARD? SOMETIMES VIOLENT. UNPREDICTABLE. BUT NOT ARBITRARY. WHEN HE ERUPTS THERE'S A REASON. HE'S LOYAL. PROTECTIVE. GOT HIMSELF TASED OVER A STRAY DOG. I THINK IF I KNEW HIM BETTER I'D KNOW HIS TRIGGERS. FRIENDS WITH OLLIE. I WONDER HOW FAR HE'D GO TO PROTECT HIM? "THINGS WORSE THAN DEATH." WONDER WHAT THAT MEANS? HE SEEMS LIKE A GENTLE GIANT. BUT GIANTS CAN HURT PEOPLE BY ACCIDENT. STILL, NO OTHER KID WOULD HURT OLLIE WITH SOMEONE LIKE LEONARD PROTECTING HIM.

WHAT ELSE? THAT STRAY DOG. HOW'D HE GET IN HERE? I GUESS IT COULD HAPPEN. EVERY BODEGA IN QUEENS HAD A STRAY CAT THAT CHASED THE RATS.

OFFICER WRINGLE. IF HE DIDN'T HAVE A UNIFORM AND A WEAPON HE'D BE HARMLESS, BUT WITH THEM, HE'S DANGEROUS. DENIA FLINCHES EVERY TIME HE SHOWS UP.

A door bangs open. I put the pen and notebook down.

Clop-crunch. Clop-crunch.

The sound of boots on gravel. Officer Wringle is back. No Leonard.

I close my notebook and walk toward him. He's rounding us up like junkyard puppies, taking us back to our pens.

"Where's Leonard?" I ask.

He focuses on me and then walks closer until I smell the pastrami sandwich he had as an early lunch.

"If you'd like to find out, I'm happy to take you to him." The threatening grimace on his face tells me to keep quiet. His nose scrunches. "Get in line."

1. SAVAGE

The jumpsuit is not as stiff. I'm breaking it in. Am I being broken in too?

The lobby holding area walls are the color of dirty snow. Old cameras dangle from the ceiling. Do they even work? A vending machine, all lit up, sits in a corner, probably for the guards. The barred windows are few and far between, turning every view into a grim grid of confinement.

Uncle Aldo's all buttoned-up in his blues, in the middle of a pow-wow with the warden and Officer Wringle. The warden's pulling a tiny black suitcase, probably skipping town for a night or two.

Wringle's strutting, chest puffed out. Warden's pointing at Wringle a lot.

What if she's leaving him in charge while she's away?

Uncle Aldo's holding the door for the warden, suitcase trailing. Her heels click-clack, echoing until she's in the parking lot.

Wringle vanishes into his office, slams the door.

Uncle Aldo looks around, eyes hunting. Then, a twitch of his mouth, like he's restraining a smile when he sees me.

I'm propped against the wall of the holding area, arms crossed. A line in the floor, faded, separates tiles laid at two different times. I shuffle. Uncle Aldo struts. We meet in the middle at the dividing line.

"You did it. Day one's almost in the bag."

A snort slips out of me. "So soon? Guess all good things must come to an end."

He chuckles—a sound that doesn't belong here, too warm, too human. "How did it go?"

"I'd say it was the best day of my life. If I was born yesterday." Sarcasm drools from each of my words.

Uncle Aldo's lips part into a half smile.

"It could be worse. I'm alive at least. Anything on Ollie?" I shift my weight as I change the subject.

"I'm going to make house calls tomorrow. Talk to people who know him outside of here. See what I can find."

I fish out the notebook, then tear out a couple of pages and hand them over. "Sorry it's so sloppy. I wrote as neat as I could. I bullet-pointed what I saw at the top."

He takes the papers, and his cop mask slips. He's concerned.

*BIG LEONARD AND OLLIE WERE FRIENDS, OFTEN PLAYED VIDEO GAMES TOGETHER

*BIG LEONARD IS THE ANGRY TYPE

*STRAY DOG

*BRUISE ON DENIA'S ARM

*DENIA'S REACTION TO THE SECURITY GUARD

*PEA-KNUCKLE IS A STUPID GAME

"Thanks for this. I like the way you spell pinochle."

"It's the only way I know."

"Makes more sense. Pea-knuckle should be spelled your way."

A guard slams a door down the hall, and I jump. Our little bubble pops. "I'd better go. Don't want anyone to see us together too long. I have a reputation to hold up. Hardened criminals can't be seen with the boys in blue."

Uncle Aldo's got a crinkle of worry between his brows. "You're no hardened criminal."

I stick my chin up. "True. And you're definitely no boy."

He throws back a make-believe glare. "Hey, you saying I'm old? Get out of here."

"I'm trying my best to get out. But the fence has razors on top. I'm going to start digging as soon as I steal a spoon. Should be out in about fifty-two thousand, four hundred, thirty-three spoonfuls."

"I don't want you in here a minute longer than you have to be. I'm

1. SAVAGE

working on it. You know you can trust me." Uncle Aldo's voice is lower, a promise, or maybe a prayer.

My throat pulses. Trust isn't easy, not here, not anywhere. But this is Uncle Aldo. So I nod, once. "Yeah. I'd hug you, but like I said, my reputation and I don't want to wrinkle my new outfit. Night, Uncle Aldo."

"Night, kid."

I pivot on my heel, ready to strut back to the world of locks and bars. Walking away, back straight, head high, every step saying I'm more than this jumpsuit, more than these walls, more than razor-blade fences. I'm Vickie from Queens, and I'm not gonna be broken. Not by this place, not by anything.

I stand in the middle of my concrete coffin, wearing the night clothes they issued. The fabric's even rougher than the jumpsuit and smells of chemicals and not giving a crap. My hair's wet from the shower, water droplets trailing down my back like ice fingers. But that's not what makes me shiver.

Something's off.

The same eerie sense I had in Queens when our apartment got robbed. We didn't have much. But the guy that broke in, Frank, took more than stuff. He took a piece of my peace, my sense of safety.

I survey my cell. The bunk is as I left it, the bedsheet stretched tight, not a wrinkle. Officer Wringle made sure of that. My tennis shoes are tossed in the corner, haphazard and forgotten. I'm wearing my shower shoes.

My gaze falls where I keep my one photo on the far wall — Ma, Uncle Aldo, and me.

Gone.

Panic flares. I search, hoping the picture fell. But I know someone's been in my cell. Who? One of these messed-up kids? Or one of the messed-up staff?

It's only a photo, but since I have nothing else to latch on to, it's more than a pic. I feel naked without my momento, like I've lost a shield.

Lesson three in prison: *They can take anything from me, anytime.*

I sit on the bunk. I should've hidden the photo instead of putting it on display. Anything that means something becomes a weakness, a target.

The anger slow burns. I'll find out who stole my only reminder of home.

Denia is most likely. She's got motive. I didn't hide my dislike of her. And she sleeps in the cell next door.

Trouble is, these kids don't need motive — the moaning, the acting out, the fights. If there are motives, they aren't the kind that make any sense.

I lie on my bunk.

Shadows dance in the dim light, creating monsters out of nothing, so I close my eyes.

Sleep is miles away.

My mind races, thoughts chasing each other in circles.

I think of Ma and Uncle Aldo.

I don't need a photo. No one can take my thoughts.

I'm Vickie. From Queens.

I'll find my photo. And I'll find a way out of this nightmare.

DAY TWO

CHAPTER 54
Time Bombs

VICKIE

Kids in juvie, they're like ticking time bombs. Except some don't tick. They explode without a countdown. Each one duct taped to their own messed-up reality.

I sit at a table in the corner of the cafeteria, my back to the wall, watching, scribbling in the little notebook Uncle Aldo gave me.

I've gotta be careful, on alert. But a different way than when I lived in Queens. Fights in my old neighborhood were motivated. The logic made sense. Here the fights break out like power surges in an overloaded outlet—fists flying, feet kicking, all desperate rage and nothing to lose.

Even at night, I don't know when the next scream or moan will shake the walls. Even during the quiet, I'm waiting for someone to bust in. Even now, I know I'm not safe.

Today's early morning matchup is Crazy Cara and Skinny Mike. Cara's got this wild look, always twitching, her eyes darting around like she's seeing ghosts. When she walks, it's a jerky dance—her body can't decide which way to go. And Skinny Mike, picking fights, out to prove something. He struts around, chest out, but his eyes, they're scared. When he throws a punch, it's more desperation than anger.

I'm not afraid of punches. But I save my energy for fights that matter.

Or fights I can't avoid.

Oh no.

I spot Denia before she spots me.

She struts in like no one else exists. Her eyes dust the room, landing on me with a glint, eager to pull me into her world.

I'd disappear into this cinder-block wall behind me if I could. I focus on my notebook. Like a little kid, I hope if I don't look at her, she can't see me.

My body tenses. I brace for the sound of her goat voice.

"So, are you a reporter?" She cocks her hip, folds her arms.

"Nope." I don't look up. I don't need her drama.

She slides into the seat next to me. I flash a glare to her. Her eyes narrow, her challenge clear in her forward lean, invading my space. "Snitches get stitches. Anything about me in there?" Denia grabs for my notebook, hooking the corner in her fist.

I move so close to her, I'm almost Eskimo kissing her pointy nose. "Let go before I pea-knuckle your face."

She releases. I'm beginning to see power in the word pea-knuckle.

As much as I want to avoid Denia, we're in prison. Like high school, I'm locked up and forced to interact with people I dislike.

If I change tables, she'll follow me.

I planned to confront her about my missing photo, but wanted to choose when. My grip tightens on my pen. I don't like surprise conversations. I push the words out. "Someone was in my cell last night. Know anything about that?"

Her breath hot on my face, a mischievous gleam in her eyes. "It was me." She admitted that fast. I guess crazy people don't know any better. "I wanted to watch you sleep," she says. "So I snuck in."

I meet her gaze, unflinching. "That wouldn't surprise me except I know you are locked in your cell, nice and tight like a ziplock baggie, every night."

Denia throws her head back, her laughter harsh and irritating.

I don't think she's the one who took my photo. If not her, then who?

I look around, searching for a distraction.

Big Leonard sits alone, slumped. What did the Troll do to him yesterday? She follows my gaze, her face softening. "Poor Leonard. All alone. No Ollie and no more visitors."

"Why no more visitors? Because of yesterday?"

Her body droops. "Oliver's real parents used to visit both of them. No one else ever came to see Big Leonard. Probably never will."

Denia exhibits empathy. Surprising.

Ollie's parents visiting Big Leonard is unusual, and I'll write this info down as soon as Denia leaves.

"Look, I really want to be alone." I hurry her exit.

"Me too. We can be alone together."

I shove a spoonful of runny oatmeal into my mouth and blow out a Big Bad Wolf breath that doesn't blow her away.

I think of other things. Uncle Aldo. He said he is making house calls today. Like a doctor fixing people. I'll bet he wishes he could fix me, but I know I'm not broken. Just a little glitchy.

CHAPTER 55
Pie

ALDO

Why would a couple take in a foster kid with a medical history like Ollie's? Out of kindness? For the money? To feel better about themselves? All of the above?

Stepping into the Franklins' home is like walking onto the set of one of those 1950s TV shows where everything's wrapped up nice and neat by the end of the episode. The kind I used to watch as a kid, that American-dream type life.

What's that buzz? I look around and spot a lamp in the corner of the Franklins' living room that's got a short. The bulb's flickering so slight most people would miss it. I'm not most people.

There's an old-person smell that probably came with the house, like mothballs and memories. Photographs in old frames line the mantel, capturing smiles that seem too perfect.

The shiny hardwood floor creaks under my size-twelve shoes.

Mr. Franklin's seated in a Lazy Boy. Lines etch his middle-aged face, deep as the Grand Canyon.

I shake his rough hand. Hands that have seen hard work, not pushing papers and stapling corners.

Mrs. Franklin's dress, all floral and neat, holds her figure in place. She wipes her hand on an apron tied around her waist, ironed, white and crisp. Her hair's done up in a neat bun, not a strand out of place. But it's her eyes. They're bright. The twinkle says she's holding on to hope.

And there's the pie, sitting pretty on the table, steam dancing off it, putting on a show. The scent of apples and cinnamon wafts, making my stomach do flips.

We exchange pleasantries, and soon I'm perched on a firm but comfortable chair, tasting a first bite of fresh-baked hospitality. A slice of heaven in this house that's working too hard to be perfect.

"How's the pie?" Mrs. Franklin's expression is expectant. She waits for my verdict.

The crust is flaky, crunchy but soft. The right balance of sweet and salt in the filling. "You know, even though cops are notorious for their sweet tooths, I've never liked doughnuts. Or sweets in general. Except pie. And this is top notch."

"You made her day." Mr. Franklin shifts in his seat. There's a grimace he tries to hide. I know someone in pain when I see them.

"Time for your medication." Mrs. Franklin is on her feet in a domestic blur, her dress swaying as she heads to the kitchen.

I pounce on my opportunity to approach a delicate subject. There's been hurt here, physical and maybe more. "How's the recovery from—the injury."

"I'm fine." His eyes tell me he's lying. "How's Ollie?"

"Missing. That's why I'm here."

"Oh no. Poor boy." Mrs. Franklin's voice drifts from the kitchen, a mix of worry and disbelief.

"It's my fault." Mr. Franklin's voice crackles like an old record with too many scratches.

Mrs. Franklin hands him a pill and a glass of water that sparkles in the light. "Don't say that. You couldn't have known." The care in her movements, the gentle way she handles the glass, tells me her affection for her husband is as real as her pie.

1. SAVAGE

The Franklins, with their perfect house and their pain hidden behind smiles. And that pie. A sweet lie in a world that's anything but sweet. Maybe that's the real American dream. Someone by your side to share hard knocks with and enough time to take a breath and appreciate what you've got instead of focusing on what you don't have yet, and probably never will. A better name for The American Dream is The Great American Distraction.

I put down my fork. "What makes you say it's your fault?"

Mr. Franklin expels a grunt, shifting before he speaks. "He had only been with us a week and played video games from the time he got up until the time he went to bed."

"He didn't even want to go outside. It's not healthy." Mrs. Franklin wrings her hands like she's washing them under the faucet. What's she scrubbing clean?

There's tension between them. Understandable. Not easy sharing your imperfections with a stranger.

Mr. Franklin's eyes are distant. Part of him is with us, but most of him is somewhere else. Maybe back in that moment. "We'd tried to coax him, bribe him, until finally, I unplugged the TV and took the controller. That's when he stabbed me."

Mrs. Franklin eases closer. "With the dinner knife from his *half-eaten* steak." From the words she emphasizes, Ollie's *half*-eaten steak is as heinous as the stabbing. I make a mental note to never criticize her food.

"Removing the video game didn't warrant his reaction." I offer validation. A way to connect and keep them talking.

"Of course not." Mrs. Franklin's voice strains.

Mr. Franklin continues, more present now. "But what I didn't know is that his mother was in and out of manic episodes. Father was depressed all the time. Still, the father was the most solid thing the kid had. They used to bond, playing video games. Probably good for them both."

"I see."

"So, when I took that controller—"

"We were taking away his only connection to his father." Mrs. Franklin finishes Mr. Franklin's sentence the way old married couples do.

The picture is coming through clearer for me like the image shaken out of a Polaroid.

"I could see in Ollie's eyes how he wished he could undo stabbing me. He looked like he was in more pain than me." Mr. Franklin chuckles, grabbing his right side, just above the bandage.

I push off from the arm of my chair and stand. Mr. Franklin attempts to stand out of politeness, but I gesture for him to remain seated. "Thank you both for your time. And hospitality."

"He's a good kid. I hope you find him." Mr. Franklin's bottom lip quivers. His wife is in place behind him, rubbing his shoulders to soothe his emotions.

"Would you like a piece of pie to go?" Mrs. Franklin asks.

"You know, I'd better not. My wife doesn't like when I eat another woman's food. She can smell the scent on me." I grin, pulling out my tiny bottle of Listerine from my front shirt pocket. "That's why I keep this with me at all times. Happy marriage insurance."

Outside the closed front door, I'm not sure if the heaviness is from the apple pie or the weight of the task of finding Ollie, but I'm tired already and I'm only halfway through the day.

CHAPTER 56
Sidekick

VICKIE

Denia is stuck like a piece of toilet paper I can't shake from the bottom of my shoe. She stands beside me in the lobby holding area, a couple yards from the security office.

The fluorescent lights buzz overhead, puking out a hollow glow on the bolted-down furniture.

The other kids, my fellow inmates, move through the lobby like ghosts. My interactions are cautious, each of us wrapped in our own cocoon of survival. Three of them sit at different tables scattered throughout the room.

In the far corner, the door that leads to the offices, the inner workings of this place, is closed. A barrier between us and the people who thumbs-up or thumbs-down our fate.

Officer Wringle's inside the security office. It has a separate entrance. The door's cracked open, leaking bits of his phone conversation. "We're out of cyan and black ink. This joint's falling apart. How am I supposed to copy these visitor logs? By hand? Can I borrow some? Be right there."

He hurries past us in a huff.

I giant step my way to the door.

Denia's molten gaze burns through me. "You can't go in there."

She's a terrible sidekick. All kick and not on the side of anyone but herself.

If my eyes were fists, she'd be flat on the floor from the glare I give back at her. "Snitches get stitches." I echo her words from the time she wrestled for my notebook.

I enter Officer Wringle's weird, creepy office. Animal heads on the wall. Smells like cat piss and beef jerky. Perfect lair for a troll.

The visitor log sits on top of an old copy machine. I flip the pages back a couple days.

"What are you doing?" Denia's voice is annoying even when she whispers.

"Just keep an eye out for the Troll."

"There. Mr. and Mrs. Green visiting Oliver. And Big Leonard." Scanning back a few pages, no other visitor entries for Leonard. Confirms what Denia said. I go back further in the logs. There are several more visits with Ollie and his parents.

Why's Leonard meeting with Oliver's folks so often? Leonard hates adults. Why's he making an exception for them? The puzzle's not fitting right. Wrong pieces jammed in the wrong places.

Officer Wringle enters. Denia gasps.

Thanks for the warning, Denia. Worst sidekick in the history of mystery solving. Wringle pushes by her. He clamps on to my arm with his large, sweaty hand. "What are you doing in here?"

Best lies are marinated in truth. "Came to report my cell's been broken into."

I wait to see if he's dumb enough to buy my half truth.

He releases my arm. "Didn't you hang your Do Not Disturb sign?"

I hate pretending to be stupid. But I need to finish the sales job. "They took something. My photo."

"You think someone wants a picture of you? Have you seen yourself?"

Real original. Not the first time someone insulted the way I look.

"Get out of my office," Wringle snarls.

Denia's already gone. I leave. The air from the slamming door behind me blows past.

What is Officer Wringle hiding?

I never told him I was in my missing photo. It's possible he saw it in my cell yesterday during bed checks.

But there's another possibility. A more dangerous possibility. A possibility that would mean he's messing with me. Taking things from my cell when I'm not there. Or worse, while I am there. Sleeping. Watching me.

What if the Troll took my photo? And what if that is only the beginning?

CHAPTER 57
Freeze Frame

ALDO

I knock for a second time.

No answer.

One hour after my conversation with Ollie's foster parents, the Franklins, I stand on the cracked concrete slab porch of the home of Ollie's biological parents.

My stomach growls. Pie is no substitute for a meatball parm.

A short, stout woman with greasy brown hair and thick glasses creaks open the door. Ollie's mother. I recognize her from the file. "Yes?" Her voice quivers like a leaf in a storm.

"I'm Officer Bartolucci, ma'am." I offer my badge. It catches a faint glimmer of light from the cloud-covered sun above. "I'm here about Oliver."

Mrs. Green opens the door and leans to inspect my badge; she's so close her breath is warm on my hand.

I stiffen so I don't recoil, hiding my discomfort.

"I'm sorry. My eyesight is poor. " There's inadequacy in her tone.

"May I come in?" I ask as gentle as I can to soothe her.

"Oh dear." A flicker of uncertainty darts through her eyes like a restless toddler going from room to room. "Now is not the best time."

"I won't be long."

She considers, then moves aside, and I enter. Inside, the clutter's like a map of the Greens' lives — piles of clothes, magazines, and wires tangled like thoughts that can't find their way.

Mr. Green sits on a couch, lost in a video game. His fingers dance over the controller with the agile fingers of a concert pianist. He pauses the game and locks eyes with me.

I see the game freeze on the television just a few feet away from him.

"Hello, Mr. Green." I speak less like a cop and more like a guest. But I'm betting they don't get many guests.

His face is blank and heavy, all the expression drained. A man battling his own mind. I didn't have to read his file to see the weight of his depression hang on his body like a heavy winter coat.

"I wanted to introduce myself and let you know we're doing everything we can to find Oliver." I don't have to fake my sincerity. The situation's serious. Life threatening considering Ollie's epilepsy. Worst case, Ollie's had a seizure. And I'm looking for a body and not a boy.

"We just want him here with us." Mrs. Green's voice is so low I strain to hear her.

"They should've never taken him from his home." Mr. Green's monotone is colored with a bitterness that's been fermenting.

Mrs. Green's hands shake. Could be her medication. Lithium for her manic episodes. "We were never very good about taking our own meds. But I always made sure Ollie took his. The pharmacy's just down the block. We've been diligent about taking our meds for two weeks now. Our social worker said she thought Ollie would be back with us within a couple months. Then this incident happened at his foster home. Next thing we knew, he was in juvenile hall. It was terrible for him in there."

The room's got a feeling of desperation. The curtains are closed like they're keeping whatever hope is left trapped inside. Afraid it will escape with too much interference from the outside reality.

"I understand. I have a couple questions if you have a moment?" There's no response, so I keep going. "Would you describe Ollie as accident prone?" I phrase things as careful as I can inside this emotional minefield.

"Are you kidding? You have to have top-notch reflexes to be as good at gaming as he is." Mr. Green's tone is all proud father, bringing life into his face for a moment.

I notice a second controller on the couch beside Mr. Green. Probably Ollie's. Sad and sweet he leaves it out. I don't mention the bruising I saw in the photos in case the Greens weren't made aware. Now's not the time.

"We should've been there for him. He should've been here with us." Mr. Green's tone is firm.

"We would do anything to have Ollie back." Sobs punctuate Mrs. Green's words.

"Like any good parent." Mr. Green underlines his wife's words.

The vibe in the room shifts. Mrs. Green's fingers twist and untwist the hem of her housecoat. Like a mouse looking for a way out of a maze. Too much pressure for her. If either of them breaks, they won't be any help now or in the future. "I didn't mean to upset you. I know this is a difficult time. I'll leave my card in case you need anything."

Mrs. Green takes my card, her eyes lost in a distant thought. Mr. Green's attention returns to the frozen video game. A cave full of spiderwebs and skeletons is on the screen. Ironically, a safer world for him than reality.

I make my way to the door, pause, take another look around the cluttered, lived-in space. "Thank you for your time."

Reaching my car, I slide behind the wheel and sit. Stretching my neck from side to side releases the stress of censoring so many of my impulses to keep the couple at ease.

This isn't just another case. Every case involving a child makes me think of my kids—and Vickie.

Seeing Ollie's parents brought the pages in his file to life. His parents care about him. More than they care about themselves. I'm not sure that's a good thing for them or Ollie. But that's what parents do.

Mrs. Green's trembling hands. Lapses in needed medication. Struggles with mental health. And now the absence of their son.

Not easy.

I start the engine. The hum of the car, a small comfort as I pull away from the curb.

Ollie, wherever you are, hang in there, kid. I'm gonna find you.

CHAPTER 58
Holes

VICKIE

The ground is a patchwork of worn grass and dirt.

A basketball hoop stands at one end, its net frayed and hanging limp. A few benches, paint chipped and faded, offer a cold, hard seat for reflection or regret. Birds circle above. But fly away, uninterested.

I sit alone at a table in the prison yard, the metal surface cold under my hands. A handful of others distract themselves in other ways, but I ignore them.

My chest tightens. A familiar anxiety. Like when I wait up for Ma to return from one of her late night dates. I like to put together Dollar Store puzzles to distract me from checking the clock; the biggest one I've tackled so far is one thousand pieces.

Spaces not filled. Pieces not placed.

Questions with no answers.

Makes me anxious. But better than being anxious about Ma staying safe or Ollie staying alive.

I release my thoughts into the notebook, hoping my chest will feel less heavy.

DAY 2

JUNE 12TH

DENIA ACTS CAGIER THAN USUAL AROUND OFFICER WRINGLE. WHY?

BIG LEONARD DOESN'T TALK AROUND ADULTS, BUT JOINED OLLIE ON PARENT VISITS. WHY?

SOMEONE TOOK MY PHOTO FROM MY CELL. WHY?

A sliding, dragging sound draws my attention.

Big Leonard's prison dog, sneaky-like, slips under the chain-link razor-crested fence, ears perked, body wary and on high alert.

So that's how the mutt gets in and out. One mystery solved. My face relaxes in a contented grin.

I'm so impressed with the dog I don't notice Officer Wringle.

With a speed that betrays his girthy physique, the Troll claws my notebook from my hand. "What's this?"

"Give that back." My voice is edged like a blade.

His sneer grows, challenging me. "What are you going to do about it?"

I should challenge him to a game of pea-knuckle. "It's mine," I say. Defiant.

His laughter is empty. "Nothing belongs to you in here. You don't even belong to you."

I lunge for the notebook.

He shoves me, hard.

The ground meets me with a rough welcome. I use both hands to push myself up, when a biting zap jolts through me. My body seizes.

I've been tasered.

Time slows, sound dulls.

"Write about that in your little book." Wringle's words twist in my ears.

Crumpled on my side, I drool.

Gloating glee infects every muscle in his face.

Growling. Barking. The prison mutt pounces, biting and pulling Wringle's arm. With a powerful swing, Wringle throws off the dog.

A pained yelp resonates through the yard.

"I'll have my gun ready next time. Should have shot that mutt when I first saw him." Wringle scuttles away holding his arm.

Barred windows barely let light inside the lobby holding area, their griminess turning the outside world into a blur of muted colors and indistinct shapes. Doesn't stop Crazy Cara from staring out of one of them. Whatever she sees in her mind's eye makes her laugh.

I wish I had a better imagination. Life at juvie, maybe life everywhere, would be a lot easier. But, I've never been good at pretend.

Standing across from Uncle Aldo, his eyes pinch into me, like he's peeling back my tough layers. "What's wrong?"" Concern is poured into his words.

I'm still tremoring from being tasered.

"Nothing." I shove my hands deeper into the pockets of my orange onesie to steady any shake.

Uncle Aldo pulls me around the corner. More privacy. "If anyone's giving you problems. If they're mistreating you—"

"I can handle it." The words sharp, a little too sharp. But if I tell Uncle Aldo about Wringle, he will worry.

Or worse.

I've never seen Uncle Aldo lose control. And don't ever want to. Everyone has a breaking point. And the more controlled someone is, the more they are holding back. Uncle Aldo is always in control.

I need to get the spotlight off me.

"I've got some bad news. They took my notebook." I pull a couple of crumpled pages from my pocket. "But not before I tore these out."

He takes the pages, scanning them. "Good work. This info is a big help. Just—"

"I know. Stay out of trouble."

"I was going to say, just remember I'm here for you." His words cover me like an electric blanket and warm me from the outside in.

The sound of boots in the hall snaps me back. Officer Wringle. I straighten up.

"I've gotta go. We'll talk soon, all right?" Uncle Aldo's jaw is tight with concern as he turns. I watch Uncle Aldo drift toward the door.

Officer Wringle rounds the corner and goes in his office.

The lobby might as well be empty now, just me and the echoes of a handful of conversations that aren't mine.

I leave the lobby, turn the corner, fall back against the wall. The concrete's unforgiving, but real. Solid. Steady.

I swipe at my eyes, with my stiff sleeve.

DAY THREE

CHAPTER 59
Napkin Notes

VICKIE

I slouch in my chair, the metal cold against my back. A chill seeps through my orange jumpsuit. A dozen kids gobble down their breakfast. Denia and Big Leonard finished a few minutes ago.

My tray is untouched in front of me.

No notebook today, but who needs it when I've got napkins and a pen? I scribble words loosely strung together.

Officer Troll lurks.

I don't care if he sees me writing. I want him to know I'm not afraid.

DAY 3

OFFICER WRINGLE: TASER-HAPPY, NOTEBOOK THIEF, DANGEROUS

DENIA: BRUISE ON HER ARM SCREAMS A STORY, ALWAYS JITTERY AROUND WRINGLE

OLLIE: MISSING. SEIZURES. BRUISES

LEONARD: GENTLE GIANT, OLLIE'S ALLY

DOG: GUARDIAN ANGEL. ESCAPES THROUGH HOLE IN THE FENCE

OLLIE'S PARENTS: VISITING BIG LEONAR.

I chew the end of my pen.

Where's Ollie? Playing hide-and-seek with the adults? They say he's tiny, skinny. Could be hiding anywhere, outsmarting every grown-up in this facility. Or did he escape, through the doors, past the fences?

My gaze lands on Leonard, alone, sorting scraps for the dog.

Then, insights flood my brain so fast, my eyelids flutter.

I stand, beelining toward Leonard.

With every step my shoes stick to spots of who-knows-what on the floor, but my thoughts are quick.

"Hey, Leonard." I speak low. "We need to talk."

Big Leonard looks up, his eyes deep pools of secrets.

"I know it was you." My eyes meet his, trying to pull the truth from him. "You helped Oliver, didn't you? Through the hole, under the fence."

Leonard looks away, then back at me.

"Why?" I press. "Ollie's bruises? No accident, right? Denia's got them too. She's no klutz, and neither is Ollie."

Leonard's eyes flick to Wringle, who's now elbows deep in doughnuts in the cafeteria line. "Had to," he whispers, "to keep Ollie safe." Desperation paints his words.

"Where's Ollie now?" Urgency bubbles in my tone.

His lips pinch together.

"Don't you get it? Ollie needs his pills. He might already be dead. Don't you care? Unless—" An idea hits me, sharp and sudden.

"Wait. Where are you going?" Leonard's words don't stop me.

I need a phone. Gotta call Uncle Aldo.

Wringle's busy pigging out. Now's my chance. I slip out the door.

The holding area is down the hallway and around the corner. Deserted.

I slide into Officer Troll's office. The door closes with a soft click, sealing me inside this bizarre animal trophy room. Dead heads, their glassy eyes stare down. The largest one, a deer with antlers like twisted branches, seems to follow me. But there's no time to be creeped out.

1. SAVAGE

The government-issued desk is covered with papers. A phone. I edge close and pick up the receiver.

I dial the number, my fingers surprisingly steady. Each ring a countdown.

I glance at the door, half-expecting Wringle to burst in.

The office remains silent, except for muffled voices from down the hall and the hum of the fluorescent lights above.

"Come on, come on," I whisper to the phone.

And then, "Bartolucci residence."

"Uncle Aldo. It's Vickie." My voice shakes out the words. "I know where Ollie is."

CHAPTER 60
Refills

ALDO

I lean against my car in the Greens' neighborhood. Came here as soon as I got off the phone with Vickie. Morning mist licks my face and dampens my uniform. The drugstore across the street is a relic. A few cars litter the parking lot. Mrs. Green shuffles out of the store, her white cane tapping a rhythm of survival on the sidewalk. She wears a rain bonnet to keep her greasy hair dry. In her arms, she clutches white prescription bags.

I approach. Only twenty feet away and she's still unable to see me. "Mrs. Green," I call, not wanting to spook her. She jumps despite my efforts and turns, facing me down.

"Officer, you startled me."

"You recognize my voice."

"Of course."

"May I help with those bags?" I'm a few feet away from her now.

She cradles the bags. "My prescriptions. I told you we've been good about our refills. I can handle them." She angles away from me. "Is there something I can help *you* with?"

"One of those is for Ollie, isn't it?"

"Yes. For when he comes home."

"Mrs. Green, I know where Ollie is. And so do you. I understand you think you're doing the right thing, but this isn't the way." I put my hand on her shoulder.

Her lips tremble like she's holding back a dam of words. "I—I just. You don't know what it's like. Seeing your boy hurt, and being so helpless. Bruises every week. We couldn't do anything. He was already taken from us. And that guard, he'd have made it worse if we told the warden."

A lump clogs my throat, thick and heavy. Officer Wringle was the one responsible for the bruises on Ollie. I'm sure of it. How many other kids has he hurt there? "Take me to Ollie. I promise I'll help sort things out. Make sure Ollie isn't hurt further. Okay?"

Her head dips up and down. Mrs. Green walks her memorized route to her door. I shadow her and she shuffles up the stoop. The door creaks open under the direction of her gentle push.

The sound of video game gunfire blasts, a sharp contrast to the quiet of the street. Inside, Ollie and Mr. Green sit together on the couch, their fingers a blur on their game controllers. Ollie's sucked into the virtual world, using the controller I saw beside Mr. Green during my last visit.

Ollie's and his father's focus is so absolute, they don't notice me. "Why were you gone so long?" Mr. Green's eyes are glued to the screen, his face full of joy.

I step farther into the room, tidier than yesterday. "Hello, Oliver."

They both startle, pause the game, stare. I raise my hands. "Relax. Everything's gonna be okay." The words are as much for me as them, a reassurance.

CHAPTER 61
Broken Shield

VICKIE

The line clicks dead, and I release a breath I didn't know I was holding hostage. Uncle Aldo will handle things from here. My shoulders drop an inch. I hang up the ancient landline in the security office. A clunky sound echoes in the tiny room.

No more puzzles to distract me from my own reality. Just me stuck in a cage. Locked doors. Watchful eyes. No escape.

My eyes flick to Wringle's desk, where his coffee mug sits like the king of a paper mountain. And winking at me from under the mess, my notebook.

I dig it out, reclaiming a piece of myself. Underneath the notebook is the photo from my cell. My only keepsake from home—me, Uncle Aldo, and Ma back when laughs were easy.

The idea of Wringle's sticky fingers groping my belongings makes me gag. The thought of him creeping into my cell anytime he wants squeezes me from the inside out. Even locks won't keep him out.

I pocket my treasures and turn, but I'm blocked by Wringle's bulk in the doorway.

"I was. I am—I need to get back." The words stumble out of me, but my feet are glued to the floor. My heart's racing, and my palms sweat. I can't dodge past him. He's a wall, an unmovable force. I'm cornered.

Wringle's smug grin infects his round, stubbly face. "The little mouse went looking for cheese and got herself caught in a trap. Did your uncle send you?" He inches closer, the door clicking shut behind him, trapping us in this stale, coffee-scented box.

"What are you talking about?" My words come out sharp, like shards of glass. I shift my weight, fists clenched, ready to defend myself.

Wringle jabs a finger toward his eyes, his gaze locked on to mine. "Nothing gets by me. I read your notebook. Little mouse spy." His words slither in the air, venomous and full of accusation.

"I'm leaving. Move." I step forward, every muscle in my body tense, ready to spring.

"Put out your hands." Wringle's voice booms in the cramped space.

"Why?" I bite back, electric defiance surging through me, my skin a prickling mix of fear and anger.

The cop stick in his hand thunders down on the desk. "Now."

I don't move. He grabs my right forearm and squeezes hard enough to cut off circulation. This is how Denia and Ollie and probably others got their bruises. He's more than a bully. He's a coward. Hurting kids because he can.

I give in before my arm breaks, jutting my hands out in front of me. The cold steel of the handcuffs snaps around my wrists, the chill biting into my skin. Panic surges.

Clank. Wringle unlocks the gun rack and grabs his shotgun.

His push is forceful, his hand heavy on my back—each touch stings like a snake's strike.

My heart pounds against my rib cage. "Where are you taking me?"

"You need discipline, little mouse." He shoves me toward the side door, his eyes glinting with sadistic pleasure.

"I could scream." My warning's an empty threat. Screams aren't unusual here.

"Good. I'd like that. Makes it more fun." His words are a cold suffocating fog. "And who's going to help you? I'm the boss here."

He marches me down the hallway. My rage and fear battle each other.

The Troll unlocks the side door exit and sunlight floods in, blinding me. I blink against the glare, my eyes adjusting. He gives me a shove, and I stumble, catching myself last minute.

Parking lot's a stretch of asphalt, lined with cars, some battered and bruised. Sun's rising, casting long shadows. Air's sharp against my skin.

I'm pushed again, harder this time, and I'm on the ground beside a car. The smell of fresh-cut grass mixed with the scent of motor oil makes my head swirl. Every muscle in my body tenses.

He unlocks his truck and rummages in the glove compartment, pulling out a rattling box of ammo. "I'm gonna show you what I do with troublemakers." He pops two long red cartridges into the shotgun. "These are high-powered." His voice oozes satisfaction. "Perfect for taking down big game. Or little nuisances."

My pulse pounds. I'm cornered, powerless. "You see, Vickie, hunting's not just a sport. It's an art. You have to select the right tool. These shells spread out on impact. More damage. More pain."

The shotgun clicks as he loads it, the sound echoing in the empty lot. "It's all about control," he continues. "You take aim, and you have the power to end something. Anything."

I swallow hard, my throat dry. Fear's got a grip on me, but I won't let it show. I stare him down, my gaze steady. "You think a gun makes you powerful?" My voice is a low hiss.

Wringle smirks, his eyes narrow. "I know it does." He steps back, the gun now aimed in my direction, his finger teasing the trigger. I scurry backward against the front wheel of his truck, panting. "Looks like you agree with me." He laughs.

In my head, I'm screaming, cursing. But on the outside, my face is stone, unflinching. I won't give him the satisfaction of seeing me break any further. He leans over the hood of the truck, pointing the gun away

1. SAVAGE

from me and at the fence 200 yards in front of us.

What's he doing? I'm not the little nuisance he referred to.

The mutt from the yard trots on the outside of the fence, sniffing. Wringle's eyes gleam. "My dad taught me how to hunt." His voice drips with pride. "It's all about patience and control."

He's going to shoot the stray.

The dog, clueless and curious, finds a gap and shimmies under the gate.

"Just a little closer," Wringle taunts.

I can't let this happen. I leap forward, my cuffed hands swinging, and bash the gun. The shotgun jerks, and a loud bang shatters the air, my ears ring. The bullet dings the truck as the gun skids across the hood.

Wringle swings at me. All blubber and fury but makes contact.

I taste blood in my mouth. He winds up again. I duck, feeling the air brush past as his fist misses. It's us now, him with his bulk and me, all spitfire and survival.

Still not a fair fight as long as he has weapons and I'm still handcuffed.

In a flash, Wringle reaches for his taser. But I'm quicker. My cuffed hands lash out, smack the taser. It clatters into the gravel. No gun, no taser.

All he's got now is his cop stick.

Whack.

Pain explodes across my back, my knees give out. Vision blurs. The air around me swirls.

He's winning.

Tires screech. Words from a familiar voice. I strain to make them out.

"I said drop it, Wringle!" Uncle Aldo. His gun drawn, pointed at Wringle.

Wringle hesitates, stick still raised, but his eyes flick to Aldo. My uncle. On the edge of losing control.

I see my chance. I use my remaining strength, roll, snag the taser from the gravel, and zap. The prongs hit Wringle square in the chest.

Wringle's down.

He convulses, dropping like a sack of bricks.

I'm panting, feeling like I've been through a war. Every inch of me screams, but there's this wild triumph coursing through me.

Uncle Aldo's by my side, asking if I'm okay. I nod, too winded to speak.

He cuffs Wringle. Saying those words about rights you see cops shout on TV and that I've had recited to me several times.

CHAPTER 62
Punches and Pokes

Three hours later, the yard's buzzing like someone shook a beehive. Blue uniforms swarm. Uncle Aldo is in his element, orchestrating the chaos.

The warden's back. Her nails sharper and shinier. She sports a new hairdo, shorter and fancier.

Uncle Aldo's eyes find me. "You doin' all right?"

"You know me." My smile is half-hearted, but all I've got.

"Yeah, I do. Proud of ya. Just a second, then we can get outta here." He slips back into cop mode and returns to the badge brigade.

Uncle Aldo promised he'd get me out. And he did. He's worked out something with the judge.

Chaos surrounds me. I look around the yard. Strange, thinking I won't see these walls, these faces, anymore. Ever again.

Kids are huddled in groups, whispering, watching. Some look relieved, others confused. Like someone froze juvie life in place, and nobody's sure what comes next.

Wringle, cuffed and flanked by two officers, looks smaller, less menacing. Seeing him under control is satisfying.

The warden's voice, sharp, slices through the murmurs. She's all about damage control, painting a pretty picture over a filthy wall. Her new hair sways with each dramatic gesture, but her eyes are all self-preservation.

Denia, with her all-too-familiar smug walk, approaches. "Since you're leaving, can I poke you goodbye?"

"Sure. If you want a goodbye punch in the face."

"I'll pass." Denia looks over in Wringle's direction. The mark on her arm is purple now, fading around the edges.

Denia has a way of getting in between the layers of my skin, but she deserved better than what Wringle did.

"Good luck. I wish I could say it's been fun." She grins, then takes a few steps toward the hallway. "Hasn't been — terrible." Denia looks over her shoulder, tossing her last parting words back at me, then releases her ridiculous goat laugh.

"That girl's laugh is gonna haunt my dreams," I mutter to myself.

I spot Big Leonard, the giant of a guy who's more teddy bear than grizzly, and walk over.

He pats the prison mutt. "You're heading out, huh?" His voice is soft and cuddly.

I take a seat next to him. "Yeah, my uncle Aldo pulled some strings. Some fancy-schmancy rehab place for troubled teens like yours truly."

His eyebrows quiver. "Thank you."

"What did I do? You're the hero. What you did for Ollie. Helping him get out. You're a good friend."

"You're a good friend too." Leonard's voice is thick with raw appreciation.

"Learned from the best, didn't I?" I look at the ground, not sure how to say goodbye. Doesn't seem fair, me leaving and him locked in here with no one to even visit. "Is there anything I can do for you? Before I go?"

He points at the dog. "Take him with you. Just until I— Just until..."

I don't know anything about being a pet owner. And I'll be away for a while at that fancy jail. But it's also not a terrible idea. Uncle Aldo could watch him for a few weeks. While I'm away. "You sure?"

"It's what's best for him." He leans close to the dog, whispering something that sounds a lot like, "I'm gonna miss you, Candy."

I freeze in place. "What did you say?"

"That's what I call him. Reminds me of a dog I had when I was little. When I lived with my pop-pop." Leonard's voice gets distant, like he's traveling back in time.

"What happened to Candy? And Pop-Pop?" Candy's an unusual name for a dog. Only heard it once before. My neighbor's dog has the same name. And his missing grandson called him Pop-Pop.

"Pop-Pop died. Charlie told me."

"Who's Charlie?"

"He picked me up in my yard. Took me for ice cream on my fourth birthday. Said he'd bring me back. Never did. Trusted him because he had on a uniform. Phone company. If I was a dog, guess I would have been a better judge of character."

"Why didn't you tell anyone?"

"What does it matter? Charlie told me Pop-Pop died. Charlie died a few years later. Heart attack. Been bouncing from home to home ever since. I guess I'm not lucky when it comes to family." Leonard shrugs, a small mountain shifting.

Taking a deep breath, the words roll out. "Leonard. I've got something to tell you."

CHAPTER 63
Repairs

TWO WEEKS LATER

My neighbor's house isn't as creepy anymore. Big Leonard's only been home a couple days, but he's been busy with yardwork and repairs. The bittersweet smell of sanded pine and fresh paint wafts from the fence splitting our yards. I'm sandwiched between Uncle Aldo and Ma, who's fluttering around like she's hosting a party. Maury and Big Leonard stand in their mowed yard.

"Do I call you Big Leonard or Hugo?" I fold my arms on top of the fence.

Big Leonard shrugs. "Big Hugo." A smile splashes across his face.

"Can I get you two something? A diet Pepsi? Or I could make punch." Color floods Ma's cheeks. "Look at us spending time with neighbors. Just like in Queens, right, Aldo?"

Uncle Aldo nods, hands in his pockets. Goodbyes are hard for him. Hard for me too. Thanks to him, tomorrow I leave for the fancy prison. It's got to be better than juvie.

"We can't stay long. Just wanted to wish Vickie luck on her journey." Maury's voice is rich with gratitude.

Ma fidgets with her hands. "She'll be back soon."

Big Hugo looks down at his feet, then meets my eyes. "Thank you again, Vickie. For everything."

1. SAVAGE

"How are the two of you adjusting?" Uncle Aldo asks Maury and Big Hugo.

Maury slings an arm around Hugo's shoulders. "One day at a time. But what did I always tell you?"

A grin spreads across Big Hugo's face. "A little love goes a long, long way."

Maury swivels his head from one side of his yard to the other. "We're going to be okay. And the house and yard have never looked better."

Ma clasps her hands, her eyes shimmering. "These are good times. Maybe we should play the lotto again, Vix. I think our luck is changing."

Two dogs named Candy play. The younger one runs circles around the other.

"Vickie, you went looking for one missing person and you found two — Ollie and Hugo." Uncle Aldo elbows me with a playful jab. "Impressive."

Maury's face brightens, his eyes crinkling. "Make that three missing people. I've been missing in action too long. And Aldo, I appreciate what you said in the hearing on Hugo's behalf. Made a difference."

"Least I could do." Uncle Aldo fidgets. He's as uncomfortable with compliments as I am.

I help him wiggle off the hook. Change the subject. "How's Ollie anyway?" First update I've asked on him in a week.

"Ollie's settled into his new foster family's house. His parents are visiting every day, and if all goes well, the judge thinks he can go home in a couple weeks." Uncle Aldo rocks forward on his toes, then back on his heels.

Shifting my weight, I put my hands in the back pockets of the fancy sweatpants I haven't worn in three weeks. Paper crinkles. I pull it out and open one corner at a time. The missing-person flyer with Hugo's face on the front. I hold up the flyer, comparing Big Hugo to the image of his younger self. "Guess we don't need this anymore." I scrunch the paper in my fist.

Uncle Aldo places his hand on mine. "Keep it. A reminder that solving mysteries is just one of the many things you're good at. Couldn't have put things together without you."

Rosemary presses both her hands to her heart. "My daughter. A hero."

"I'm just Vickie from Queens."

"You're not just Vickie from Queens." Uncle Aldo ruffles my hair. "You're one hell of a niece."

Heat rises from the collar of my shirt and I can't contain the smile that erupts. "Watch the hair. Do you know how long it took me to get that I-don't-own-a-comb look?" I kick at a clump of grass and slide the paper into my back pocket. "I'd better get going."

Ma's eyebrow shoots up. "Where are you off to on your last day at home?"

"Just gotta sort some stuff out before I go. You know, loose ends." My tone is casual. Uncle Aldo wouldn't like the payback I have planned for a couple of kleptos.

CHAPTER 64
Mirrors

My sneakers scuff the polished floor at Talmadge's. The air's heavy with the scent of expensive perfume and new clothes. The store's the same since I was here last.

I inch close to the jewelry counter, and under the bright lights. I thought about being the better person like the judge suggested. Letting things go. I've changed. But I haven't changed that much.

Giggles from the earring aisle. Blonde and Blonder. The girls who got me sent to juvie.

I hover around the counter, adjust each of the small freestanding display mirrors to get the perfect view of the duo.

The saleslady's eyes flash with recognition. "Don't I know you? You're the girl—"

"Yeah."

"I almost lost my job because of you. Do I need to call security?"

"Yeah, you do. But not for me." I point to the mirrors, angled at Blonde and Blonder. "Learn to use your mirrors. They're not just for the customers."

Following my gaze, the saleslady peers into the closest mirror and gasps.

The two rich girls shove shiny stuff into their bags like it's a sport.

The saleslady lifts the phone and whispers a single word into the receiver. "Security." Then she looks at me. Like she really sees me and isn't looking past me or through me.

And I see a woman who's probably more like me than like her customers. She's an outsider too. But she's learned to fake it better than me. "Thank you," she mouths.

I take a detour on my way to the door, swinging by Blonde and Blonder, waving just as a lone security officer swoops in. The girls' faces are even paler than usual. Mouths open, hands shaking.

Stepping outside, the sun's blazing, but the warmth inside me burns brighter.

My problem was never about fitting in to juvie or this fancy store. My challenge was fitting in my own skin, feeling at home in my bones. Not just saying it, but being one hundred percent me. The best Vickie Bartolucci I can be.

I stride down the street, feeling like I've dropped a heavy backpack I've been lugging. My sneakers hit the pavement in a steady rhythm, a new confident beat.

I think about Uncle Aldo, who's as steady as concrete. The cop in our family, who showed me more about justice and fairness than any judge in a courtroom.

Then there's Ma, who loves me with everything she's got to give. Getting up early to wish me luck job hunting. Saying prayers for me. All the hugs.

And Ollie and Big Leonard and Candy, who've taught me about friendship and loyalty through the way they're there for each other.

I'm not the same girl who walked out of Talmadge's a week ago, framed and furious. I'm Vickie Bartolucci, a girl who survived juvie, uncovered truths, and found herself along the way.

My bedroom's a chaotic mix of me, like my mind spilled out and decorated the place. My desk, cluttered with laundry to fold, the bookshelf crammed with everything but books, and sneakers tossed in the corner.

I plop down on the bed, and remove my big purchase for the day—a large, faux-leather album with *The Scrapbook Chronicles* engraved on the front and a roll of Scotch Tape. The book's like the one Nona Bartolucci keeps all her old photos in, so she never forgets everything she's been through.

I thumb through the blank pages, then grab my Great Detective cassette from my desk, remove the photo insert and tape it onto the blank paper, then turn the page.

I saunter to my nightstand and remove a press clipping from the drawer. The familiar headline looms: "Priest Confesses to Murder in 30-Year-Old Cold Case—Convent Scandal Uncovered." I Scotch Tape the clipping into place and turn the page.

Then I retrieve the missing-kid flyer from my pocket. I smooth it onto one of the album pages. A sense of pride swells. Big Hugo was a cute kid. And now he's home. I helped find him, helped bring him back. Helped bring Ollie home too.

I give the book a pat and close it. Then rifle through a cup full of pens and highlighters on my desk and fish out a Sharpie. With the marker, I cross out *Scrapbook* and scribble in *Vickie*. "The Vickie Chronicles." I say, making it my own. "Much better."

CHAPTER 65
Blueberry Hill

We're driving, Uncle Aldo and me, the car sliding through a countryside that feels like an eighties horror movie. Maine's got a weird way of mixing beauty with the feeling of being watched.

The lake glistens a few hundred yards away, the surface like glass, almost too pretty, too still. Trees tower over the road, their limbs full of needles and leaves, stretched out, snatching at the car. The radio fights to keep a station. Uncle Aldo fiddles with the dial. He gives up and clicks the knob off. "Your ma woulda come, but—"

"I know." The words stick like thorns in my throat but I understand.

"You got a good head on your shoulders. You're dependable. Reliable. You remind me of me. You'll be all right. My girls could stand to be a little more like you. They're just good at trying to look pretty. His voice drifts, a half-laugh slips out. "I pulled a lot of strings to get you in here. Don't waste this opportunity."

"Opportunity? Uncle Aldo, they won't even let me have pants with drawstrings, and sweats are the only kind of pants I got." My shoes tap on the car floor, releasing some of my pent-up tension.

"You're worried about drawstrings? Trust me, this is better than juvie. You think rich people would send their kids to a place that wasn't top-notch?"

"I know."

We turn down a tree-canopied road. Only the sound of the tires on the road. We turn and pass a large stone sign tangled in ivy—*Welcome to Blueberry Hill.*

"When you make putz choices, kid, you pay putz prices for a long time. But you're turning things around. New chapter. Take responsibility for your life. Worry about your goals. You got too many talents to waste." His words are urgent.

My face heats. Still not comfortable with compliments. "I'm nothing special."

"Are you kidding me? If you think you're a nothing, that's what you're going to get—nothing. You're somebody. *Sàngue.* My blood. You think we're a family of nobodies? Do I look like a nobody to you? Huh?" His tone's desperate and pleading—makes me want to turn away. So I do.

"No, Uncle Aldo."

We wind around a circle drive. His fingers drum the wheel. "You think the Queen of England don't wake up and think she was a nobody sometimes? She gets up and does the job she's was supposed to do. You don't let bullshit in your head mix up your feelings."

He puts the car in park in front of a large, castle of a building.

A silence hangs between us.

"Sorry I let you down, " I whisper. The tightness in my chest makes it hard to squeeze in a breath.

He blinks away a hint of tears. "Sorry? What is this, a Hallmark convention? You don't need to apologize to me. This is your life. It starts here."

He taps his temple and then his chest. "Head and heart. Connected. Capisce?"

"Yeah."

He holds a hand to his ear. "What was that?"

I roll my eyes, play along. "Come on. What is this, a Hallmark convention? Capisce."

"Oh, you do comedy now? Get outta here."

We slide together for a hug.

I grab the laundry bag containing a few clothing items and a small plastic bag I packed with a few other essentials, mostly candy and my favorite sandwich, in case I don't like what they have for lunch. Pastrami, with good mustard and cheese. The type of bread isn't important to me. The filling matters most.

I open the car door, taking in the imposing façade of the Blueberry Hill Home for Troubled Youth. The cold scent of old stone mixes with freshly mowed grass.

From a window on the fourth floor, a girl's eyes pull mine toward her like she's sending me an unspoken message. She looks sad, trapped behind glass.

"You're my sàngue. Remember that. Find the bright spot." Uncle Aldo's shout jolts me back.

Near the front steps, a boy strums a happy tune on a guitar. His eyes drift to me, a playful glint in them. "G'morning." He's got chiseled features, long dark curls, and an English accent.

"Think I found my bright spot," I murmur to myself.

A stern nurse, dressed in a white uniform, beckons at the top of the stairs. I swallow hard and grab my bag tight.

Life changes in an instant.

I climb the steps. One thought creeps into me like the ivy that strangles the welcome sign—this ancient mansion looks like the perfect place for a murder.

DID YOU ENJOY *DARK TRIALS*?

Please take a moment to support the author by leaving a **review on Amazon, Goodreads and/or BookBub.**

And the adventure continues in *Dark Masks*, book one in The Vickie Chronicles series.

Order Here

Turn the page for exclusive freebies.

GET A FREE PREQUEL NOVELLA

Be the first to read *Dark Cycles*, a free prequel novella from the author.

COFFEE SHOPS

Special thanks to the coffee shops that provided an extra-vibey backdrop for the writing of *Dark Trials*.

Please support those who so generously caffeinate creatives.

Café Cluny
284 W. 12th St., New York, NY 10014

Common Good Harlem
2801 Frederick Douglass Blvd., New York, NY 10039

Lucille's Coffee and Cocktails
26 Macombs Pl., New York, NY 10039

Sadie's Coffee
324 S. Garnett St., Henderson, NC 27536

Think Coffee
208 W. 13th St., New York, NY 10011

ACKNOWLEDGMENTS

Thanks to every member of the IN Studios Family, past, present, and future. May we continue to inspire the creative best in each other.

I appreciate the beautiful minds of my editors, Suzanne Purvis, Kylie Maron-Vallorani, as well as my proofreader Joanne Lui. Thanks for ensuring it all made sense.

A special thank you to my mentors at 5 Star Books, Veronica Mixon and Jennifer Jakes.

To all who added visuals to the book, thank you: our illustrator Katerina Prenda, photographer Ismael Fernandez, video editor Erick Ricarte. You made everything look and sound pretty, including me.

Thanks to those who participated in readings and improvisation workshops, or purchased the book, or simply sent well wishes.

A special acknowledgment of my beta readers: Richard Johnson, Mindy Kaplan, Caren Skibell, Gabriele Schafer, Jonah Alexander, Annette Saunders and Kylie Maron-Vallorani.

Thank you Elaine Gutang, Toren Savage and Erick Ricarte for the administrative support.

Special appreciation goes out to our IN Studios members who stoked each other's creative flames with this particular project: Timothy Coleman, Adrian Danila, George Davis, Vavaria Etheredge, Travis Himebaugh, Richard Johnson, Mindy Kaplan, Ellen Ko, Kylie Maron-Vallaroni, Elizabeth Parish, Kenya Sophia, Gabriele Schafer, Caren Skibell, Sherry Taveras, Lara Gordon Jonah Alexander, James Lacey, Peter Previte, Annette Saunders, Alistair Ganley and Rodney Umble, to name a few.